Praise for Water Against C

"Passes the Bechdel test."

- *Nanamé Prothar*

"Mildly amusing."

- *Mykolnos Lorimer*

"A dazzling display of pronouns."

- *Athera Barandion*

"I could have sworn I was more awesome at the time...."

- *Cordela Shent*

R. A. KLEPSIS

THE AMULET

AND THE DRAGON

BOOK TWO OF THE CORDELA CHRONICLES

An engineer27 Publication

Klepsis.com

Foreword

Just like its predecessor, Water Against Chaos, the story presented in The Amulet and the Dragon is based on events that occurred in an actual fantasy tabletop role playing campaign. At this point of the campaign, the players took charge of the direction of the adventure, with the Game Master along for the ride. We hope you appreciate the shenanigans, drama, and antics of the group as detailed here. Once again, in creating this book, we took few liberties with the story. Though it may be difficult to believe, rest assured that everything is related here just as it happened around our table.

The following were all involved some way in bringing The Amulet and the Dragon to completion, even if they don't know it, and we offer them our eternal gratitude: our non-role-playing family members; the staff of NaNoWriMo; members of the Fort Writerdale and Palm Beach Wrimos groups; the original creators of the Rowan Grouse and her crew; Sugar Boy; Bob Thomas; the Orionid meteor shower; Google Docs; Literature and Latte, producers of Scrivener software; Emily's World of Design for our cover art; IngramSpark for self-publishing help.

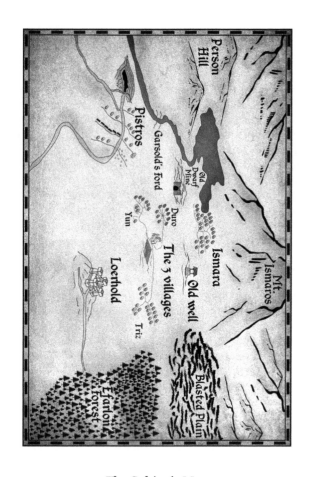

The Sphinx's Map

Part I

Prologue

WILHELMINA was the first person awake in the Beaver Lodge Inn, as she usually was. Everybody called her Willie, including her father except when he was in a particularly serious mood, and she preferred it that way. Looking out the window of her room, she saw an absolutely clear sky illuminated by the first light of dawn, and she anticipated that today might bring the first signs of spring after the weeks of cold winter that Palmyra had endured. She made her way out into the common room at the front of the inn and gently pushed open the double doors that led to the street. The air that entered from outside was chilly but definitely contained the promise of the first fine day in a while.

Inhaling deeply, she drifted over to the hearth and added some kindling to the banked coals from the night before that still glowed gently, blowing a bit to catch them. She added some larger wood, then filled a kettle from the water bucket and hung it over the growing fire. She would have to fetch some more water from the well in order to cook some meal for breakfast for the Inn's guests and residents, but that could wait. For now, while she waited for the kettle to boil, she began to sweep the winter's collected dust out into the street.

A bleary-eyed and somewhat disheveled half-elven woman came forward from the residence wing into the common room and sat heavily on a chair near the hearth. "Good morning, Cordela," Willie said cheerfully. "You'll have to wait a few minutes for coffee or tea. I just put the kettle up a few minutes ago."

"Thank you," the woman stifled a yawn. "And good morning to you, too."

The sounds of an approaching horse drifted in from the

street, followed by sounds of rider dismounting, and finally by the rider himself. He wore some kind of blue uniform with gold trim, and had close-cropped hair under a narrow-brimmed hat. He briefly saluted Willie. "I bring a message for Miss Cordela Shent," he announced.

"That's me," Cordela levered herself out of the chair by pushing on the table.

"Excellent. I am also looking for Miss Valory Smith."

"I'll fetch her," said Cordela, pulling her robe a bit tighter around her. She vanished back down the hallway she had emerged from.

Willie paused her sweeping. "You must have ridden all night. If you are hungry, you can stay for breakfast. I'll be serving in about an hour. If you would like a hot drink, that will be ready in a few minutes."

"I was certainly up and out before dawn, but not quite all night," explained the messenger. "I would take you up on the hot drink, but I have several more stops to make here in Palmyra, and I really mustn't delay. Thank you very much, though."

Cordela returned with a similarly disheveled but taller woman. Her black hair was in desperate need of brushing, and she still had a crease on her cheek from where her pillowcase had pressed into it. "This is Valory," Cordela said.

"It is my privilege, honor, and duty," began the blue-clad rider, "to deliver to you these missives from his Highness Prince Prothar, esteemed and beloved ruler of Kandahar." He handed each of them a scroll of vellum. Each was wound with a blue ribbon that matched the courier's uniform, and was sealed with wax imprinted with a design that Willie assumed was the emblem of Kandahar.

The two women muttered their thanks, and the Prince's messenger saluted them and briskly turned about. Before he had even finished mounting his horse, Willie had turned to the two recipients with wide eyes. "A royal message! You two are certainly special. What does it say?"

Cordela read aloud from her scroll. "Prince Prothar, ruler of Kandahar, cordially invites you as esteemed guests to his marriage to Princess Nanamé of Ishtar, to take place on the day of Midspring in the current year of his reign, at midday. Reception at the Kandahar Gathering Grounds to follow."

"Woo!" exclaimed Willie. "Royal wedding. Very exciting."

"Princess Nanamé," Valory began, "isn't that the Princess that ..."

"That was abducted and Stonefoot had to negotiate her release," finished Cordela. "Yes."

"What am I going to wear?" Valory's forehead furrowed. "And I'll need to bring a gift. I'm not ready for this!"

"Settle down, Valory." The half-elf took her friend by the hand. "Midspring is nearly eight weeks away. We will have plenty of time to get you prepared for this event."

Willie giggled and stood her broom behind the work counter, then went to the hearth to check on the kettle.

"I'm glad the Prince found his Princess," Valory calmed down and caught her breath. "I'd like to think their courtship was very romantic, but it is probably a political marriage more than anything else."

"I hope it was some of both," replied Cordela.

"Maybe there are still princes out there for us, Cordela?" Valory mused wistfully.

"Could be," replied Cordela.

One

CORDELA Shent was a cleric of the Daughters of Isis. As part of her service to the order, she was occasionally assigned missions or tasks at places outside the city of Palmyra where she lived. These were occasionally interesting, exciting, or fun. This particular mission in nearby Kandahar was none of those. She was assigned to guard duty and recruitment activities for the Temple of Isis there, still under construction. Cordela allowed that this was appropriate, since she had been involved in the founding of the temple. She and her friends, in Kandahar on a completely different mission, had unmasked an impostor who had imprisoned the real Prince and usurped the throne of Kandahar. After releasing the Prince from his captivity and helping him to defend his principality from imminent attack, his gratitude toward her order was considerable. He summarily granted a charter within the city, along with a generous parcel of land on which to build. Cordela's involvement in the founding of the temple didn't make "guarding" it from the occasional passerby any more appealing.

At least she was able to check up on the construction, which was well under way. A shipment of blindingly white stone had arrived the same day as Cordela, and the masons were fashioning an impressive facade. Cordela learned that this material was known as Pistros Stone and was quarried in the eponymous village a few days' travel to the north. It was prized throughout the region for its luster, strength, and versatility. The structure would be beautiful when complete.

The head of the new temple, Daughter Parolas, seemed to be getting along well in the sometimes rough and tumble environs of Kandahar. She had managed to attract a core of adherents who provided fairly generous support. It didn't hurt that the followers of Isis had been so instrumental in averting the potential disaster of the invading army from the west. Cordela found the residents of Kandahar very receptive to her recruitment efforts, even when she ventured into The Warrens, the seediest part of town. She wasn't sure if it was the battle scars she now wore, or that people there recognized her as a Hero of Kandahar, but she noticed that people were much more deferential and respectful to her than they had been on her first visit to Kandahar. That, at least, raised her interest in her mission.

Today, though, she had a slightly different assignment. The Daughters of Isis, along with several other of the more well-regarded religious orders, had been asked to provide security support to bolster the efforts of the Royal Guard for a major event that day. It was scheduled for midday, the time when the Prince usually made his appearances before the public on the balcony of the Royal Residence. Cordela was tasked with keeping the roadway alongside the Gathering Ground clear for some kind of procession, and was detailed a group of acolytes to assist. Cordela's patience with the inexperienced acolytes was nearly exhausted when a large convoy emerged from the forest, and as it approached trumpeters sounded a fanfare and heralds proclaimed the arrival of the royal family of Ishtar. The crowd was well behaved, and Cordela was able to watch the procession as it passed her. Sitting in the main carriage next to a stately dressed man she saw a very pretty young woman. Cordela guessed that this must be the princess that had been abducted by the Sultan of Samarkand, an incident that had almost incited a war between the two cities until her friend Stonefoot the dwarf had intervened. That altercation had proved to be just one aspect of the machinations of Tillingast, a follower of gods of chaos who was attempting to awaken them by creating lots of chaos everywhere. Cordela had been instrumental in ending the life of Tillingast, and had averted the existential threat to the world through her perseverance and will. She ought to be *in* this parade, not directing traffic out of its way. But Isis demanded what service she chose, and all Cordela could do was grumble and try to get the herder to keep his goats off of the road.

The procession made its way into the Royal Residence, and soon the Prince appeared on the balcony beside the Ishtar royals. He introduced them and stated that they were his esteemed guests and he hoped to formalize a treaty relationship between Kandahar and Ishtar. Cordela thought she saw him glance at the Princess briefly after that statement.

Thus it was that when the messenger wearing the uniform of the Kandahar Royal Guard appeared in the lobby of the Beaver Lodge, Cordela was not terribly surprised that he brought wedding invitations for herself and Valory. Clearly, the treaty negotiations had included a marriage proposal.

Two

RIZO Malkin was a cold halfling. He was also tired, hungry, cramped from sitting on the hard ground, and his throat was sore from maintaining a chant for the last eighteen hours. But he was trying not to think about all that and concentrate on what he was doing. What he was doing was attempting to cast a magic spell that he had learned from the elderly wizard Lanthanum in Amorium that, if successful, would summon a magical animal companion known as a Familiar. The spell procedure was very detailed and exacting. He required a brazier of brass with enough charcoal to last a full 24 hours. The coals had to be either gilden or acacia — he picked gilden — and must have been fired with wood aged at least one year. Then he needed incense compounded of sandalwood, sage, myrrh, and cinnamon, also enough for 24 hours. And he needed to learn the chant. From practicing, he knew that it took about 20 minutes to complete the chant once. He might have lost count, but he thought that the repetition he was on was number 54. Almost time to add more coals to the brazier. After two more iterations he would add incense. He was pretty sure he had done everything correctly, but after 18 hours and no familiar, he was beginning to think maybe he had forgotten something.

This wasn't what Rizo had in mind when he enrolled in magic school. He didn't mind his life before, which consisted of doing odd surveillance jobs, breaking and entering, light pilfering of targeted valuables, and the occasional heist. Then, he had met Cordela and realized that "doing good" could also be fairly remunerative, and people thanked you for doing it as well. His stealth, dexterous hands, skill with setting traps, picking locks and the like could also be used in ways that he could talk about in polite company. And he saw how Cordela and her fellow Daughters of Isis used magic to achieve their noble goals. If he had some magic of his own it would nicely supplement his other talents. And that

9

thought, carried through on its natural course, had ultimately led to him sitting on the hard, cold ground of this field in the dark of night, chanting the same thing repeatedly while trying to keep the brazier in front of him lit. Rizo added more coals. That would warm things up for a bit, at least. He renewed his chant. Number 55, maybe.

He had started this process in the late morning, after a brief line of squalls had moved through the area. The skies behind seemed clear, and he had hoped that they would stay that way. That particular hope had been fulfilled, and the weather had cooperated with his plans. The day had been the warmest of the past several weeks. But the night had grown chilly after sunset, and after sitting relatively motionless for so many hours, the cold began to seep into Rizo's bones.

He had selected a large open field at the northern edge of Palmyra for the ritual. The spell instructions had recommended to cast it in a natural area, to make it more likely that a creature would answer the summons. This field fit that purpose, and also provided plenty of visibility to see anyone that might be approaching. It was used in more temperate seasons as a drill ground by the Palmyra home guard. His last visit here had been when the army that he and Cordela had been leading camped here overnight on their way to confront their antagonist Tillingast. Since he expected to be concentrating on the spell chant, he enlisted Bowe, his fellow student at the Palmyra Institute of Magical and Necromantic Arts, to be his lookout. Although he and Bowe could not have contrasted more in looks, the lanky young man was a valued and capable study partner for Rizo. The infrequent times that Rizo spared a glance in his direction, he could see that Bowe was also cold, and bored. At least he could get up and move around.

At this point in his magical training, Rizo thought he had learned enough to be useful — some would say, enough to be dangerous. Not enough, however, to unlock the secrets of the ruby amulet he had recovered on his last adventure. And he didn't get along with or trust any of the head wizards at the PIMNA magic school, or he might have asked for some help. He didn't truthfully fit the mold of "wizard."

Wizards loved sitting in darkened rooms, poring over dusty manuscripts seeking out and learning obscure magical formulae. Also, they seemed to enjoy using magic for frivolous pursuits, or just for its own sake, not as a means to an end. Bowe had more of what Rizo considered the wizarding temperament, but even he was more of a utilitarian practitioner than most of the students, and the professors as well, to tell the truth. It was why they got along so well, and why neither of them really fit in. Rizo focused again on his chant, eyes softly closed. The fire would need more incense soon.

Rizo's problem was that he didn't really have much of a plan about what to do after magic school. Missions to save the world didn't land in his lap on a regular basis. So regardless of how profitable those opportunities might be, he couldn't rely on them for steady income.

He was going to need some way to sustain himself in the lifestyle to which he would like to become accustomed. He had in the past done some under-the-table work for the Wolliers Guild — the group that oversaw the wool trade in Palmyra, and thus essentially ran the city — but after becoming a local hero they decided he was too well known to be effective in carrying out clandestine activities on their behalf. He had few ideas about how he could apply his now rather considerable skills to bring in enough gold.

When he opened his eyes again, the sky was beginning to illuminate with rays of predawn sunshine. Finishing up the chant for the 56th (or so) time, he reached into his sack of ground incense to add more to the fire. Bowe, to the right of Rizo, seemed to have nodded off in the chair he had thoughtfully brought along. Rizo caught a hint of movement to his left. Instantly he was up, dagger drawn, to confront the unexpected visitor. His sudden leap startled Bowe, who tipped over in his chair and landed with a thud. In the gloaming, Rizo saw a small black creature sitting on its haunches.

"Meow," it said.

"It's a cat," Rizo observed.

"Yes, it's a cat," Bowe shoved himself up onto his knees. "He's been there for at least an hour. I thought you knew."

"Knew what?"

"Isn't he the Familiar you summoned?"

"Maybe. Why didn't you say something an hour ago? I could have stopped the chant and we could both be someplace warmer."

"I don't know how the spell is supposed to work. I assumed you needed to keep going or you would have stopped." He stood and brushed off his robe.

"Well," Rizo sheathed his dagger and addressed the cat. "If you are my familiar, how would I know?" As he said it, he heard, or rather felt, a response in his mind. It was not in any language he could comprehend, but he nevertheless understood the concept of 'friend.' The cat licked a paw and drew it across an ear.

"Do you come with a name?" he asked. The presence in his mind supplied syllables. "Iko-Iko?" The cat stood and approached Rizo. "Well, it's not much of a name, as names go." The cat glared at him with a steely look. "But I guess it will do. What do you say to getting inside out of this chilly weather?"

Iko-Iko leapt up to Rizo's shoulder in one bound.

"Right. We'll get going as soon as we clean up. I'm eager for breakfast."

Three

BORDINI was going through his normal daily exercise routine when the stranger appeared in the arena. He recognized a fellow fighting man immediately, although his features were a bit off. Clearly, not a local.

"Sorry for interrupting your practice," the fellow started. "My name is Garynd DiMarco and I'd like to ask you what you know about Cordela Shent."

"Never heard of her," Bordini shrugged. "Someone I should know?"

"I heard a story that she broke up a fight in here that you were involved in." DiMarco placed an ornately booted foot on Bordini's step stool.

"Broke up a fight?" Bordini scratched his head. "No one breaks up fights here. People have money riding on them. They'd be pretty upset if the fight ended without a winner."

"Right. That's how I heard. People were pretty upset."

"Oh, yeah. I remember that now. It was back when the Prince — I guess they figured out it wasn't the Prince after all — had me fighting people instead of monsters. They brought over this halfling for me to take care of. Sneaky little fellow. Gave me a couple of scars for my trouble."

"That's the time I'm interested in. What happened to stop the fight?" The stranger leaned forward, keenly interested.

"Well, I was just about to put the big hit on the little guy, when suddenly this place lights up like daytime. Before my eyes can adjust this lady is swinging in on a rope, grabbing the halfling, and swinging out again. The light vanished as mysteriously as it had lit up, and in the confusion they got away. You're saying that the lady was this Shent woman?"

"That's what I hear. I'm trying to track her down. I gather she's been seen around here lately."

Bordini shook his head. "Not by me. I lost money on that fight. If you see her, tell her I'm looking for payback."

Captain Kirloo was a very busy woman. The Prince had just announced that he would be marrying the princess from Ishtar in just about eight weeks time, and as the head of the home guard she had quite a lot of security arrangements to take care of. She was a little peeved that the Prince was bringing in that dwarf to lead the security detail, but the bride's family had specifically requested him, and at least he was a competent and trustworthy individual, someone that Kirloo knew and could respect.

Not like this stranger that had just arrived in town and now somehow thought that he could occupy as much of Kirloo's precious time as he liked asking probing questions about a Hero of the Realm. He shared his name readily enough — Garynd DiMarco, or so he claimed — but he set off all of Kirloo's warning bells. He spoke smoothly, but with an accent she couldn't quite place. His clothing seemed to have been haphazardly collected from all over. And he looked like a ghost from the North — light skin, light hair, extremely tall and muscular, and with creepily blue eyes. Just seeing him set her on edge, and she stiffened. "What do you want to know about Cordela Shent?" she had asked when he approached her.

"Mostly I'm interested in her role during the battle of Kandahar. Any particularly heroic acts? Was she the key to victory?"

Kirloo had made a show of stroking her chin in thought while she considered how busy she was and how much to tell this stranger. "Well, she was instrumental in slowing down a charge on our undefended flank that might have proved disastrous without her quick action. Other than that she played mostly a supporting role by coordinating the medical troops."

"Any idea where I might find her now?"

"She was in town some weeks ago, but I assume she returned home a while ago."

"Any idea where home is?"

Kirloo hesitated again. She considered that whatever this guy was after, Cordela could probably handle him. "Palmyra, last I checked."

With a quick "Thank you" Garynd DiMarco turned and went on his way. Kirloo sighed in relief. She'd managed to get rid of him without spending too much time. She really needed to figure out how many different duty details she was going to need to cover the various venues for the wedding related activities.

Four

ONCE Cordela was dressed and had thanked Willie for the tea, she stopped by Valory's room. "I'm heading to the temple, and then dropping in on Rizo. The others should have received their invitations by now."

"Okay." Valory was brushing her hair. "I need some breakfast. I'll try to catch up to you later."

Outside the Beaver Lodge, the sun was rapidly warming the late winter day. Cordela made her way through the enormous tetrapylon that dominated the center of Palmyra toward the section of town that housed most of the temples and religious centers of the city. The Temple of Isis was kind of her second home here in Palmyra. She spent many days and even more parts of days there, performing religious service, helping to train new acolytes, maintaining and cleaning the building, and studying in the temple's modest but worthwhile library. Among the followers of Isis she was treated with nearly as much respect as those who had been there far longer than her — almost as much as she felt she had earned. As soon as she entered, an acolyte accosted her with a question about a charm necklace she was working on.

"These glyphs are not quite right," Cordela pointed out the offending symbols. Why these newcomers couldn't just read how to do things like this in the library, as she had done, was a mystery to Cordela. After all, she might have to hurry off to save the world again, and then who would the acolytes lean on for crafting help? Cordela took a breath to bolster her patience. "This one is derived from a bull symbol and must have more pronounced 'horns.' See, like this," she pointed to an example on one of the decorated pillars that supported the mezzanine. Cordela had come to see her friends, not to provide instruction. As a senior member of the Daughters of Isis, she shouldn't be bothered with such trivialities.

As she sent the new adherent on her way, Cordela was hailed by a stout dwarf and a tall dark human man, both armed and armored. "Stonefoot! Markham! Just the men I wanted to see," she gave each of them a quick embrace. "I expected you two had been assigned guard duty today."

"We've been here all week," Markham intoned. "We just saw you yesterday."

Cordela nodded. "But that was before Prince Prothar sent out invitations to his wedding by royal courier. I trust you both received yours?"

"No." Markham frowned. "I was not part of your Kandahar expedition, and even though I participated in the battle, I suppose I was not outstanding enough to draw the Prince's attention."

"I'm sorry," said Cordela. "Maybe I'll bring you as my guest, if you are interested." She turned to the dwarf. "How about you, Stonefoot?"

"The missive I received was more than an invitation." The dwarf's beard quivered and creases appeared near his rock-hard eyes. "It seems that the Prince wants me to be the head of security for the event."

"Putting you to work again? Don't you ever get to just have fun?"

"Apparently, the bride's family specifically requested my services."

"You must have really impressed them during the negotiations with Samarkand," Cordela tapped his arm and smiled. "Well, I guess I don't need to ask what you will be wearing. The armor you have on now will do nicely for security."

"I will probably shine it up for the occasion."

"Good idea," agreed Cordela as she turned to go. "If Valory comes by, tell her she can find me at Rizo's place. See you later."

To get to Rizo's apartment, above the Woolly Thinking tavern, Cordela had to return back through the tetrapylon. It was a lot more crowded now, and Cordela's thoughts drifted as she made her way slowly through the traffic. She would need something impressive to wear to the Prince's nuptials, and she would need a gift. She wondered what might be appropriate, welcome, needed by the Prince, and in her price range. Guests of state might have significant resources at their disposal and could present impressive even if not entirely practical gifts. But she was just a lone adventurer, and not an immensely wealthy one either. It turned out that saving the world from being turned into a chaotic sludge, while it helped pay the bills, was not sufficient to make one wealthy. And a substantial portion of the income she did come by was donated to her religious order. She tried to think of something that would be meaningful and embody the relationship she had with the Prince, but also not too expensive. Nothing occurred to her.

She was so preoccupied in her thoughts that she nearly walked right past the Woolly Thinking tavern. When she entered, the bartender greeted her.

"Good morning, Miss Shent!" he said while shining an ale tankard. "Anything to wet your tongue today?"

"No thank you, Mr. Thinker," she waved him off affably.

"The amber ale is a great way to start your day." He was always selling.

Cordela just shook her head and made for the staircase at the back of the tavern that led to Rizo's apartment.

At the landing atop the stairs she raised her hand to rap on Rizo's door, then hesitated. He usually heard her coming up the stairs, somehow identified her by the rhythm of her footfalls, and yanked open the door just as she was about to knock. But not this time. She grew concerned that perhaps something had happened to him, then thought that perhaps he was just out somewhere this morning. She knocked anyway, but expected either to turn around and leave immediately, or to force the door in a probably vain attempt to rescue Rizo from whatever mess he had gotten himself into. To her surprise, he answered the door.

"Hi, Cordela," he offered, waving her in. He hefted a large bronze brazier off of a chair at his dining table which was otherwise covered in half-scribed scrolls and unusual spell ingredients such as wool batting, sand partially loaded into small sacks, and pieces of chalk carved into interesting shapes. "Have a seat," he said.

As she took the offered seat, among the wizard detritus on the table she noticed Rizo's invitation, still sealed and bound with its blue ribbon. "I see you got your message from the Prince. Aren't you going to open it?"

"Should I? I mean, is it good news?"

"I guess that depends on your point of view. I took it as good."

Rizo heaved a weary sigh. "I will. I've just been busy this morning." He looked around his apartment in a distracted way. "In fact, I've been busy for the last 20 hours."

"Doing what?"

"Summoning my Familiar." He pointed at a bureau that had drawers overflowing with various pieces of leather, vellum, woodcarving tools, and other odds and ends. The top of it was as cluttered as his dining room table if not more so. As Cordela looked at it, a wooden mortar leapt off of it, seemingly of its own accord, but as Cordela looked more closely she saw in the dim light the outline of a completely black cat.

"A cat? That's very You, Rizo," Cordela said. "Congratulations. I guess you were able to comprehend Lanthanum's scroll then?"

"Uh huh."

"Have you named him yet?"

"He arrived with his own name. Iko-Iko."

"Did he now?" Cordela raised an eyebrow. "Does he answer to it? Here, Iko-Iko!"

The cat ignored her. "He comes to 'Hey now' for some reason," Rizo explained.

Cordela looked puzzled for a second, then shrugged. "Hey now!" she called. The animal bounded off the bureau, covered the short distance to where she sat, and leapt into her lap. She stroked his head and back while he gently purred. "He seems friendly enough," she smiled.

"Well, let's see what important news Prince Prothar wishes to share," said Rizo, retrieving the sealed scroll from his tabletop. "Prince Prothar, ruler of Kandahar, cordially invites you..." his voice trailed off as he read the rest to himself. He looked up. "So, our Prince has found a princess." He looked back at the invitation. "Say, isn't that ..."

"Yes," Cordela cut him off. "And get this. Her family is insisting that Stonefoot handle the security arrangements for the event."

"You don't say. Well, I'll have to see what I can do to make things less secure," Rizo grinned one of his most mischievous grins.

"Don't make things too hard for our friend Stonefoot," Cordela protested. "Or ruin the Prince's special day."

"Serves him right for inviting me," Rizo quipped. "Besides, he might suspect me of being an impostor if I didn't make some trouble. You know me, I'm incorrigible."

"Don't let me incorrige you." Cordela shook her head.

Rizo lifted Iko-Iko off of Cordela's lap and cradled him gently. His mischievous grin faded. "Listen, Cordela. I need to ask a favor of you."

"Sure. What do you need?"

"I've been working on figuring out this amulet I pinched from Tillingast's study for weeks. I tried all of the

20

identification magic I know, and all I can get is that it's magical. It won't give up any more of its secrets." Iko-Iko meowed and squirmed out of Rizo's arms. "And I've exhausted the contents of the PIMNA library. None of the books mention anything like it."

"What can I do to help?"

"Can you get me into the Isis library? She does have magic as one of her domains of influence. Maybe your library has something I can use."

"Well, I hate to disappoint you, but I've been all over that library, and there isn't anything that might tell you what that amulet is."

Rizo was crestfallen.

"But you know what?" Cordela stood. "The library at Odin's temple has a lot more of the type of book you are looking for. And it is very well indexed."

"Can you get me in there?"

"I think so," Cordela flipped her hair back over her shoulder. "Want to go now?"

"No, right now I'm busy."

"Doing what?" Cordela looked around. "Cleaning up?"

"No," said Rizo. "I need a nap."

Five

CORDELA made plans to meet Rizo outside the Temple of Odin the following morning. She left him and his new companion with nothing planned for the rest of her day. As she passed through the tetrapylon she encountered a fellow holding a placard that advertised a tournament that afternoon at the armory. She thought wistfully of her cousin Zoro Burke that had competed in and won such a tournament just days before his demise at the end of a kobold's javelin. She resolved to enter as a tribute to him.

First she needed dinner, and to change into clothing more suited to fighting than the woolen shift she was wearing. So she headed home.

"Welcome back to the Beaver Lodge," Willie greeted her as she stepped in.

Cordela blinked as her eyes adjusted from the bright sunlight outside. "I live here, Willie. I don't need the hospitality treatment."

"I know, but I need to get back in practice. It's almost shearing season, and the inn will soon be packed again."

"Okay," Cordela smirked. "You can practice by getting me something to eat."

Willie giggled. "Coming right up, Miss!"

Dinner consisted of the last of the previous season's root vegetables, roasted with herbs, and some leftover oatmeal from breakfast. Cordela left a few coppers for Willie, then rushed to her room to change.

She selected one of several tight fitting green tunics that she owned, and some black leather leggings. Her well-worn boots and a belt completed her accouterments. She used the belt to bind her tunic at the waist so that the overlong article of clothing flared out at the bottom like a skirt. That generally kept the lewder elements from gawking at her curves, a distraction she didn't enjoy dealing with. Her suit of scale mail she left in her closet, since the armory would be providing standard padding to all entrants. The padding was generally sufficient to deflect any serious damage from the wooden and padded weapons used in the tournament. Finally, she brushed out her hair and tied it into a tight bun which she pinned with a crossbow bolt. Zoro had given it to her shortly before he was killed. Since then, she had always worn it into combat. Giving herself a look in her hand mirror, and tucking in a few stray hairs, she nodded smartly. She fished out a small coin purse from her locked chest, briefly running her fingers over the barely visible glyph on the lid that she had placed there to keep out the unauthorized. She verified that the purse contained enough for her entry fee, then closed and locked the chest.

On her way out she met Valory in the common room. "I've been chasing you all morning," the taller woman complained with a smile.

"I thought I left you enough bread crumbs to follow my trail," Cordela replied.

"You did, but I don't think Rizo was very happy to have his nap interrupted."

"Ooh, I didn't think of that. Oh well, I'm sure he got right back to it after you left. That guy sleeps like he's under a spell."

"What are you all dressed up for?" Valory scanned Cordela head to toe and nodded.

"I'm competing in the armory tournament this afternoon. Want to come cheer for me?"

"Sure. I want to grab some dinner first, though."

"The turnips are really good. See you soon!"

"Good luck!" called Willie from behind her counter. Cordela waved and was out the door.

Six

THAT afternoon, after Willie had just come from the stables to make sure that all the horses had adequate provender, Cordela and Valory stepped back through the main doors of the Beaver Lodge. Cordela looked somewhat the worse for wear, and Valory looked a bit glum herself. The pair were involved in an animated discussion.

"I didn't get enough time to rest after the bout with the skinny fellow," Cordela complained. "That Son of Set had a whole round to recover from his last fight."

"At least you took care of that dwarf — um, lady? — without much trouble." Valory smiled.

"Sure. That was a pretty easy fight." Willie could see that Cordela wasn't mollified. "But I beat that cleric of Set once. I shouldn't have had to fight him again."

"Well, those were the rules. You had a tough draw. Your first match was against that Giant. What a rough way to start."

"Thanks, Valory," Cordela sighed, "but your sympathy doesn't win me any trophies."

"I cheered for you."

"I appreciate that. It sounded like you had a whole squad there yelling."

"I guess you're pretty popular." Cordela just shrugged.

Willie took advantage of the pause in their conversation. "Welcome back to the Beaver Lodge," she presented her cheery hostess demeanor despite the disappointing tournament results. It wouldn't do for the face of the Beaver Lodge to be anything but welcoming and pleasant. "I guess the great Cordela Shent isn't so invincible after all."

"I wouldn't go that far," Cordela held up her hand, palm toward Willie. "This was just practice, after all."

Valory shook her head.

"But, I was one point away from advancing to the second round. So not too bad a performance overall."

"Well, that tournament draws some pretty fierce competition, owing to the size of the prize purse. You look like you could use a washing up, though. Would you like me to put on a kettle for a hot bath for you?"

"Sure," Cordela nodded, brightening a bit. "First, I'm going to look in on Elri, since I'm already filthy."

"Good thinking," said Valory. Willie agreed. Cordela's pet pig loved to wriggle in dirt and mud when he could.

"Are you going to have supper ready early, Willie?" Cordela said over her shoulder on her way to the stables. "I'll need some extra sleep tonight, and I'm supposed to meet Rizo first thing in the morning."

"So you can research his mysterious amulet?" said Willie slyly.

Cordela turned back to face her. "How do you know everything, Willie?"

"I have two ears," she said, pointing to them with each hand.

Cordela just shook her head. "Do you want to come say 'Hi' to Elri, Valory?"

"Right behind you," she called.

Willie giggled to herself. She didn't need to mention that Rizo had been there for dinner while Cordela was at the tournament and had told her the plans. A good spy never revealed their sources, after all.

Suppertime was more crowded than it had been for weeks.

Willie had to keep herself circulating and couldn't spend a lot of time with Cordela and Valory. But every time she stopped by, they seemed to be talking on the subject of wedding gifts for the Prince of Kandahar.

"I really think I ought to find something more personal, that he'll know it's from me every time he looks at it," Willie overheard Valory saying.

"I've been thinking the same thing," replied Cordela. "But it should also be practical. You know, something he really needs. But what does a Prince need that he doesn't have already?"

Willie could see their point. There were plenty of things she'd like to get as gifts, but then again she wasn't royalty. She didn't have any advice, but at least she could keep her ears open for any ideas that floated by.

As she planned, Cordela was gone to bed early. Willie wasn't sure Valory had retired or gone out again. But she didn't see her again that night.

Willie barely saw Cordela on her way out in the morning, but she returned with Rizo for dinner early in the afternoon.

"Did you two find what you were looking for in the library?"

Seven

RIZO was already waiting outside the Temple of Odin when Cordela arrived. The weather had remained mild, chilly at night but clear and sunny during the day, and Cordela found she could dispense with her heavy overcoat. She was thankful for that, since the library of Odin tended to be stuffy and uncomfortable. "Been waiting long?" she asked her friend and erstwhile research partner.

"No, just got here a minute ago."

"Great." She started toward the temple entrance. "Just let me do the talking until we're inside," she advised.

They were met just inside by a priest and two guards adorned with Norse-style horned helmets. Cordela wondered whether they were authentic or just an affectation.

"Ah, Miss Shent. The hero of the Battle of Kandahar," the priest began with a lilt. "To what do we owe the pleasure of your presence?"

"I need to consult your excellent library for a very pressing matter." Her voice was smooth and practiced, with barely a hint of the sarcasm induced by priest's lugubrious tone of voice. "Would you be so kind as to let me and my associate pursue our research here?"

"Of course. No doubt you seek a way to avert some grave threat to our world."

"Perhaps I hope to resolve the issue before it becomes a threat." She emphasized the word 'threat' ever so slightly, while leaning forward a bit in an aggressive but not quite menacing way.

The briefest of frowns flitted across the face of the priest, replaced quickly with the condescending smile. "You and your companion may follow me." Without checking to see if they did, he wheeled about and strode deeper into the temple.

Cordela beckoned to Rizo to keep up, and led him after the priest toward where she knew the library was.

"The librarian will assist you as needed. Please leave everything as you find it." With that, the priest drifted out of the room.

The librarian on duty was a man Cordela had worked with before. "Greetings, Justfreed. Do you have an index of magical talismans mentioned in the library's collection?"

"It may not be quite complete. The Odiner who had been working on it passed away some years ago, and none have taken up the work since."

"We'll start there," she said, more to Rizo than to the librarian. To Justfreed she said, "Can you retrieve it for us?"

"I will meet you at the reading desk." While the leather-clad librarian moved off to fetch the catalog, Cordela led Rizo past a statue of Odin's eight legged horse to where the reading table was situated beneath a skylight that provided copious illumination for examining books. She caught a blur of black motion out of the corner of her eye. "Is your cat in here with us?" she whispered to Rizo.

He nodded.

"Well, make sure he stays out of sight. I'm not sure Justfreed would be too happy to see a clawed animal in his precious collection."

Rizo waved off Iko-Iko discreetly just before the librarian arrived with the reference book.

"Thank you," Cordela nodded to Justfreed.

"I'll be nearby if you need anything else."

"All right," Cordela lifted open the heavy leather cover of the book. "I guess we'll start with 'Amulet'."

Rizo flipped a few pages. "There must be hundreds of 'amulet' entries."

"Well, we just need to go through them one by one and see if any resemble yours by description."

"That sounds very annoying."

"That's 'research,' Rizo," Cordela rolled her eyes. "We can probably eliminate some without having to find where they are referenced. Like this one," she pointed. "'Amulet of Hrymyr.' That one is a mythical object that belonged to the Norse god Hrymyr. It was supposedly destroyed in a battle. So it probably isn't the one you found."

"Probably not," Rizo agreed. "So let's scan down the list and see if there are any more likely candidates, and we'll look those up first."

"Did you bring anything to use to take notes?"

"Ummm..."

"I thought not. Never mind, I have." She brought a cloth bound notebook, pen, and inkwell out of her pack. The two of them went through the list of amulets, and also looked up charms and talismans. Eventually they had a list of about thirty promising leads. Cordela handed her notebook to Justfreed so that he could fetch the works cited in the catalog.

He returned with a stack higher than Cordela's forearm was long, and excused himself to go get more from their list. Cordela and Rizo split the stack between themselves and began their task which occupied the rest of the morning.

Most of the leads went nowhere, of course. Either they were in a language that neither of them could make out, were mere mentions with no description that could help them determine whether the item mentioned was Rizo's, or they had descriptions that were clearly not the amulet they were interested in. Just when Cordela was going to suggest they break for dinner, she read a description in Gilberto's Magical Compendium that seemed to fit. "Rizo, how about this," she summarized aloud from the book, "Amulet of al-Azhar. Walnut sized ruby, platinum setting, runes inscribed on the setting. Sounds like your amulet, doesn't it?"

"Sure does!" Rizo was visibly excited. "What else does it say?"

"Not much. Gilberto claims he saw it in a volume called The Travels of Mooreham Dunne." Cordela called to Justfreed. "Do you have this book here?"

The librarian looked at the title in the open book in front of Cordela. "Perhaps. Wait here."

Some ten minutes later he returned with a small volume, barely more than a pamphlet. "Be careful with this one. It is rare and we have not had a chance to copy it yet. And obviously it was not catalogued by our deceased brother."

Rizo gently opened the thin book and gingerly turned the pages. "Bullseye!" He had stopped on a page with a hand drawing that Rizo might have drawn himself while looking at his amulet.

"What does the book say about it?"

"Well, this isn't a reference work," Rizo shrugged, turning back a few pages. "It seems to be a travelogue. He's got information about weather, plant life, local festivals ..."

"Can you find where he mentions the amulet?" Cordela looked over Rizo's shoulder and saw that the book was written in very neat Greek, which she understood but with some difficulty. Rizo seemed to be zipping through it.

"It says he passed through Tibiscum," Rizo paused on a page and began to read aloud. "There I met a man who was known throughout the town as a sorcerer of great power. Since I had need of his services, I paid a call on his place of business. Having met with many magicians of all sorts, I immediately gauged the man to be a fraud of very high caliber. When I challenged him, he confided to me that the source of all his power was a trinket or charm that he called the Amulet of al-Azhar, a modest representation of which follows on a subsequent page drawn by my own hand. He said that he acquired it in faraway Lycia and learned its secrets from the monks of Mortekap, near legendary Ismara. Sadly, he was not able to provide the services I sought ..."

"Tibiscum?" said Cordela, "Never heard of it. I wonder how the book came to be in Palmyra."

"Well, never mind that. This is exactly the information I need," Rizo jotted some notes onto his paper.

"Except for one thing?"

"Right," he looked up. "Do you know where Ismara is?"

"I don't," Cordela pointed to her head. "But I'm pretty sure they have a geographical reference here where you could look it up."

"You're really pushing this research thing, aren't you?"

"Why should I have to do all the work?"

"Fine," Rizo humphed. "Justfreed, do you have an index or catalog of places, like the one for magical things?"

"Yes," Justfreed sauntered over. "Would you like me to fetch it for you?"

"Please. Oh, and we're done with the rest of this material," Rizo took in the entire reading table with a gesture. "Do you want some help replacing it where it belongs?"

"No thank you," the librarian replied. "I'm very particular about how my books are shelved. Just stack everything neatly, larger books on the bottom. I'll collect them later."

"How was that?" Rizo cocked his head to the side in the manner most annoying to Cordela.

"Very polite," Cordela allowed. "I could have told you he

wouldn't want help reshelving, but it was nice of you to ask."

"Let me know if you need anything else," Justfreed said as he deposited a large tome on the table in front of Rizo before heading back into his stacks.

"Let's see," Rizo cracked open the book about at the halfway point. "Ismara. Idumea, Intblausus, Ircumnassus, here it is. Ismara. Reputedly magically infused city in the far north adjacent to the Forlorn Mountains. Little independent evidence of its existence, might be purely myth."

"Well, Dunne did call it a legendary city. Still, I think I remember seeing it on Valory's map. So I think it is probably a real place."

"At least we have a direction to go," Rizo closed the book. "But that will have to wait. Right now, I want dinner."

"Yeah, I'm pretty hungry too. Let's go."

On their way out of the temple, Rizo called "Hey now!"

Iko-Iko scurried out of his hiding place, glared briefly at the lugubrious priest — who looked agape in horror that such a creature might be corrupting his temple — and leapt onto Rizo's shoulder who did not even break stride as he sauntered out onto Temple Row.

Eight

CORDELA and Rizo arrived at the Beaver Lodge for dinner early in the afternoon.

"Did you two find what you were looking for in the library?" Willie looked up from her washing to greet the newcomers.

"It was a very fruitful venture," Rizo smiled broadly.

"We got what we needed," Cordela was more muted.

"Fantastic! Anything to share?"

"Not until I get some of that World Famous Beaver Lodge lamb stew," Rizo plopped into a seat and glared as though he would wait until the end of time for his dinner if need be.

"Coming right up!" Willie smiled, dropped her rag, and danced over to the hearth to scoop out a generous helping for the halfling. "Same for you, Cordela?"

"Sure," she had a seat, more gingerly than Rizo.

"So?" Willie sat down next to Cordela after she had served them. "What did you get?"

"Well, this amulet has been around," began Rizo around a mouthful of hot stew.

The pair related their experience in the library, including the priest's reaction to Iko-Iko's unexpected presence. Midway through their tale, Valory joined them after finishing her duties at her temple. She brought Markham with her.

"Hey, hope we're not too late for dinner," Valory sat across from Rizo and motioned for Markham to sit to her right.

"There's plenty of stew," Willie rose to get two more bowls. "Rizo and Cordela were telling me what they found today at the library. You said you were heading north, right?" Willie asked.

"Right. That seems to be where we need to go," Rizo soaked up the last of his stew with a piece of bread.

"We'll probably leave first thing tomorrow," Cordela said.

"I don't know if I can be ready that soon. Will we be back in time for the wedding?" Valory interjected.

Cordela looked at her askance for a moment. "I didn't want to just assume you were going with us, Valory. But since you volunteered, thank you very much, we'd be glad to have you along. And I'm sure this trip won't take seven weeks, so we'll be back with plenty of time before the wedding."

Valory looked about as red as Willie had ever seen her. "Maybe we'll find something nice for the Prince and his bride on the way," she said meekly.

"And how about you, Markham? Are you interested, and available?" Cordela looked in his direction. "We could use an extra sword, in case we run into ruffians or any other trouble."

"I would certainly accompany you," Markham looked at Valory briefly. "Of course, I'll need to be excused from my duties at the temple."

"Let me know if Daughter Soussi gives you any trouble," Cordela offered.

Willie set the bowls of stew on the table. "Sounds like fun. I can't wait to hear about it."

"Thank you for the stew." The man's voice was as dark and strong as he looked.

"Well, I need to go," said Rizo. "I need to request a leave of absence from PIMNA for however long we'll be gone."

"Meet here first thing in the morning," Cordela said. "And bring the — the thing with you."

"Right-O," Rizo left with a little wave.

Valory blew on her stew. "I'm sorry Markham. I just invited you for lunch, and somehow you got roped into a whole quest."

"Well, temple guard duty is not very exciting." Willie thought she caught a hint of some shared expression between the two of them as she returned to her washing. She had four more bowls to clean now, and she still needed to prepare supper. As much as she liked chatting with the guests, and felt it important to stay on top of the goings-on of Palmyra, keeping the Beaver Lodge running was a full-time job. She needed to work.

Willie briefly saw the group in the morning as they set out on their quest. "Good luck! I'll be waiting to hear all of your stories when you get back."

She didn't see Cordela or Rizo again for nearly three weeks. When Cordela strolled in wearing a big smile, Willie had a feeling she was in for an epic of a story.

Nine

AS Rizo entered PIMNA, he could tell that some kind of commotion was occurring in the courtyard and he steeled himself for whatever was going on. A student literally flew past him, intercepting a ball that looked to be on a collision path with Rizo's head. The student used some sort of woven racket to swat the ball away toward another group of students who were also floating some eight feet off the ground, then rose back up to their height, clearly under the influence of some sort of flying spell. Apparently all the participants were using flying magic to play this fast paced sporting event. This was just the sort of frivolous use of magic that irked Rizo, and was typical of the PIMNA students, and many of the wizards Rizo had met. Rizo was trying to figure how to get past the game without being hit by a stray ball — or student — when the headmaster came out of his office.

"Wasteful! Just wasteful!" he berated them. "Do you green slimes have any idea how much those very rare spell components cost this magic school? And for what? A silly game! I should set all of you to cleaning the potion lab for a week."

It took the headmaster some time to bustle off all the misbehaving students. He had yet to earn their respect, since he had only recently taken over the post. The previous headmaster had abruptly left the magic school under somewhat mysterious circumstances a few months before. It was made clear to all, though not in so many words, that it was best not to ask too many questions about the prior holder of the chair. Rizo was curious about another thing, however. "What sort of spell components?" he asked.

The headmaster straightened his posture and pronounced in a professorial tone, "Flying magic generally requires the use of rare feathers as a spell component. The magic will be particularly potent if feathers of a magical creature are used. Particularly sought after are feathers of rocs, harpies, pegasus, and perytons."

"Where do we get our feathers from?"

"Well, we have to buy them," the headmaster said matter-of-factly. "And they are quite expensive! As you might surmise."

"Hmmm," Rizo thought to himself, his money-making instincts kicking in. Here was an opportunity to turn bad wizard habits into a steady income. Then he remembered what he was here for. "Headmaster. I need to request a leave of absence. I'll be gone perhaps two weeks."

"Mr. Malkin," the headmaster patted him patronizingly on the shoulder, "you are well advanced in your studies. I think we can grant you some time off. It is well earned."

"Can I go too?" Bowe, wearing brown-stained wizard robes, appeared out of a classroom adjoining the courtyard.

"Sure," Rizo said. "You'll have to get leave from the headmaster, too, of course." Bowe, at least two feet taller than the diminutive halfling, looked down at Rizo and then back up to the headmaster.

"Yes, well," began the headmaster, "I suppose. You have proven to be an exemplary student, if not a terribly proficient wizard." Bowe frowned. "You are also granted two weeks leave." The headmaster moved his hand deliberately from Rizo's shoulder and tapped the side of his own nose before continuing across the courtyard.

"Congratulations, Bowe," Rizo looked up at his taller friend. "You may have gotten yourself into something more than you planned for."

"What's the trip for? Exciting adventure?"

"Come over to my apartment and I'll fill you in."

In the greater privacy of his apartment, Rizo explained what their quest was about. "Are you sure you're interested?" he asked seriously.

"Absolutely," Bowe said. "Not much is really going on here at PIMNA, and from your stories it sounds like traveling with you would be a blast."

"I'll be glad to have you along," Rizo said. "Be ready outside the Beaver Lodge at first light. See you tomorrow. Oh, and you'll have to bring your own horse."

After seeing Bowe out he set about getting himself ready for the trip. He would need some provisions, a water canteen, his bedroll, his bandolier of throwing daggers and the enchanted one he received as a gift from the Daughters of Isis, his spellbook, and the ingredients he would need to cast the spells. He packed some vellum and special compounded ink for writing magical scrolls, and also some regular ink and paper. He wasn't about to let Cordela berate him for not having note-taking supplies again. He took his lock picking tools since they were handy to have. He had been busy studying magic for the past few months and hadn't practiced his other skills. He hoped he would have a chance to exercise them. He considered leaving his firestarters, since he could create magical fire if needed, but since he had limited use of spells, he brought manual backup with him just in case. Stowing everything economically in his backpack and belt pouches, he felt he was ready to go. Time to get some decent sleep. He suspected it would be a while before he would have another chance to enjoy it.

The adventuring party assembled in front of the Beaver Lodge. Cordela and Valory had brought their steeds out from the stables behind the inn. Cordela sat astride Moon, a brown mare with a crescent-shaped white patch on her forehead. Valory rode a pinto stallion that looked a bit big for her, but Rizo knew from experience that she was a capable rider who could handle the mount. Markham's roan gelding looked sturdy enough, while Bowe sat a bit uneasy on his grey mare. Rizo was not too concerned about Bowe though. His gangliness made him a bit awkward in the best of situations, but it didn't reflect on his ultimate effectiveness or ability to take care of himself. Rizo rode a sturdy pony that he had acquired as a gift from Prince Prothar. Iko-Iko rode just in front of him, seemingly as sure-footed atop the pony as anywhere else. Willie sent them off with some fresh biscuits that she must have been up baking in the wee hours. Thus mounted and provisioned, they began their venture at an easy trot. The Palmyra marketplace was just beginning to stir as they made their way northward through town, and they refrained from conversation in the quiet city. As the sun heaved itself upwards into the sky, the road from Palmyra became more crowded. Rizo noted the contrast to the last time he had traversed this road, on the way to confront the evil necromancer Tillingast and his other-worldly servants. Then, the road had been nearly empty except for a few refugees from unnatural wolf attacks. Months later, commerce and travel had returned to normal, and many were taking advantage of the break in weather to head to Palmyra or points beyond to visit or trade. Rizo felt it was a good time to break the silence of their group.

"I'm thinking we'll make our first stop in Ishtar," Rizo announced. "It's about a day's easy ride, and at least we know there is a nice inn to stay at."

"And not too expensive, as I recall," Valory chimed in. "Good thing, too, as I'm down to my last few gold pieces."

"How can you be?" Cordela's tone was incredulous. "The Prince rewarded us all pretty handsomely after the incident with the ogre and the battle."

"Well, I had some ... expenses," Valory cringed a bit.

"I have a way for you to earn some coin," Rizo suggested. "PIMNA is in serious need of feathers from magical beasts, as spell components. They'll pay serious gold for good quality material."

"What sort of beasts?" Valory inquired.

"Pretty typical flying monsters. You know, harpies, rocs, perytons ..."

"What's a peryton?"

"It's a sort of deer or stag with wings," Cordela said. "It is said that some can mimic human speech."

"How can you know about so many beasts and monsters?" Valory turned in her saddle to look at Cordela. "I know you haven't encountered them all."

Cordela's tone dropped a half-octave. "I read about them in the temple library."

"I guess if I spent more time in the library and less shopping, I would know some of this stuff. And I would have more than two gold pieces to rub together." Valory sighed, "But then I wouldn't have quite as many shoes."

Markham cut in, "Valory, no one could spend even half as much time in the library as Cordela does."

"Guilty as charged," Cordela waved her hand over her head. "Can I help it if I'm a bookworm?"

"You don't look like a worm to me," said Bowe, visibly confused.

The group arrived in Ishtar toward evening, which was relatively early at this time of year. The city's streets were still bustling with people doing their last minute errands before the merchants began to close down their stalls for the day. Rizo saw many hand-lettered signs with messages like "Best wishes to the royal couple" and "Good luck Nanamé." Clearly, the people of Ishtar were excited about the upcoming nuptials.

"I'd like to check the market to see what sort of gifts Nanamé's people are thinking about for the wedding," Cordela said.

"Good idea," Rizo agreed, although he was skeptical. "We'll go on and rent some rooms at the inn." Ultimately it was just him and Markham that went on ahead.

"You are from the far south, right?" Rizo asked his dark-skinned traveling companion as they rode toward the great statue of Ishtar that dominated the main square of the city.

"Yes," he replied in his usual smooth tones. "It is known as Tamilnadu. It has a fairly distinct culture, people, and language."

"But not much opportunity for a fighting man, I imagine."

"Not much, but some," Markham gestured toward his chest. "But my personal geas is what brought me northward. I experienced a — not quite a vision, but a presence — that called me to serve Isis."

"Seems like Luxor would be a closer place to serve than Palmyra."

"Well, how I got to Palmyra is an entirely different story."

"I guess it will have to wait," Rizo looked up. "Here we are. The Temple Inn. The stables should be just there. Book five stalls for the mounts. I'll get some rooms for us."

Rizo selected a larger room for the men, and a smaller one for Cordela and Valory. Three gold pieces paid for both rooms. Rizo assumed another would cover the price of the stables.

When Rizo emerged from the inn, Markham was already done in the stables, and Cordela, Valory, and Bowe had arrived. They were all talking to a heavily-armored stranger at the edge of the large square in front of the temple of Ishtar. Rizo joined the little knot of people in the deepening twilight.

"Here he is," Cordela began an introduction. "Rizo, this is Galahad. Apparently, he heard about our battle at the Rabbit Cave. He wants to join us."

"It is a pleasure to finally meet you, Sir Rizo," the man bowed deeply, which still only brought his head to about the same level as Rizo's. "And to be more precise, I wish to pledge my service to you and the Lady Cordela."

"'Sir' Rizo? Just Rizo will do," Rizo coughed slightly. "What sort of service, and for how long?"

"As you wish, Rizo," Galahad straightened up. "I'm afraid the only type of service I am qualified for is that which is delivered via sword and shield. My oath is for a duration of one quest or mission."

"Well, you certainly look qualified to join our quest," Rizo allowed. "How is it that such a formidable warrior as yourself is available?"

"I heard of your leadership of the forces of Order while I was assisting an extended family of pegasus who were attempting to evade predation by a bunch of rocs," Galahad explained. "It was from them that I first heard of the Lady Cordela. Since then I have heard much of your great confrontation with your chaotic foes, and I swore an oath to provide some small service if I am able. While awaiting an opportunity to fulfill my oath, I have taken on some less significant quests, and one that by happenstance brought me to Ishtar at this moment. My chance meeting with the Lady Cordela at the market finally gives me such opportunity, and it will take precedence over my prior commitment. Those on whose behalf I undertook the mission will understand."

"Well, if Cordela approves, I see no reason to keep you from your oath. I hope you have other accommodations in Ishtar, however, as I have only rented enough space for the five of us at this inn."

"That will not be an issue. What time tomorrow do you plan to depart?"

"We will probably not be ready for an hour or so after sunrise," Cordela said. "So you should be here by then."

"Very well." Galahad bowed again. "I look forward to the pleasure of your leadership."

After Galahad had departed, Rizo asked, "Anyone interested in supper?"

There was general agreement, and after they had stabled all their animals they found a nearby restaurant called Manna Innana. The fare was hearty but simple, and two gold pieces fed them all adequately.

Ten

WILLIE had just sat down to mend some bedsheets when the tall stranger came in from the street. She set her needle down and approached him and began her spiel. "Good afternoon, sir. You have missed dinner I'm afraid, but we have tea, warm ale, or pea soup to tide you over until supper. It is not quite shearing season, so you have your choice of rooms. I'm Willie. Welcome to the Beaver Lodge."

The fellow looked around the common room. He had an odd look about him, and Willie wasn't sure if it was how light his hair was, the angle of his nose, or his piercing blue eyes. "My name is Garynd. I'm looking for Cordela Shent," he said finally in a too smooth voice.

It was not unusual for people to arrive at her inn looking for guests by name. It was more unusual for two people in one week to be looking for the same guest. And this fellow already had Willie on edge. She decided that 'neutral hospitable' was an appropriate attitude. "There is no one here by that name," she said with a smile, which was true if somewhat evasive.

"I have heard that she stays here on occasion," the man was still smiling, but Willie wasn't sure that her nonchalance was deceiving him.

"Do you know her?" Willie tried misdirection.

"Not personally," Garynd said. "But her renown has been spreading and has drawn my attention."

"Has it?" Willie could not keep a look of surprise from crossing her face. "Well, perhaps you will find her. Can I get you anything?"

"No, thank you." He turned to leave. "If you do see her,

45

please don't mention that I'm looking for her. I'd like it to be a surprise."

Justfreed was examining a newly arrived grimoire to decide if it were worthy of inclusion in the collection of the library of Odin when the head priest came in trailed by a tall, northern-looking fellow and began speaking without introduction.

"This man is looking for that couple that was in here the other day. You know, the ones that brought *that beast* in here."

Justfreed rolled his eyes. How that man got to be in such a position of authority in the temple of Odin with such a fragile and sensitive disposition was a mystery that Justfreed knew he would not solve if he read every single tome in his library.

"By the wisdom of the All-knowing Father," began the stranger, "I apologize for the interruption."

He certainly seemed like a Northern man, Justfreed thought. He even spoke as a disciple of Odin.

"The ones I am looking for would be a half-elven woman and a halfling man," the fellow continued. "I think they might have been here within the last few days?"

"Yes, I remember them," Justfreed replied. "They were researching magical talismans as I recall."

"Did you happen to overhear where they were going next?"

"They said something about dinner."

"Besides that."

"Yes, they talked about heading northward. I think they mentioned Ismara?"

"Ah, the legendary city of magic. That is very appropriate," he said. "Thank you."

"May the Eye of Odin watch over you, brother," Justfreed gave the traditional farewell before turning back to his book. He wondered for a moment what the stranger wanted with Cordela and her halfling pal, whether it was good or ill, and whether he might have put them in danger by directing this stranger after them. But only for a moment, and soon he was absorbed in the book and had forgotten about the encounter.

Eleven

RIZO was awakened the following morning by a gentle knocking at his door.

He bounced out of bed to find Cordela outside of the door to the room he shared with Bowe and Markham.

"Valory is making pancakes for breakfast. Tell everyone that if they want them hot and fresh that they should come soon."

Rizo nodded to her and gently closed the door. The thought crossed his mind that if he didn't wake the others, he could have all the pancakes for himself. But he considered that he might have to rely on Bowe or Markham that day for his life, and he would be better served if they had a good breakfast. He gave them every opportunity to get moving before he followed Iko-Iko down the hall.

As soon as he entered the room Valory shoved a plate of pancakes into his hand. "Eat up!"

"Thanks." Rizo dug in with gusto. After a few cakes, he deliberately asked, "Do we know if this Galahad fellow is what he claims to be?"

"I think so," said Cordela, finishing up her own plate. "Valory cast a spell to try to ascertain his motives, and he seemed to be on the level. Right Valory?"

"As far as I can tell," the black-haired woman called from the hearth, "his intentions are as pure as a mountain stream."

"Sounds good to me," said Rizo, still chewing. He slid the cat his last pancake and set his empty plate on an armoire. "I'm going to see what's keeping the others."

Rizo found his two roommates packing their last few items. "Good. You're almost ready. I was afraid I'd have to eat all these pancakes myself."

"You make it sound like that wouldn't be your preference to begin with," Markham smirked.

"Why?" Bowe asked as he slung his pack over his shoulder. "Does Valory make decent pancakes?"

"Only the best in Palmyra," Markham replied.

Rizo liked Valory's cakes, but he wasn't sure he agreed with that assessment. After all, she had Willie for competition. "It was more of a threat, really." He snatched up his own pack. "Let's go."

Just as they approached the door to the women's room, Rizo overheard Cordela.

"Well, it's on the way to Ismara, so I say we should head for it. I'll see if Rizo agrees."

"Agrees to what?" he poked just his head into the room and smiled crookedly while raising his eyebrows to convey maximum innocence. Cordela looked forward and blew a stray hair off of her forehead. Satisfied with the level of annoyance he had induced, Rizo brought the rest of himself into the room and allowed Bowe and Markham to follow him in.

"Where our next way point should be," Cordela was rolling a map and stowing it in a scroll case.

"I hope it's breakfast," said Bowe before Rizo could say anything.

"Coming right up!" chanted Valory.

"I see why you and Rizo get along so well," Cordela deadpanned.

"You seem to have already decided without me," Rizo said as soon as Bowe and Markham were busy chewing.

"Have you ever heard of Eridu?"

"Is it a person, place, or thing?"

"Place. It's on Valory's map, and is in the general direction of Ismara. We don't know anything about it, but it seems to be on the way."

Rizo was pretty sure that if Eridu was a town of any significance he would have heard about it. But he didn't know any other places directly to their north. "Sounds like a good plan. How far is it?"

Cordela pinned her hair bun in place with her ever-present crossbow bolt. "We should be able to reach there today."

"I hope they have a decent inn."

She put a fist on her hip. "Did you forget to pack a bedroll?"

"No," he waved off her insult. "It's just that I spent the night before last outdoors and I'm not ready to do it again so soon."

Cordela let it drop and turned to finish packing.

Rizo grabbed his empty plate from the armoire. "Hey Valory, any pancakes left?"

"You'll have to wrestle your cat for them," a little laugh accompanied the declaration.

Galahad was already outside waiting for them when they had finally finished breakfast and gotten their horses out of the stable. He sat atop a nearly blindingly white gigantic war horse. The horse was laden with wilderness survival gear, weapons, armor, and at least two barrels of what Rizo hoped was ale. The huge animal seemed to barely notice the load.

Cordela immediately approached him. "Are you ready to ride, sir?"

"Indeed I am, my Lady," he replied, raising his forearm in salute.

"Today we make for Eridu," Cordela continued. "Do you know the way?"

"I have seen a road so marked," Galahad's clear voice carried easily over the morning bustle of the temple square, and Rizo could imagine the man in command of a battlefield. "But I have never traveled it. I would not swear that it led anywhere."

"We won't hold you responsible for that," Rizo thought he heard Cordela stifle a giggle. He wasn't sure what was funny about a road that might lead nowhere. "Lead on," she instructed the knight.

Galahad seemed to have no problem navigating the streets of Ishtar. A few turns that kept to major thoroughfares brought them to a road that led northeastward out of the city. Once clear of the city traffic, they could ride three or four abreast and carry on conversation, which included narratives on what people had done during the fight against Chaos.

For several leagues there was constant if thin traffic on the roadway. They even saw official patrols from Ishtar and Samarkand, establishing a presence and maintaining order. Travelers appeared to have business in or originate from various villages along the way.

However, the population on the route eventually dwindled, and they saw fewer and fewer fellow travelers. Eventually they passed what must have been the last village served by the road, and they were alone on the highway. Soon beyond that they noticed a marked decrease in the level of maintenance of the roadbed, and their pace of travel slowed as they had to look harder for the markers that indicated whether they were even on the road. They also needed to slow so that their horses could find sure footing in the overgrown gravel. Late in the day they passed the ruin of a stone wall and gatehouse, and they realized that they had arrived in what must have once been the glorious city of Eridu. A few stone slabs indicated the sites of what were probably once fine manors.

"It looks like we're a hundred years too late," Cordela said.

"Boo," Rizo grumped. "No inn."

The only feature of long lost Eridu that still seemed to be somewhat standing was a tower some 40 or 50 feet high, and perhaps a little more than that across at its base. It seemed to have a square cross section with rounded corners, although whether the rounded corners were designed that way or worn such by wind and weather was impossible to say. Since it was the only landmark visible, they headed for it. As they approached they could see that there were two additional sections of the tower that had fallen nearby, brought down by warfare, banditry, or nature.

"That looks like a doorway in the base of the tower," Rizo hoped that maybe they could still spend the night under some sort of shelter. "Let's check it out."

"Not so fast," Cordela cautioned. "Someone might already be using that abandoned building."

"Not so abandoned, in that case," Rizo chided. "We'll have to check it out carefully."

The group left their horses to graze nearby, and arming themselves against potential resistance they entered the base of the tower.

A deep and throaty but feminine voice emanated from the deep shadows. "Who dares invade the sanctum of Arnesher the Great?"

"It is I, Cordela Shent, renowned throughout the world." Rizo slapped his forehead. One knight in Ishtar had heard of her, and suddenly she is "world renown."

"Never heard of you," replied Arnesher. "Are you tasty?"

"Um," was the only response from Cordela.

Rizo decided to help her out. "She'll certainly leave a bitter taste in your mouth." Whoever or whatever Arnesher the

Great was, she sounded big enough to eat one of them.

"What is it?" asked Valory, tight-lipped with concern. "I can't make it out."

"Well, unless all of the Egyptian and Greek legends I've read are mistaken," Cordela found her voice again, "that is a sphinx."

Naturally, Cordela had no problem seeing in the dim light. But that didn't help the rest of the group. Bowe tried casting a spell that would provide some illumination, but the sphinx somehow countered it with a spell of her own. "Not so fast, human. I'll decide whether I allow you to gaze upon my beauty." Rizo was impressed with the power of Arnesher's magic, but skeptical that she was all that beautiful.

"Really, you've never heard of me?" Cordela did not seem ready to drop that subject just yet. "The hero of the Battle of Kandahar? Victor at the Rabbit Cave? Savior of the entire world?"

"All very impressive, I'm sure. If you are concerned with puny human goings on. But I see that you are an Elf. Surely you have a much longer view? Unless, of course, living among these short-lived beings has constricted your perceptions?"

"My view encompasses all living things, be they great or small. My concern is for the enhancement of order, providing a place for all things."

Rizo wasn't sure that Cordela was winning this exchange, or even keeping up her side of it. But he knew he didn't like sitting in the dark, vulnerable to this sphinx or whatever allies she might have lurking in the dark. So while Cordela was keeping her occupied he gave old-fashioned stealth a try. The sphinx undoubtedly had as good or better low light vision as Cordela, so he used some nearby rocks for cover and crept around to the side of where he thought Arnesher's voice was coming from.

"You have intrigued me, Cordela Elf-woman. I have decided that I shall not make you my next meal."

Someone exhaled. Valory, maybe?

"But," the sphinx continued, "Your halfling friend trying to sneak around behind me looks like a very tasty morsel indeed, even if he is barely a mouthful."

Rizo froze as the chamber was suddenly illuminated by light that emanated from somewhere above the enormous creature. He could now clearly see her golden fur and her feathered wings that blended with the gold of her body and gradually faded to white at the edges. Ivory fangs glistened in her incongruously human-looking mouth. Blonde hair flowed down her back and neck, barely revealing her cat-like ears. And he was much too close to the fangs for his own comfort.

"I have read that sphinxes are very fond of riddles," Cordela spoke up, "and halflings are famous for being expert riddlers."

"That's such a stereotype," Rizo complained.

"Hmmm," mused Arnesher. "Nevertheless, I demand a riddle that can befuddle my enormous intellect, or else you — and all of your friends — shall be dinner."

"Great job, Cordela." The common halfling reputation was started by a couple of performers and didn't apply to most of his folk. He really didn't know any riddles. "What happens if I don't live up to the stereotype?"

"You'll be surprised at how the threat of being dinner can focus the mind," Cordela said, not quite encouragingly.

"Fine," Rizo planted one foot on a stone and clasped his hands together behind his back. This could go amazingly, or horribly, he thought. To gain some time and some confidence he made a show of screwing up his eyes as if deep in thought, while he waited for something superbly clever to occur to him. Nothing did. Arnesher licked her extended claws, one by one. Still nothing. Cordela's eyes began to widen and her breath quickened. Rizo cleared his mind and went with the first thing that came into it. "Okay. Here is my riddle to you, Arnesher the Great." He put one hand on his knee. "What has the body of a lioness, the wings of an eagle, and the face of a woman?"

Cordela buried her face in her hands, shaking her head. "Ugh," she muttered under her breath.

"Sounds hideous," said the sphinx.

Cordela's head snapped up. "What?"

Arnesher spoke again. "I know of no creature that matches that description," she intoned.

"Then my riddle has confounded you." In truth, of the two it was Cordela that looked more confounded. "As you agreed, you must spare all of us," Rizo smiled. Sometimes his plans worked so well even he was amazed.

"You have GOT to be kidding me!" Cordela's ears were twitching slightly.

"This was fun," Rizo stood back from the rock. "Perhaps we'll play again sometime. Now, though, I think we ought to be going."

Cordela's jaw hung slightly open and her hand, palm upward, waved aimlessly.

"Leaving so soon?" said Arnesher. "I was just getting to know you." She scratched an ear with a gigantic paw. "You may go. But first, I demand to know what brought you here to trespass on my domain."

"Well," Rizo considered offering a less truthful tale, but quickly settled on a mostly accurate one. "We are on our way to Ismara in the north."

"What business have you there?"

"We wish to learn secrets from the monks there. There is a problem, however." Rizo tried to sound plaintive. "We don't know exactly how to get there. That is the main reason we stumbled into here and interrupted your privacy. We're awfully sorry about that."

"How interesting. Monks certainly hold many secrets. They also make a decent snack," the sphinx giggled and licked her lips. "But it just so happens that I may be able to guide you toward Ismara."

"That would be most helpful." Rizo was skeptical that the creature was actually going to be of use, particularly after its riddle-solution failure. But he waited to see what she offered.

"It will, of course, cost you. Perhaps another riddle?"

"I — I will do the riddling this time," Cordela put her hand in front of Rizo.

"As you like," he shrugged. "But I thought I was doing pretty well."

Cordela seemed to be counting to herself. Then she took a deep breath. "Here is my riddle."

> Warehouse for wisdom,
>> Chamber for thought,
>> This thing with gold
>> Cannot be bought.
>> This thing once lost
>> Is what you miss most.
>> Elders and sages
>> About it will boast.

She turned to Rizo with a smug look. "That's a real riddle," she whispered.

"Hmmm. Somewhat clever, I suppose," drolled Arnesher. "At least it rhymes."

"But can you solve it?" Cordela turned back to the sphinx.

"It's Your Mind," she said. "Simple. Easy. Somewhat dull." Cordela gaped.

"Real riddle," Rizo muttered under his breath.

"I guess I can provide a modicum of help in return for that weak effort."

"Weak —" Cordela began, but Rizo cut her off.

"Any assistance will be appreciated, Great One."

"I have a map — or rather, had a map — of the area to the north of here, which includes Ismara," Arnesher sighed. "Unfortunately, it was recently stolen by a clan of bugbears. They also stole a golden bejeweled scepter that I am particularly fond of. If you track down these bugbears and convince them to give you the map, you will advance your goal of successfully navigating to Ismara." A plaintive tone not heard before entered her voice. "If you bring me back my scepter, I would be very well disposed to provide you additional help, including rewarding you from my remaining treasury."

"Where might we find this band of bugbears?" There was always a catch. Still, it was a much better deal than being supper, and they might get valuable guidance on how to find their destination.

"They dwell in an underground lair. The entrance to it is just on the other side of this tower." She pointed with a paw. "However, they do not appreciate riddles as I do, so you will have to find some other way to convince them to yield their pilfered goods."

"Great advice," Cordela's voice had a sarcastic edge. "Anything else?"

"Here. Take this." The great cat claws proffered a small glass vial toward Cordela. "It is poison antidote. It may come in handy."

"May?" Cordela accepted the vial, but Arnesher yielded no more details.

Twelve

THE entrance to the underground dwelling was just about where the sphinx said it would be. Rather than the natural cave-like structure that Cordela was expecting, this appeared to be a well constructed tunnel. The rectangular entrance was framed with sturdy stone columns, and although the relief designs carved into them had been gently smoothed by hundreds of years of weather, the columns themselves were solid.

"The daylight has almost run out," observed Valory. "Are we going to wait until morning to go in there?"

"It looks pretty dark in there," said Rizo. "I don't think it's going to matter what time of day it is."

"Well, what are we going to do with our horses? Is it safe to leave them out here all night?"

"I am not concerned for my mount," Galahad offered. "He is very capable of looking after himself." He untied a small sack from his mount's saddlebags.

"I'm not worried about anyone stealing them," Rizo reassured Valory. "This place is a long way to go for a common horse thief. And I would think that the predators to care about are probably in there where we are going."

"That's comforting."

"We'll make sure they are well fed before we go in," said Cordela.

"As you say, Rizo," Galahad remarked, "it is very dark in there. We're going to need some light."

"Well, Bowe can summon some magic light, can't you?" Rizo

turned to him.

"The sphinx countered my one light spell." The tall wizard shrugged. "I'm out until I can sit down, rest, and study my spell book."

"How about you, Valory?" Rizo turned back to her. "You can sometimes make magical light, right?"

"Sometimes," she replied. "But for this trip I asked for extra healing power, knowing how good you are at getting into trouble. I have an old fashioned oil lamp, though."

"Better keep it handy. Anyone else?

Cordela breathed a heavy sigh. "At least I can make some contribution." She grasped her red stone star-ankh symbol that she always wore at her neck and tapped it against her metal shield. It instantly burst forth with intense light. As she moved the shield, the light shot from it like the beam of a lighthouse.

"Very impressive," Rizo said flatly, reclining against one of the entry pillars.

Better than your stupid riddle, Cordela thought.

"Has anyone wondered," Bowe's voice cracked a bit, "Um, I mean, how did bugbears manage to steal from a sphinx?"

"Yes, I have given that matter some consideration," Galahad paused while tying his sack to his belt. "I feel that we ought to be more concerned about the fortitude of these bugbears."

"My guess is that this sphinx might be a super genius, but lacks sense," Rizo stood away from the column. "Not too difficult to outsmart, even for a bugbear. Let's head in."

Beyond the entryway was an irregularly shaped room that extended perhaps 30 feet into bedrock, sloping sharply downward. About halfway along the right hand wall a door hung slightly ajar. Another awaited them at the far end of the room.

"Someone keeps this place very tidy," Valory observed. "There is no dust or dirt on the floor that would show tracks that we could follow."

"That's a good observation, Valory," Cordela complimented. "Unfortunately, it means finding our targets will be that much harder."

"Well, just look sharp for bugbears," Rizo advised. "Let's see what's through that door at the end."

The heavy door required the efforts of both Markham and Galahad to pull open. As they did, there was a flash of fur as something came darting through the door. Cordela had her flail ready, but could not hit the fast-moving creature. Dodging out of her reach, the beast bit Valory on her leg.

"Ahh! What is it? Get it off!" she cried.

"It appears to be something from the weasel family," Rizo said calmly.

"A very big weasel," Markham added. Cordela had to agree. It was at least four feet long, not including the tail, and about as tall as Rizo.

"It won't let go!" Valory tried swatting it with her mace but couldn't get a good swing because of the awkward angle.

"That's great Valory," said Cordela encouragingly. "As long as it's biting you, it can't go after anyone else."

"But it HURTS," she complained.

"Just try not to move too much. We'll take care of it."

Bowe approached. "I'm going to try to put it to sleep." His incantation was brief, and when he concluded, nothing happened.

"How long is it supposed to take?" Valory gasped.

"It should be instant."

"Let me just hit it!" Cordela swung Tadlusa, her elven flail, and connected hard. With a yelp, it let go of Valory's leg and snarled at Cordela. Galahad's sword brought down the weasel from behind.

Rizo studied the dead animal. "Definitely a giant weasel. You know, this pelt could be worth quite a bit on the market, if we can get it off in one piece."

"Excuse me?" Valory interrupted. "Wounded party member over here. Concern appreciated."

"Just make use of some of that healing magic you prepared," Rizo advised. "I thought I was the one always getting into trouble."

Cordela helped Valory up after she had cast her spell. "Are you all right now?"

"Yes. Now what was Rizo saying about a valuable weasel pelt?"

It took them half an hour to skin the weasel. Galahad demonstrated unexpected expertise, and he and Rizo were able to guide Cordela and Bowe. With the pelt neatly folded, they were ready to resume their hunt for the map thieves.

"Let's see what that weasel was guarding," Cordela shined her shield into the room beyond the open door.

"What do you see?" Valory asked from behind her.

"Nothing. Just a big empty room." She lowered her shield and turned back toward her fellows. She saw Rizo unpacking some paper, pen and ink.

"We had better make a map," he explained. "The last thing we want is to get lost down here.

"Good thinking." Cordela nodded approval. "And I see you learned to pack writing supplies." With at least two rooms, and possibly many more, the map would help them to keep their bearings. Rizo passed through the door and Cordela watched him carefully note the relatively larger size of the new room, as well as the doors in the far and right hand wall.

"What's through that door?" Rizo indicated the far wall.

"Do you want me to open it?" Cordela was the closest to it. "Look what happened the last time."

"You open it," Rizo said. "Galahad and Markham, stand by in case something comes out. Bowe and I will stand back and throw daggers or spells."

When they were all in position, Cordela pushed in the door. Nothing came out. She shined her shield in. "Another empty room. Smaller, but just as empty. And no other exits."

Rizo duly noted that on his map. "This place is crazy. It seems to have no sort of plan or order."

"Almost like the architect just laid it out randomly," agreed Cordela. "We should shove the weasel carcass in that empty room before it starts to attract scavengers."

That done, Rizo suggested they go through door drill #1 again on the other door that led out of the large room. Nothing emerged from that door either.

It opened to a wide hallway that extended to the left and right from the doorway. "Which way first?" Rizo asked, peering first one way then the other. At least he asked.

"Step aside," Cordela brought up her shield and illuminated the hallway to the left, then to the right. To the right the passage continued to the limits of her light. To the left, she could see a stairway descending from where the hallway ended. "I'm guessing that down is where the bugbears are more likely to be hiding. Let's go."

Cordela led the group to the top of the stairway. It was framed by pillars similar to the ones she had examined at the entrance, but the relief work was not weathered. As she took the first step, Rizo grabbed her by the arm and said, "Wait, Cordela. Something doesn't look right to me. Can I borrow your staff?"

Cordela unbound it from her pack. He was in one of his more serious moods — she could tell, because he wasn't trying to annoy her — so she didn't question what he was up to. Rizo prodded the steps with the metal heel of her staff. The first step produced no result. Neither did the second. But the third step shifted slightly as he poked it. A harder poke and there was a grinding noise as every step pivoted to form a completely smooth ramp designed to spill the occupants at the bottom.

"Nice spotting Rizo," Valory said approvingly.

"The seams along the edges of each step gave it away," Rizo explained. "They were well-fitted, but not quite well enough."

"Well, I guess we're not going down there after all," said Cordela. She retrieved her proffered staff from Rizo and bit her lip in disappointment.

"Maybe," Rizo allowed. "But there has to be a mechanism to reset the trap around here somewhere. We just have to find it."

"Okay, everyone look around for a lever or handle or something," Cordela instructed. She examined one of the pillars that framed the stairway. She thought that there might be a discontinuity in the design that was carved in it. "Hey Rizo. What do you make of this?"

"Shine your shield on it," he approached the pillar. "Could be a seam," he ran his hand up and down the stone, eventually settling on the pedestal at the bottom of the pillar. He put gentle pressure on one stone, which levered out a whole section of the pillar. Cordela and Rizo stood looking at a series of pulleys and ratchets that would have made any engineer proud. In the center of it was a glass cylinder that had about an inch of water at the bottom. Rizo scratched his head while staring at it for a while. He stuck his head as far into the cavity as it would fit, looking up and down.

"Can you disable the trap?" Cordela asked.

"Maybe. Most of the mechanism is pretty standard, but I'm trying to figure out what this glass piece is doing here."

"Out of your area of expertise?"

"I don't think so. I might be a little rusty, having spent my time recently studying magic. Hmm. Hey, Valory," he turned to the human woman. "You mentioned a lantern?"

"Yeah, it's right here." A minute of fiddling with the wick and striking the firestarter and it was burning brightly. Cordela still had no idea what Rizo had in mind. He set the wick to about the longest setting that would still burn steadily, and held the lantern against the glass cylinder in the trap mechanism.

"It doesn't seem to be doing anything," Cordela remarked.

"Patience," counseled Rizo.

After some time, the heat of the lamp caused water in the cylinder to evaporate. As it did, the float in the cylinder dropped and triggered a set of pulleys with counterweights. They activated with some grinding noise.

"See if the stair trap has reset," said Rizo.

Cordela saw that the steps had rotated back into their original position. "Nice job Rizo."

Bowe also came forward to congratulate Rizo. "The noise startled the spells out of me when it started resetting."

"It has an ingenious mechanism that resets when the sun comes up and evaporates a pool of water," Rizo described. "So the trap is always ready to spring again at the start of a new day. By using the lantern to speed the evaporation, we didn't have to wait."

"Okay," Cordela said. "Let's see what this trap here is guarding. Watch that third step!"

They were disappointed when all they found at the bottom of the stairs was another empty room.

"I don't get it," Rizo complained. "Elaborate trap designed to dump intruders down here, and there's nothing here."

"Well, there are a lot of cobwebs," Galahad observed. "Perhaps there used to be spiders here that would attack the victims."

"Aha, cobwebs. I need some as spell ingredients," Rizo began to collect the webbing, joined by Bowe.

Cordela looked all over the room for hidden doors and the like, but came up empty. "There is really nothing here. Get your webs and let's go."

With Rizo and Markham in the lead this time, they ascended the stairs and ventured past the door where they had entered this hallway. Cordela hazarded a peek into the empty room on the other side of it, just to be sure they weren't being followed. The room looked just as empty as it had the first time they had passed through it. Maybe a hundred steps beyond, Rizo stopped at a doorway in the end of the hall, holding up Valory's lantern.

"Problem Rizo?" Cordela asked, trying not to sound annoyed.

"It's just more hallway through the door."

"So?"

"Who puts a door in the middle of a hallway?"

"Perhaps they found the need to seal off parts of it occasionally," Markham speculated.

"This place makes no sense whatsoever," Rizo concluded.

"Let's keep moving," Cordela urged. "We need to find these bugbears."

After another hundred paces the hall ended in a larger circular room. Other than some broken furniture, its only content was a metal banded wooden chest. Cordela bent to open it and found that it was locked.

"Rizo, do your stuff here" she stood making way for him.

He squatted and examined the lock closely. "Hmmm. See here, near the keyhole? There are a whole bunch of pinholes facing the front of the chest."

"It looks kind of like a honeycomb."

"I think it's trapped," he announced. "I'm guessing any attempt at picking the lock will release poison needles, giving the picker a bad day."

"Can you disable the trap?"

He shook his head. "I'm not going to try. As I mentioned, my skills are rusty."

"Well, there's more than one way to get into a locked chest," Cordela said. She brought her flail down on the lid between two metal bands. She barely gave Rizo time to dodge out of her way before she sent wood splinters flying.

She looked inside, pulled out a sturdy canvas bag. "Look! Money!" That would certainly help out Valory.

"We'll count it later," Rizo advised. "Let's find these bugbears."

A curved passageway led out of the round room. Cordela led the way this time.

"More webs," Markham noted.

"Maybe we should find another way," Galahad sounded nervous.

"Bowe and I have had our run-ins with spiders," Rizo tried to assure him. "Should be no problem, right Bowe?"

"Well, as you recall, our last encounter didn't end quite as well for one of us," Bowe reminded him.

Cordela agreed. "I was the one who had to patch him up after that incident."

Rizo smiled. "He looks okay to me."

"Umm," Bowe was pointing farther along the passageway.

"So, that's a really big spider," Cordela added.

Its legs nearly straddled the entire width of the corridor. Eight eyes reflected the light from Cordela's shield redly. Markham, Cordela, and Valory prepared to meet the approaching threat. Galahad stood frozen in place. Cordela saw Rizo trying his best to meld into the wall.

"Keep back. I don't want you to end up a spider snack," he said, shooing Iko-Iko off of his shoulder and back up the corridor. The black cat complained, but darted away.

Markham slashed at the gigantic spider with his sword, but it was not deterred. "Watch those pincers!" Cordela advised the soldier to avoid the beast's primary weapons. Valory was knocked over by a hairy foreleg. Rizo sprinted through the space it left behind while Cordela moved to defend her fallen friend. Dagger drawn, Rizo lunged at the unarmored abdomen. Vital fluids gushed from the deep gash.

Bowe had been hanging back waiting for his opportunity to do something. As the spider turned to face Rizo's attack, he slipped between Markham and Cordela chanting the words of a spell. Bowe grabbed the nearest spider leg, sending sparks flying from his hand. The spider recoiled immediately. Markham was able to use his sword more effectively then, and the monstrous arachnid did not resist much longer.

"Are you all right?" Markham helped Valory back to her feet.

"Thanks. I guess that thing was pretty hungry."

"Well, it must have found plenty to eat down here to grow that big," Cordela mused. "Maybe it had some deal worked out with the bugbears?"

Thirteen

THEY had been exploring the underground complex for hours. They still saw no signs whatsoever of the bugbears they were after. They had run into a giant weasel, a gigantic spider, two very large staghorn beetles, and a puddle of semi-sentient jelly that dissolved one of Rizo's sandals. He was beginning to think that the sphinx had sent them down here just to get rid of them, and there were actually no bugbears and no map.

"Well, decision time," called out Cordela. They had arrived at a place where the corridor branched. Both directions looked equally promising to Rizo, which is to say not promising at all. No one seemed very keen to address Cordela's implied question. Rizo didn't have any good advice to offer either. He himself had thought many times in the past that he would love to have some unobtrusive way to sneak around, scout, and gather intelligence. He was just rehearsing that same desire to himself when he suddenly realized that he had exactly what he had been wanting, dozing peacefully and softly purring on his shoulder.

"We should have Iko-Iko scout out the passageways ahead," he said. At the mention of his name, the cat's head snapped up.

"Sure," Cordela agreed. "Make sure he knows not to put himself in any danger."

"What do you say, Iko-Iko? Are you up for a little reconnoitering?" The cat jumped down and made his way toward the branch on the left, then looked back over his shoulder. "Sure, you can do that one first. Fine."

Iko-Iko was gone for several minutes, during which time everyone just sat down to rest or had a drink. When he returned, Cordela asked, "How do we find out what he saw?

He doesn't talk." She scratched her head. "At least, I've never heard him talk."

"He gives me impressions," said Rizo. "Images, sensory intuitions, or emotional notes." He bent down to stroke the cat's back. "What did you see that way?" he asked Iko-Iko. After a moment, he said to the others, "It seems like he didn't see much that way. I'm going to have him try the other branch." With a motion, he saw Iko-Iko off down the other passageway.

"You know, I haven't minded traveling with Iko-Iko," said Cordela. "But if he actually proves useful I may need to raise my opinion of you."

Ordinarily, Rizo would respond to such a jibe. But in this moment he was more concerned about Iko-Iko. They really hadn't been apart from one another since he had done the summoning ritual. He wasn't sure if Iko-Iko could take care of himself if he met more of what they had already run into in this complex. He breathed a sigh of relief as the cat's black body slid back into view. This time, he got a distinct impression of a source of light, and something with a strong scent.

"Iko-Iko detected something down that passageway. It smells bugbeary," he announced.

"Great job, Iko-Iko," Cordela said, saluting the animal. To everyone else, "You heard the cat. Bugbears thataway. Weapons ready. I don't expect them to be too friendly."

Galahad asked Cordela, "For one who respects all living things, you certainly seem to be doing a lot of killing."

"Well, if it's a choice between respect and not being eaten, I tend to choose not being eaten," Cordela responded. Then, more thoughtfully, "For beings that can understand, I try to make their choices clear when I can. Particularly when I know I have the weight of force on my hand. I hope you are not regretting your oath of service."

"Not at all. Your philosophy mirrors my own in many ways. I also accept the necessity of killing sometimes. After all, mortality is a fact of life that we all must accept."

Rizo wasn't sure he was ready to accept the necessity of mortality just yet, but he certainly had no qualms about inducing it in others, if they deserved it. But before he could give his opinions on the matter, they had to curtail their discussion, as they had reached a door that emanated dim light from beyond it. They wordlessly agreed that Markham and Galahad would enter first, followed by Cordela and Valory. Hoping for surprise, they kicked in the door and burst into the room. The inhabitants were not surprised. Rizo saw five very large and hairy bipeds, each one as broad as two halflings, as tall as five or six, and heavily armored. They held their heavy looking spiked clubs at the ready. Their heads looked something like dogs, but with rounded ears protruding from their heads. Although he had never met one, these things fit all the descriptions of bugbears he had ever heard.

"Return what you stole and no one needs to suffer," Cordela was saying. Rizo had heard her deliver more commanding speeches in the past. It probably wouldn't have mattered. These bugbears didn't look like they were in any mood to negotiate.

The largest one replied in a gruff voice, "Why should we do that when we can just kill you and take more of your stuff?" Rizo wondered if the bugbear had any voice that was not gruff. At any rate, Cordela had made the offer, and it had been declined. It was more than they would have gotten from Rizo. It was five on five, but Bowe was less than useful in hand-to-hand combat, so Rizo looked for some way to even things out. The webbing he could conjure might slow one or two of them down for a second, but if they were as strong as they looked it wouldn't hold for long. His best bet, as usual, was probably to fire some magical force missiles at the enemy, but he thought these guys looked tough enough to stand up to that. Instead, he ran up behind Markham and whispered, "Don't be alarmed," before casting a spell that caused him to double in size.

"Whoa," he said. "Now who's intimidating?"

There was no time for any other remarks before the two groups began to trade blows. The magically enlarged Markham was seen as the biggest threat by the bugbears, so two of them teamed up on him. He was hard pressed to deflect and dodge their spiked clubs, but it allowed Cordela and Valory to coordinate their attacks on the one that had spoken up before. They appeared to be handling him just fine. Galahad faced off against one of the beastly fighters. That left one for him and Bowe to try to keep busy.

Bowe tried his sleep incantation again, with about as much effect as he had against the weasel. Rizo used a spell that caused fire to shoot from his fingers, which had only slightly more impact. He motioned for Iko-Iko to get safely out of the way, and drew his dagger. "I guess we'll do this the old fashioned way."

What he really wanted was for Bowe to stage a more frontal attack, so that he could take the bugbear from behind and potentially do a lot more damage. However, his hardened leather vest was not going to provide much protection from those spiked clubs, and Bowe's wizard robes offered even less. So instead Rizo was just going to have to rely on his ability to duck. He was doing pretty good at making the monster miss while making him pay for even trying, but eventually the bugbear got in a lucky swing that knocked the wind out of Rizo and sent him flying. The foe was about to follow up with what might be a killing blow when Bowe distracted it with a handful of magical projectiles that darted from his fingers and homed in on his target. The bugbear recoiled, which gave Rizo time to roll away from the club as it came swinging down towards him. He could tell that he was bleeding from a few puncture wounds, but not too badly. He tried to be a bit more careful for a time, but that just made him miss more. Eventually he was forced to take more chances, and that brought him back within range of the spikes. The club whizzed past, fingerbreadths from his head. Rizo avoided the attack, but the effort left him off balance. The bugbear recovered before he did, and brought the menacing club on a return arc, directly at Rizo's temple. He tried to duck, but he could tell he wasn't going to be fast enough this time. This was going to hurt. With a clang, the spikes smashed into Galahad's shield. He had dispatched his bugbear opponent, sustaining a few dents in his armor, and had arrived to help Rizo and Bowe.

Rizo acrobatically adjusted his ducking maneuver into a tuck and roll, ending behind the bugbear. With Galahad making the frontal assault, Rizo could take his time exercising his particular ability to find the most lethal spots on an enemy in which to place his dagger. The bugbear succumbed quickly.

With their enemy down, Rizo and Galahad moved to assist Markham, who despite his expanded volume was still just one sword against two clubs, and was having trouble. Again, Galahad engaged and Rizo looked for opportunities to deliver unexpected and damaging blows. Soon, Cordela and Valory were also available, and the remaining foes did not stand long.

"Is everyone okay?" Cordela asked as soon as the fighting was over.

"I took a hit, but it looks like Markham got the worst of it, him being such a big target," quipped Rizo. "Hey now!" he called, and Iko-Iko appeared out of some concealing shadows.

"I'll help Markham," Valory stepped to him. "It would be easier if he were normal size?"

Rizo ended his magical effect with a thought. "Better?"

"I kind of liked being big," Markham said.

"It would have worn off anyway in a few minutes," Rizo informed him.

"I like you your regular size," added Valory as she began to examine his wounds and apply healing magic where necessary.

Cordela threw a spell on Rizo's punctures and said, "Now to find that map. Let's look around."

A thorough search of the room the bugbears recently

inhabited turned up some unappetizing food, armor in need of repair, a dull knife, and a few copper pieces. "If they have anything of value, they've hidden it very well," Valory complained.

"These tunnels seem to have plenty of hidden compartments, like the one that held the trap mechanism," Rizo offered. "Look for unusual seams or wear on the walls."

Cordela spotted the telltale signs of a hidden door first. "Right on, Rizo," she called. "I can see that the stonework here doesn't quite match up. How to get it open, though?" She shoved first one side and then the other, but it didn't budge.

"Keep in mind that the bugbears were big. There might be a release higher up on the wall." Rizo scanned the wall but didn't see anything. "Shine your shield over there, Cordela."

With the extra light Rizo was able to discern a bit of unusual wear on a cornice near the high ceiling. "There, see?" he pointed.

"Right," said Cordela. "Hey Markham, give me a boost up there." Just a tap on the release was sufficient to trigger the counterweighted door to swing open smoothly.

Valory was the first to peek inside. "Yep, this is where they stashed their stuff, all right," she called from within the doorway.

In addition to the map they were seeking and a very gaudy scepter, the bugbear stash also included a gold medallion stamped with the profile of a long dead ruler, some silver pins and brooches embedded with emeralds, and a few bags of gold coins. The map was an artistically drawn view of the territories to the north, including Ismara. "So, perhaps it is not so mythical after all," remarked Rizo.

"Assuming it is accurate," Cordela concluded, "it looks to have enough detail to help us find our way there."

Fourteen

"WELL, if it isn't our adorable little party of adventurers," Arnesher announced laconically. "Had enough of the rats and spiders already?"

"Oh, we got your scepter for you, Miss Sphinx," Rizo retorted. "We didn't even need your poison antidote, thank you very much."

"You can keep it," she purred. "Humans can be so fragile." She rose to a seated position from where she was lounging. "But you recovered my scepter? Color me surprised but pleased. Best news I've heard in months." She yawned resignedly, "I suppose you'll want some token in exchange for it."

"Not at all," Cordela held the atrocious piece of bric-a-brac up toward the leonine monster. "We'll hang on to the map which looks very useful. That's exchange enough."

"But," Rizo continued, "we are definitely interested in discussing some other exchanges."

"Indeed?" The sphinx's eyes widened as she accepted the proffered scepter. "What did you have in mind?"

They had discussed on the way out of the underground complex what to do with all the extra treasure they had acquired while searching for the map. Rizo had suggested that they might not want to carry thousands of pounds of metal coins all the way to Ismara with them, and that the sphinx might have useful or at least more portable items that she might be willing to trade for the currency. The others quickly agreed, except for Valory who wanted to earmark some of the gold for a royal wedding gift.

To their relief, the horses had been near where the party had left them. Moon didn't seem to mind carrying her share of the load of treasure the short distance back to the sphinx's lair.

"Hmmm," the sphinx looked askance at the bags and bags of money. "Coins are useful for trade, and sometimes have historical interest value, but they are kind of boring."

Cordela was ready for this type of response. "How about if I throw in a riddle as well?"

"Will it be better than your last attempt?" Arnesher asked skeptically.

Cordela paused to let the insult pass by and took a deep breath. "Well, it may not be as amazing and inscrutable as this halfling's riddles," Cordela leered, "but I hope you like it."

Walks without feet,
  It carries its home.
  In morning dew
  Through leaves it roams.

"Obscure and rhymed, just as I like them," Arnesher smiled. "Let's see, what walks without feet? A river runs, but does not walk." She scratched a cat-like ear with a claw. "A yard has feet, but doesn't walk. Hmmm. It carries its home. Like a turtle. But turtles definitely have feet. Through leaves it roams. So it must be rather small."

She smiled broadly. "It must be a snail. She has no feet, carries her home on her back, and is usually small — although I have seen some pretty big ones too."

"Correct," Cordela yielded, "but at least you had to think a bit."

"Yes. That will do." Arnesher turned and retreated to an adjoining room. She returned with a chest and a blanket which she rolled out on the floor in front of Cordela. She placed a few things on the blanket. "Now we negotiate."

In the end they traded most of the currency for a magic ring that could turn its wearer invisible, and a wand that produced magical force missiles of the same type that Rizo and Bowe could summon on command. Arnesher claimed that the wand held forty charges. And Valory insisted on passing up some potentially useful but unidentified potions in favor of a gold and ruby bracelet, "For Princess Nanamé."

They re-emerged from the sphinx's lair to a rising sun. It had been quite a long night, and the group was in need of rest. They took shelter in one of the collapsed pieces of the tower. A few hours of rest was enough to refresh them.

Rizo was already up and studying his spellbook when Cordela roused herself. Bowe got up shortly after and joined him.

Later, when the others had also awakened, Cordela announced, "I'm going to try to get to the top of the part of the tower that's still standing."

"What for?" asked a still groggy Valory.

"I want to see if I can situate where we are now on this view-map."

"Are you sure you should go alone?" asked Valory.

"I will accompany the Lady Cordela," Galahad volunteered.

Rizo looked up from his spellbook. "Mind if I get some of your ale?"

"Help yourself."

As Cordela exited their campsite with Galahad, she heard Markham say, "I appreciate the care you showed tending my injuries after the fight..."

The second floor was easily accessible by scrambling up a collapsed section of wall. The collapse had also taken out part of the stairway up to level three, so that part of the climb was more arduous. Galahad and Cordela were able to belay each other with ropes and anchors, and she was thankful that she hadn't tried taking the climb on solo. The stairways up to the next few levels were more intact, and the going was easier after that. At the top, a portion of the northern wall was missing, still attached to the fallen piece some yards away, and this gave Cordela and Galahad a convenient vantage point for surveying the landscape. Cordela surmised that the dark green shadow to the east was probably the forest named on the map. To the west, the River should have been a thin ribbon, but she wasn't sure she could make it out in the distance among the slowly undulating hills. There were a few landmarks on the map that were more directly in line with Ismara, but she couldn't see any of those from the tower top. A large mountain just behind Ismara was labeled "Mt. Ismaros," but the mountains were still too far away to see. She and Galahad agreed that it seemed best to follow the forest northward, as where it ended was just southeast of Ismara.

Rather than being worn out by the climb, Cordela was invigorated. She returned to their camp in the shadow of the ruined tower section ready to get moving. Rizo and Bowe were there, having finished their spell preparation. But Valory and Markham were nowhere to be seen.

"Have you two eaten?" she inquired, digging some hard rations out of her pack.

"Yes, we're about ready to pack up," Rizo answered. "Have you figured out where we're going?"

"There's a forest a few leagues to the northeast of here. It goes all the way to the vicinity of Ismara. If we follow it, we should have no problem finding our way."

"Great," Rizo seemed unnaturally impressed. "Now we just need to wait for, or go out and round up, the other two."

"I noticed they were missing," Cordela said between munches. "Any idea where they went?"

Bowe and Rizo looked at each other and shrugged in unison.

"Well, let's pack up the horses while we're waiting." Cordela stood and brushed some crumbs off herself. The four of them broke camp in just a few minutes. They carried their materiel outside to secure it to their mounts and encountered Valory and Markham already there. They were standing close to one another. When Markham saw the others he took a step back and stammered, "y-your stallion should canter much more easily with the stone removed."

"Yes," Valory's head was bowed. "Thank you for your, ah, help with that."

"Are you two ready to move on?" Cordela asked, looking mostly at Valory. She nodded mutely.

Fifteen

WILLIE didn't see Cordela or Rizo again for nearly three weeks. When Cordela strolled in wearing a big smile, the innkeeper had a feeling she was in for an epic of a story.

"Welcome back to the Beaver Lodge," she resorted to her typical greeting by habit. Then adopted a more conspiratorial tone. "You look awfully excited. I can't wait to hear what you've been up to."

"You know the drill, Willie," Cordela winked at her. "No adventure tales without dinner!"

"You're a tough customer, but a deal's a deal," Willie was mock-serious for just a second. "Have a seat, dinner will be right out."

Willie placed a dish of noodles and steamed early spring vegetables before Cordela, then sat across from her. "Spill, girl. I want to know everything."

Cordela got through the barest beginning of her tale before her plate was empty. Willie got up to fetch her more. "Amazing! A real sphinx. Just imagine! And just so you know, I think your riddles were very clever."

Two men entered the inn then, and Willie had to leave Cordela's dish temporarily unfilled to go greet them. "Hello. Welcome to the Beaver Lodge Inn, the finest lodgings in Palmyra. I'm Willie. How can I serve you?"

"Um," said the shorter of the two men, who had a wicked widow's peak and had jewelry in his ears. "We were told to come here for an audition?"

"They're here for me," Cordela came from her table to stand by Willie. "I forgot to ask you — is it okay if I use the Beaver

79

Lodge to audition some musical entertainers?"

"Sure. The music might bring in some extra guests. No problem."

"Thanks Willie." She turned to the musicians. "Just grab a couple of chairs if you need them, otherwise you can set up here in the front. I'll just need to hear a couple of songs."

"I guess I'll have to wait to hear the rest of your story?"

"You'll get it. Don't worry!"

Sixteen

THE Efarlon Forest initially was bright, cheerful, and open, and they rode gradually northward as small creatures fled their approach and birds occasionally screamed at them from above. After some hours the undergrowth became nearly impassable and they had to dismount. Shortly thereafter the trees crowded in as well, and Galahad and Markham had to hack a path ahead for the group. Their pace slowed again.

In a particularly dense area, Markham and Galahad needed to both focus on one particular tree and they were stopped mid-strike as a voice boomed out, "Invaders! What are you doing to my forest!"

Something very large moved toward them. They might have mistaken it for another tree if it had stayed still and quiet. Cordela thought it might be foolish to confront the giant creature, but stepped forward to do so anyway.

Galahad beat her to it. "We wish to pass through. We did not intend to inflict permanent damage, only create enough of a path for us and our mounts."

"You are not welcome with your metal implements. The way forward is even thicker, and you would just slash it for your convenience." The tree-like creature raised a bough and shook it over their heads. "I should crush you now!"

Cordela interceded with the woody thing. "We did not mean to do harm. I am Cordela Shent, who saved the world from chaos."

"I know nothing of your two-legged activities."

How did no one know about her deeds? She was going to have to find an enterprising bard or two to publicize her great achievement. Meanwhile, this tree creature seemed capable of carrying through on its threat, so she needed to try to placate it. "You know, I have healing magic. I can restore the health of anything we damaged — "

"Leave this forest," the thing cut her off. "Now."

"Fine," Cordela huffed. She looked around. "I don't suppose there is a shorter way out than back the way we came? Well, never mind. I guess we can just hack our way out. How about that direction?" She pointed to the left. "Or maybe that way is shorter?" She pointed the other way.

"You may cease waving your puny branches side to side like that," the tree monster said. "There is what you call a 'road' nearby, a gash right through the heart of the forest cut by men long ago. I will take you there. Put away your tools and follow."

As it led them through the woods, they didn't appear to be less dense, neither did any of the growth seem to move out of their way. But there was always plenty of space for them to move forward. If they had been able to find a way this easily, not only would they have made a lot more headway through the forest, they also would not have attracted the creature's attention. She wondered if perhaps there was some magic she could learn to help her find her way through forests in the future. She would have to have a chat with Isis about that. Within an hour, they emerged onto a well-marked roadway of hard-packed chalk. It ran east-west, but the creature seemed to want them to go west.

"That way is the shortest out of my domain. Go."

"Thank you," Cordela bowed slightly. "Nice to, um, meet you? And you can tell all of your tree friends that you met the amazing Cordela Shent in person."

The tree did not respond. It watched them as they mounted and rode until they lost sight of it in the distance behind them. They made sure to stick to the road even afterward. Less than two hours later they emerged from the forest. The afternoon sun was ahead to their left, casting their shadows back towards the woods.

"Which way now?" Valory asked the question that had been on all their minds.

Cordela consulted the sphinx's map for a minute. "This road we're on should be this one right here," she tapped the parchment with her finger. "There should be a place called 'Loerhold' ahead of us on the right."

"I am not familiar with that name," Galahad offered.

"Me either," said Rizo. "But it sounds fine."

Cordela rolled her eyes and then the map. "Straight ahead, then." She nickered to Moon and was off, with the rest of her group in tow.

The daylight was failing when they approached a stone castle about where the map indicated Loerhold ought to be. Rizo dismounted from his pony.

"What are you up to, Rizo?" Cordela looked askance at him.

"I want to check this place out. We're probably going to be stuck here overnight, and I want to know what I'm getting myself into."

"If you insist," Cordela shook her slightly tilted head. "I've found that you can also learn a lot by knocking at the front door."

"Take my mount with you. I'll catch up later one way or the other." He winked. "Even if it's just to save all your skins." He slipped away into the gloaming.

"Or maybe we'll visit you in their prison," Cordela told the evening breeze. Valory chuckled.

They rode ahead. Although Cordela's shield had not been as noticeable during the day, it was still glowing brightly and helped to illuminate the carved stone sign that let them know that they had indeed arrived at Loerhold. Beyond the sign a short driveway led to a gate in the castle wall. The sign, the gateway, and what she could see of the castle were constructed of Pistros Stone. Loerhold seemed very sturdy and built for defense. A narrow moat between the gate and the end of the driveway was spanned by a wooden bridge that could be drawn up by the metal chains affixed to the rounded guard towers adjacent to the gate. An iron portcullis descended across the opening and fitted into holes in the stonework floor. Heavy iron-clad wooden doors beyond could also be closed against attack, but they were slid partially open to reveal a well-tended courtyard beyond. An armored guard with a lit lantern awaited them at the opening. He called to them from inside the portcullis, squinting at Cordela's beaming shield.

"Good evening. What brings you to Loerhold so late in the day?" His voice was somewhat gravelly and gruff but not hostile. His features were distinctly elven.

"We were traveling through the forest nearby, but one of the residents there insisted that we leave," Cordela lowered her shield a bit so it wasn't shining directly into the guard's face. "We followed the road here. Can you house us for a night? We will be on our way again in the morning."

The elven guard laughed. "Graybark can be rather cranky with uninvited guests." He held his lantern up to illuminate the strangers a little better. "Where are you going that you thought traversing the forest was a good idea?"

"Our destination is Ismara. Have you heard of it?"

"Oh, yes," the guard replied. "I guess the forest goes nearly there. You are fortunate that we happen to have a vacant guest house. I'll need your names to announce you before the Lord of Loerhold."

Cordela provided everyone's name. The guard showed no recognition when she mentioned her own name — maybe it was time to take spreading her legend into her own hands. She omitted Rizo for the time being, in case he wanted to make his own entrance later.

"Wait here," the guard instructed.

Seventeen

THE eastern side of the castle was extremely dark, shadowed as it was from the last rays of daylight in the western skies. Perfect for Rizo to approach unseen and plot his best ascent route up the castle wall. He was still without sandals since encountering the ooze under Eridu, so any of a number of paths would do. There were occasional passes by guards atop the wall, so he chose the route least likely to be spotted. He began his climb as soon as the last guard walked back toward the front gate. If they stuck to their patterns it would be at least five minutes before he or another guard would be back. More than long enough for him to cover the thirty foot vertical distance. Iko-Iko clung tightly to him during the climb, but as soon as he had dropped onto the narrow walkway atop the wall his familiar hopped to the stone and headed to the right. A flyover from the main part of the castle joined with the walltop there. Rizo could see that architecturally the flyover was a support buttress adding structural rigidity to the outer wall, but it also served as a functional foot path between the outer wall defense and the castle proper. It was a good idea for defense, but it also left the castle vulnerable to invasion along the same path. Rizo, at Iko-Iko's suggestion, was about to take advantage of that very vulnerability.

The high parapet on the outside was replaced by a low retaining wall on the flyover, and Rizo had to keep low to be sure he was hidden from any eyes elsewhere on the wall tops. There seemed to be something of interest going on at the front gate, and Rizo hoped it was Cordela making a nuisance of herself. In any case, it was distracting all of the wall-top guards, to Rizo's benefit. Iko-Iko bounded ahead to where the flyover met the castle proper. When Rizo arrived, he saw that it joined a balcony that appeared to wrap around the entire upper floor of the castle. He got there just in time to see his black cat disappear into an open window that fronted on the balcony. He took a minute to be sure that the window was not being watched from outside, and by then Iko-Iko's head was protruding from the opening, wondering what was taking him so long. Rizo wasn't yet sure how much he could trust the cat's instincts. He might be getting himself into a world of trouble. Then again, he had already been in several worlds of trouble in his life, and things had worked out okay. He climbed through the window and found himself in a small bedroom. The room was very dark, but he still found that he could see reasonably well. His vision seemed to begin to deteriorate whenever Iko-Iko moved farther away. "Hey now," he whispered softly to bring the cat back close to him. He picked the cat up and examined the room. It was decorated as a child's room, but it seemed unused. Judging from the state of the neatly arranged toys, it had actually never been used by any child. It was, however, kept quite clean, and Rizo saw no dust at all on the floor or other surfaces. Perhaps the lady of the manor was expecting? Rizo tried the door, which was unlocked. It led to a walkway with a railing on the left side and a solid wall on the right. The midsection of the walkway was a wider landing or balcony with steps leading downward from either side. Light came from below the balcony. Beyond the far stairway was a door identical to the one Rizo stood near. He set down Iko-Iko and prepared to step through the door when the feline darted back into the dark bedroom. Rizo quietly closed the door, leaving a crack through which to observe the walkway. Soon a woman dressed in rough overalls came up the far stairs with a lantern and a bucket with a narrow spout. She filled oil reservoirs in sconces along the solid wall to his right, trimmed the wicks, and lit them from her lantern with a wire-stiffened piece of wick. She disappeared down a hallway, about halfway between Rizo's vantage point and the opposite door. Light began to emerge as she lit more lanterns. She soon emerged and finished her task by kindling the wall sconce just outside Rizo's hiding place. Then she headed back down the near stairway and Iko-Iko meowed the all-clear.

There were many fewer shadows on the landing now that the wall sconces burned brightly, and Rizo hugged the solid wall near the floor to avoid being seen by anyone at the bottom of the stairs. If only he had a way to hide without nearby shadows to do it in. He really needed something that would make him completely invisible. Just like, he finally remembered, ring he had acquired from the sphinx. Now how had the sphinx told him to activate the ring? He just needed to think transparently, or something. He had turned invisible in the sphinx's lair once, so he knew he could do it. He just needed to remember. He closed his eyes, concentrated on the ring in his mind, and meditated on not being seen. When he opened his eyes, he could no longer see the ring, or his hand. Ha. He made his way silently across the landing to where he could look beyond the railing at the grand entry foyer below.

He heard a man call out, "Cordela Shent of Palmyra leads a group of travelers who wish to use the guest house overnight, my lord." Peering through the banisters he saw a heavily armored elf who was speaking to someone below the balcony out of Rizo's sight.

"Paldo, please instruct your staff to prepare the guest house," said another, more distinguished voice.

"As you command," Paldo (Rizo assumed) replied, and he heard footsteps exit the room.

"Do they seem honest?" said the distinguished voice.

The elf guard replied, "I used a truth spell. I detect no deception." So, this was no simple guard. Rizo hoped he did not also have a spell to reveal the invisible.

"Very good. It has been some time since we had guests for supper. Please show them in."

With a small salute the guard exited the front door.

"It has certainly been quite some time since we had guests for supper," said a woman's voice, somewhat forlornly. "I shall be greatly anticipating the occasion."

Rizo thought he had better get to the front gate quickly before Cordela had to come up with something not quite honest to explain his presence. He ducked back into the child's bedroom whispering "Hey Now!"

Eighteen

SOME minutes later the elf was back. He retrieved his lantern from where he had placed it just inside the gate, and signaled to someone Cordela couldn't see. With some clanking and creaking, the portcullis rose out of the way, suspended between the two rounded towers of the guarded gate. "Please dismount and follow me," he instructed, holding his lantern up to illuminate them and the drawbridge under their feet.

The guard had them lead their mounts back up the driveway for a short distance, then off to their now right hand side down a sloping path that led along the front of the castle wall and around the tower on the southwest corner. Beyond that, nestled up against the wall, was a large wooden structure with a high pitched roof. The dirt path they were on led right into the large double doors of the structure. Once inside, Cordela saw clearly that it was a stable. It seemed nearly full, and she wondered if they had room for her party's horses. After conversing quietly with a stablehand, the guard led them to an area with a few empty stalls. "Your mounts will be well looked after here."

"They could use a good brushing after our time in the forest," Cordela advised.

"I'll see to it," said the stablehand with a nod.

With the horses situated, the guard led them back to the front gate. Beyond the portcullis and open door, Cordela could see illuminated by lantern light, and her shield as she swept it around, a well-tended garden within the courtyard between the outer wall and the castle itself. She saw green beans, tomatoes, and some kind of lettuce in addition to other plants that were too immature to recognize or that she was unfamiliar with. "You seem somewhat self-sufficient here at Loerhold," she remarked to the guard.

"We are somewhat removed from convenient markets, so we must be," he replied. "I trust, however, that you will not be disappointed in the fare we have for supper."

"Your hospitality is fare enough, I would say," Cordela hoped she wasn't being too ingratiating. The guard just laughed slightly.

Three grand steps led up to the main doors of Castle Loerhold. As they ascended in silence, Cordela took in the finely hewn stonework of the peaked entryway. Friendly and welcoming light poured forth. Inside, Cordela saw an impressive entry hall that she estimated extended all the way to the roof of this part of the castle. It was hung with tapestries that added an air of richness while damping the echoes of their footsteps on the flagstones. Two curved stairways rose along either side of the great room, meeting at a sort of balcony at the center. On the wall beneath the balcony was hung an enormous dragon's head that Cordela assumed was authentic. Below that a well-dressed man and woman sat in chairs that were more ornate than regular chairs, but much too simple to be considered thrones. The man wore formidable-looking armor under his rich velvet robes. Cordela assessed that it was more than ceremonial. An honor guard and what appeared to be domestic servers flanked the two seated figures.

A man in a more sophisticated server uniform stood just in front of the seated ones. "Lord Master Samtor and Lady Karela welcome you to their keep of Loerhold."

The guard who had led them in made a show of obeisance to his lord. Cordela assumed that this was just ceremonial formality, since he had probably just seen the man a few minutes before. He then turned and began to introduce her party one at a time. She was first.

"The Lady Cordela Shent of Palmyra."

Cordela made a little bow.

"The Lady Valory Smith of Palmyra."

Markham, Bowe, and Galahad took their turns being

introduced and paying respects to the Lord and Lady of the manor.

"And finally," the elf guard began, then stammered, "Um. Where did you come from?"

"I've been here the whole time," said Rizo, who most definitely had not been there the whole time. "You must have missed me behind Galahad. He's a pretty big guy."

"Allow me," Cordela cut in. "This is Rizo Malkin, currently of Palmyra, formerly of Kandahar and who knows where else, general gadfly and troublemaker."

"I am not a gadfly," Rizo pouted.

The Lord and Lady seemed to think that Cordela's jibe was all in jest, as they laughed quietly and traded amused looks. Then Lord Master Samtor announced, "Paldo will show you to the guest house, where you may wash the dirt of the road from yourselves."

The Lady Karela continued, "We will sup an hour from now, in this room. It has been some time since we had guests for supper, and I look forward to hearing of the purpose for your travels. Until then, please enjoy the hospitality that Loerhold has to offer, and ring the bell if you need anything."

The Lord and Lady then stood, and holding hands ascended the left-hand staircase. The better-dressed servant came forward then. "I am Paldo, Lord Master Samtor's personal butler and Master of the House. I will show you to the guest house."

The guest house was a wooden structure built up against the interior of the defensive wall. As they crossed the courtyard to it, Cordela saw a sandy practice or drill area on the right, and more vegetable gardens. Cordela estimated that the guest house was about on the opposite side of the wall as the stables outside. It was much more richly appointed than the stables, of course. They made use of the freshly drawn and warmed water to wash as Samtor had suggested. Cordela cornered Rizo. "So, halfling. Do you have any accounting for yourself? Where have you been, and what were you doing?"

"The commotion you caused at the gate distracted the guards enough for me to scale the wall and make my way across the flyover to the main house. Iko-Iko found us a way in via an open window —"

"Say, where is that cat of yours anyhow?" Markham interrupted.

"He ran off after a mouse," Rizo waved nonchalantly. "He won't have gone far." He turned back to Cordela. "Anyhow, the window led into a nursery, although it seems unused. From there I was able to get to the balcony you saw above the entry foyer. I was up there when that elf fellow came in to report about you. It's a good thing you were honest with him. He had you under a soothsayer spell."

"I thought he looked like more than your average guard," said Bowe.

"I hope no one saw you on that balcony," Cordela chided.

"Invisibility ring," Rizo wiggled his fingers at Cordela.

"Odd that they have a nursery but no child," Valory observed.

"I thought maybe the Lady of the house might be expecting," Rizo offered.

"If she is, she isn't showing a bit," Cordela shook her head. "Perhaps she is barren?" She was very curious, but could not think of a way to raise that sensitive subject during polite supper conversation.

"Do we think we can trust them?" Markham asked. "They certainly seem to be friendly."

"Say, Valory," Cordela turned to her friend, "can you perform that spell you used on Galahad on more than one person at a time?"

"Sure, I can discern the motives of anyone I look at for

about a minute after I cast the spell."

"You should try that at supper," Cordela suggested.

Valory nodded.

Just then, one of Paldo's assistants arrived to escort them to the meal.

The grand entry hall had been swiftly rearranged for supper. The two ornate chairs had been displaced, and a large table brought in and placed in the center of the room. The table was set with stoneware and silver utensils, and a first course of garden vegetables was already in place. The Lord and Lady were not yet present. Cordela whispered to Valory, "It's a good time to use your spell. We can see what the servants and guards are up to."

Valory uttered a silent prayer over her elmwood star-ankh and began to slowly sweep her gaze around the room. As she was doing so, Lord Samtor and Lady Karela appeared atop the stairs and Valory got a good look at them as well. All the guests were expected at that point to stand by their seats at the table, and as Cordela made her way to her place she gave Valory a questioning look. Valory responded with a shrug and a nod. The Lord and Lady took their seats, and soon everyone was enjoying the supper that was served. Cordela spoke of their desire to see the Monks of Mortekap and learn their secrets, without being too detailed about what particular secrets they were interested in. To change the subject, she inquired, "You must have a good story about that dragon's head on the wall watching us eat."

"The White dragons," Samtor sighed, "were not heavily involved in the Dragon Wars, and thus lost few of their number. Hundreds still dwell in the mountains to the north. That one there nearly took my life with his freezing cold breath."

"But you finally brought it down," said Cordela. "You must be very brave."

"I often wonder whether it is bravery or stupidity that leads us to do the things we do."

It seemed to Cordela that the way that Lord Samtor looked at his Lady after this last comment showed that they seemed to be very much in love, and also that they had experienced many dangerous adventures together. This made the mystery of the unused nursery even more puzzling.

"I have found that loyalty to friends or a cause is more motivating than either," she remarked. The lord and his lady both smiled at that. Cordela wasn't sure she believed it. However, speaking of friends, she now had a great new idea about what they might get Prince Prothar for his wedding.

Samtor turned his gaze to Galahad. "And how do you come to be a part of this venture?"

Galahad described hearing of the world saving actions of Cordela and Rizo, and his good fortune in finding them.

"So, we are in the presence of noted heroes," Karela raised her wine glass. "Loerhold salutes your accomplishments."

"Finally!" Cordela muttered to herself.

The assembled guests and Lord Samtor joined the lady in her toast. Then Galahad prompted, "Lord Samtor, you and your lady must have some heroic tales of your own."

"Perhaps too many," Samtor gently put down his glass. "Since before we were wed, Karela and I have taken on missions of urgency to protect those in need. Nothing that placed the entire world at risk, but important and necessary. In particular, the aftermath of the Dragon Wars left many powerful wizards, needed for the war, with nothing much to do. Many were of questionable character, and had only been empowered out of necessity. With the war won, they would prey upon the good people of the countryside.

"Often Karela and I were the only thing to stand between the innocent and magical predation." He smiled at his Lady then, but Cordela saw a bit of ruefulness in the gesture.

"You must have become very popular among the people," Cordela prompted.

"Yes, but we also made some powerful enemies."

"Who certainly did not go without a fight," Galahad intoned.

"Indeed," Samtor took a deep breath. Cordela saw him reach toward Karela under the table. Somehow, one of those battles had brought the two of them closer together. But also, perhaps, had cost them dearly. Could that explain the unused nursery? Before she could probe further, Bowe took up the topic of magic use.

"At my magic school, they always impressed upon us the ethics of proper use of magic."

"As they should!" agreed Karela. "I noted your unmistakable wizard garb at once. I was hoping you might give us a little demonstration."

Bowe blushed. "I'm sure I couldn't do anything that would impress your ladyship."

"Nonsense. Even I haven't seen every trick and spell. And it's really about the style and panache."

Bowe performed a few minor illusions, and Lady Karela responded with a few of their own. Cordela joined in the applause and laughter as the two magic users traded increasingly complex and ingenious tricks.

After dinner the table was moved aside, and a few of Paldo's crew brought instruments and played some tunes. Markham invited Valory to dance. Cordela watched them twirl around the room, wondering about the smile on Valory's face. Galahad offered his hand to Cordela and she accepted. On one of their rounds of the dance floor, she spotted Rizo with Lady Karela, who was performing some kind of dagger trick that even seemed to have Rizo impressed. When the song ended, she saw that they were still together, Rizo trying to learn to do the trick.

Cordela approached the two of them.

"You seem to be picking up that new move quickly, Rizo."

"He has very nimble fingers," Karela complimented.

"They have proven useful on occasion." Her gaze stayed on the Lady.

"You have something you wish to ask." It was a statement, not a question. The Lady's voice was a monotone. "Excuse us for a moment, Rizo."

Cordela sat beside Karela and leaned toward her so that she could speak softly and still be heard over the newly resumed music. "You and Lord Samtor have been married for some years. And you clearly love one another. And yet you have no progeny to carry your brave legacy."

The sadness behind Karela's eyes grew and her brow furrowed. "One of the foes my husband spoke of placed a curse upon us before we vanquished her. She promised that any offspring of our union would be monstrous in the extreme, and would grow to destroy all that we sought to protect. For the safety of the world, we remain childless."

Cordela's insides quivered at the Lady's tale. Cordela had risked much to benefit the world, but here was a woman who gave of herself every single day. "And is there no way to lift the curse? Perhaps I could help. I —"

"Your goddess Isis has dominion over much powerful magic, I know." Karela took Cordela's hand in hers. "But the curse of this enchantress came from a pact with the prince of demons, sealed in blood and souls. We searched many years for one who might nullify the spell." She shook away a tear. "Thank you. And please, speak not of this to others. My husband wishes it to remain a private matter, and I prefer not to attract undue attention to our plight."

"The world should know what you are doing on its behalf." Cordela was indignant.

"They may, someday. But for now, let them remain unaware." Karela gave Cordela's hand a final squeeze, then stood and gracefully and uprightly moved to where Samtor was admiring Markham and Valory, still dancing together. He bowed in greeting to his wife, and soon they had joined the others on the dance floor.

Eventually the party wound down, and Cordela and her friends adjourned to the guest house.

"What did your spell reveal?" Cordela asked Valory.

"Everyone seemed to have fairly pure motives," she responded. "I detected no malice or anything else to be concerned about."

"I came to a similar conclusion myself."

"I spent some time chatting with the guards and servants," Galahad offered. "To a one, they spoke in the highest terms about their master and his lady. I estimate that they serve out of unswerving loyalty."

"It is good to know that honorable men and women have not vanished from the world," Cordela did not add what she had learned. "Now we should rest. We need to resume our travel tomorrow."

Nineteen

ARNESHER the Great lounged in her lair under the fallen tower of Eridu, counting her newly acquired coins. Ooh, that one was minted during the reign of King Bionshasta. Officially, his reign lasted all of three months, although in reality it was only six days. Very rare. She placed it in a special pouch she reserved for her most collectible coins. "I really ought to obtain a better way to store these," she thought to herself.

The visit by that Cordela woman, the halfling, and their little band of adventurers the day before had been unexpected, but not completely unwelcome. She glanced lovingly at the gilded scepter that they had returned to her, once more placed in its position of prominence at the side of her couch. She could tell from the half-elf's expression that she hadn't thought much of Arnesher's prized treasure. "What do such small creatures know about art," she humphed. Her only regret was that she hadn't gotten a meal out of the transaction. She would have to go out and hunt sooner or later. At least she wouldn't have to worry about those dastardly bugbears coming in and raiding her hoard while she was out anymore, thanks to the adventurers. All told, not a bad deal.

Arnesher hurriedly stowed her coins and extinguished her magical light at the sound of someone entering her lair. "Second visitors this week," she thought. "How unusual." This one appeared to be alone. He might have been a human male, or he might have been a ghost — pale, tall, light haired. Perhaps she would not have to go out hunting after all. She allowed his stumbling hesitant approach to bring him within pouncing range and reignited her illumination. "Who dares invade the sanctum of Arnesher the Great?" she called out, as the human abruptly halted and furiously blinked as his eyes slowly adjusted to the light. She loved startling humans like that. Their limitations always amused her.

"I am called Garynd DiMarco," the man said in his smooth, nearly melodious voice. "I did not intend trespass. I seek word of Cordela Shent. Has she passed this way?"

Hmm. Polite. Also, well armed and armored. Not an easy meal. But she had something the man wanted — information about Cordela Shent. "She has indeed. I can even tell you her destination, if you can solve my riddle!" Here was a perfect opportunity to use the new puzzle that she had collected from the halfling.

"Thank you, great sphinx. I will do my best to answer you well. What is your riddle?"

Arnesher curled her lips into a smug, satisfied smile. The poor human would doubtless beg for an easier riddle. She resolved to be merciless. "What has the body of a lioness, the wings of an eagle, and the face of a woman?"

The man's head jerked back. "What?"

"Answer the riddle, if you can."

"Is this a trick question?" His blonde locks quivered as he shook his head. "Am I missing something?"

This was not the reaction Arnesher expected. "It is a riddle. Answer it!"

"You have just described yourself," DiMarco replied in a monotone.

"Impossible!" Arnesher's voice rose in pitch as her rage grew. "Insolent human! I should kill you where you stand!"

"Have you not ever looked in a mirror?" Unfazed, the man withdrew a hand-held looking glass from his pouch and extended it toward her. She snatched it from him and held it up. She indeed saw the body of a lithe lioness, an eagle's wings, and the face of a ravishingly beautiful woman.

"Why did no one ever tell me how gorgeous I am?" Her

golden locks perfectly framed her almond eyes and pear-like cheeks as they cascaded onto her feline shoulders. She extended her aquiline wings so she could admire the way her feathers gently rustled.

"Uh, have I answered satisfactorily?" Arnesher barely heard the human. "Will you reveal Cordela Shent's intent?"

"She is headed to Ismara," Arnesher did not look away from the mirror. "Now begone, human!" She dismissed the stranger with a wave of one of her perfect paws. She smiled into the mirror, appreciating the way her blazing ivory fangs stood out against her ruby lips. The sounds of the man's horse galloping away from her lair did not distract her from the radiant image she saw before her.

Twenty

RIZO was already awake practicing his new dagger-twirling trick when Cordela arose. She was just pinning her bun with the crossbow bolt when Valory began to stir.

"Up already?" she mumbled.

"I can hear someone exercising outside," Cordela told her. "I'm going to check it out."

"I'll join you in a minute," she said without opening her eyes.

Rizo looked up from his knife spinning. "I'll come along. The weather seems nice."

Two men were on the practice field going through some calisthenics. As Rizo and Cordela approached, they finished their counts. "Cordela, Rizo! You're just in time for sparring practice," one of them called. Cordela thought she recognized him from the guardhouse the night before, but couldn't be sure.

"Great way to start the day," Cordela called back. "Right Rizo?"

"Um, I could think of some better ways," he muttered. But to the men he said, "Gotta stay in practice somehow."

Valory came hurrying out of the guest house and jogged over to the practice field. "Did I miss anything?"

"Not even the introductions," said the one Cordela didn't recognize. "They call me Belcher, and my fellow here is Morton."

"Very pleased to meet you. I guess you already know who we are."

Morton smiled. "Lord Samtor insists that everyone learn the names of those he extends hospitality to. To make them feel at home." He winked broadly.

Cordela smiled. "What do you think, Valory? Think we can take on this big guy together?"

Morton frowned. "Two on one? Not really fair, is it?"

"But we're just two frail women," Cordela lilted.

"Most women I know would take offense to that remark." Morton puffed his chest a bit. "But, I kind of need practice in fighting two at once, so — let's rumble!"

"That leaves you and me, Belcher," said Rizo.

"That's not really fair either," Belcher smirked. "You're a much smaller target."

"You'll just have to aim better," Rizo quipped, picking a short sword out of the weapons rack. Belcher chuckled.

Cordela and Valory initially squared off on opposite flanks of Morton, so that he would have a hard time keeping an eye on them both. But he had excellent battle skills, and an almost preternatural awareness of his opponents' locations and actions. They could not breach his defenses. After he turned their joint attack back on them, threw them off balance, and landed a hit on both of them, Cordela decided it was time for a change of tactic. She signaled to Valory by holding two fingers in a 'V'. Valory nodded. Cordela intended that they were to both approach on the same side. As Cordela anticipated, with both of them fighting on Morton's front side he had much less room to maneuver his sword, and they began to gain ground. Valory blocked a sword thrust with her mace, and the metal rang like a bell, rebounding from the impact and slightly stunning Morton's sword arm. Cordela took the opportunity to go for his ankles with her flail, and down he went — hard.

"I yield," said Morton.

As Cordela reached out a hand to Morton to help him up,

they heard clapping from the side of the practice field. Markham was there.

"Have you been there the whole time watching?" Valory scolded.

"You fought splendidly," Markham's already dark voice seemed to have an even sultrier than usual tone. Valory's face looked flushed, but that could have just been from her recent exertions. She approached the tall warrior.

"Oof!" Cordela was distracted by a thud from nearby on the practice field, and Rizo called out, "Yield!"

"I hope he didn't go down too easy," Cordela called to Belcher.

"Not at all," he said, easily hoisting the halfling back onto his feet. "This little fellow helped me work up an appetite for breakfast!" He slapped Rizo on the back, hard enough to make him stumble forward and put a surprised look on his face. Cordela quietly laughed at his discomfiture.

"Breakfast!" bellowed Bowe, emerging from the guest house. "Best idea I've heard all day."

"You just got up," they all said in unison.

Breakfast was served in the courtyard and consisted of fresh garden vegetables, a selection of cheeses, a hearty seed bread, and fresh eggs. Cordela wondered about those, since she hadn't seen any chickens wandering about, nor heard a cock crow that morning. As she nibbled some cheese she spoke to Thonoris, the elf guard from the gate the night before.

"Are you elven on your mother's or your father's side?" he asked.

"My father, Cordono Shent," she tilted her head slightly to indicate a question.

"Can't say I'm familiar with the name," Thonoris shrugged.

"No reason you should be," Cordela assured him. "I don't think he's terribly well-known outside our village."

"You're not from Palmyra? I thought — "

"I live in Palmyra now. I grew up in a little farming village."

"I see." He chewed his green beans thoughtfully. "I passed through Palmyra a few years ago, on my way to Amorium. Not a bad place. Beautiful structure in the middle of town."

"We call it the tetrapylon. What were you doing in Amorium?"

"Oh, I was studying under a magic-user there."

"Lanthanum?"

His eyes widened. "You know him?"

"I've made his acquaintance," Cordela said sardonically.

"Well, he is an excellent teacher. But he doesn't take on many students. If you have a chance to learn from him, take it," he advised. "Even if you aren't interested in magic!"

"Thanks. Have you ever been to Ismara?"

"No, but I think our gardener has," he scanned the courtyard. "He travels all over looking for seeds." He waved to someone. A minute later a stout fellow with weathered hands joined them. Thonoris introduced him. "This is Biggs, the gardener. Ask him what you want to know."

"Good morning, Biggs," Cordela began, "We're headed to Ismara. What can you tell me?"

"Ismara, huh?" His voice was sandy but friendly. "Nice town. Nestled right up against the mountains. Very pretty. Seems to have more than its share of magical craftsmen, otherwise not too remarkable. The people there seem fairly content, and not many leave. I guess that's why it's not well known in other parts. That and the remoteness."

"Interesting. Anything else?"

"Well, there's a legend that the waters of Lake Ismara are magical. The locals pretty much scoff at that. But there is no arguing with how clear the water is. It's maybe a couple hundred feet deep, but on a sunny day you can see clear to the bottom."

"Sounds pretty."

"Something to see while you're there."

"Anything else we should know?"

"If you go through the Three Villages, there is a nice inn in Triz. I would avoid anyplace else," he made a negative indication with his fingers. "They don't really like strangers there."

"Thank you." Cordela nodded, then added, "The vegetables are superb."

Soon it was time for them to go. Their mounts were waiting for them at the drawbridge. Moon whinnied when she saw Cordela. Someone had decorated her mane with fresh wildflowers. Cordela thought it very fetching. Clearly she had been well taken care of, as had all of their animals. Lord Master Samtor was there to see them off. He made apologies for his Lady, who was still sleeping off the revels of the previous night. Rizo hoisted himself up on his pony with a quick, "Hey Now!" that seemed to magically conjure Iko-Iko from nothing and transport him up onto the pony. With copious thanks, they ventured forth, resuming their northward trek.

The first league or so seemed to be under Lord Samtor's control, as the homesteads that they passed all seemed to be displaying the Loerhold coat of arms, a device of styled, overlapping runes that seemed to be the initials of Loerhold, Samtor, and Karela. One of the homesteads had chickens wandering its yard, and Cordela guessed that was the source of the eggs. Beyond, habitation grew more sparse and at the very least did not display openly any coat of arms.

The region gradually grew hilly, and with each rise the party used landmarks and the sun to get their bearings and maintain a northerly direction. The ride was easy, even with the uneven terrain. Constant grazing, either by domestic or wild animals, apparently kept the shallow valleys from becoming overgrown.

"Watch yourself, Cordela!" Rizo shouted to her abruptly.

She dropped down to Moon's neck, just in time to avoid a four foot long dragonfly that came darting across their path. More were coming from their right.

"Markham!" Valory alerted the fighter. He got his shield up just in time to deflect the oncoming insect. The impact stunned the dragonfly, which fell to the ground, shaking its head and rubbing its large compound eyes. Markham was also nearly unhorsed, but managed to hang on.

"Thanks for the warning, dear," he smiled once he regained his balance.

The insects seemed to be barreling full speed through the valley, heedless of any obstacles. Cordela yelled at them, "Watch where you're going!"

"They don't seem to be listening," Rizo observed. "Maybe try your animal language spell?"

Cordela thought about this. Before she could attempt it, Bowe was already trying to use his sleeping spell. It didn't seem to have much effect. Either the momentum of the sleeping dragonflies still carried them at the same speed toward them, they could still fly while asleep, or perhaps they just didn't sleep. In any event, it wasn't very helpful. Cordela and the others had to stay alert, ducking when one of the insects sped through their space. The only one of them not discomfited appeared to be Rizo, who remained below the general flight path.

The fly that had been stunned finally fluttered its translucent wings and was off after the rest of its swarm. It turned out to be the last straggler, as the rest of the buzzing airborne creatures flew off to the west. "I guess we need to get in the habit of keeping our heads up," Cordela advised. They rode on.

As they crested a hill of the undulating landscape, they caught sight of a tower in the distance. "That could be the Three Villages up ahead," Cordela announced.

"Is that on the map?" Valory asked.

"Yes," Cordela replied. "According to the map and the gardener at Loerhold, each village has its own name as well. But it seems they together are known as The Three Villages."

"Is there anything to see there?" asked Markham.

"The gardener said they had a decent inn."

"That's enough for me," said Rizo. "Let's make for it."

"Well, if we continue on our current direction, we'll be there whether we want to or not," Cordela observed.

As they gradually approached the tower it seemed to grow up out of the valley it sat in, hilltop by hilltop. Eventually they could see that the tower was part of a complex that included an outdoor amphitheater and a long, low building with what appeared to be a large signboard in front of it.

The entire complex sat at a crossroads. The road was well-maintained, but seemed to be local, connecting the tower and theater to points to the east and west. There seemed to be no one there.

"I'm guessing this is a common area shared by all three villages," Rizo said. "Let's go check it out." He prodded his pony forward.

"The gardener mentioned that they didn't take kindly to strangers," Cordela called, going after him.

"Well, don't let anyone see you," he called back over his shoulder. That's easy when you've got a ring that turns you invisible, Cordela thought.

The tower, amphitheater, and what Rizo called a meeting hall were definitely not in use today. Galahad speculated that they might have agreed-upon market days when people congregated here. The amphitheater looked like it could hold a few hundred people, seated in a series of concentric squares around a stage. A bell was visible through openings in the top of the tower. The signboard had a few 'lost item' and 'recipe needed' messages posted to it. Rizo dismounted and approached the tower. "Locked," he concluded after tugging on the padlock.

"Why do you need to get in there?" Valory asked.

"He doesn't need to," Cordela explained. "He just wants to see what kind of trouble he can get into."

"Actually," Rizo put his hands on his hips, "I was hoping to get a vantage point from which to survey the area and see if I can spot this inn."

"Sorry," Cordela's voice held little remorse. "Remember, I'm trying not to incorrige you."

"Yes, good job. But, I don't need to break into their tower to have a look around the area." He immediately set to climbing the exterior of the tower. The masonry was somewhat loose, giving him plenty of hand and footholds. Partway up, Iko-Iko let out a yowl. Cordela thought it looked like Iko-Iko wasn't too happy to be up that high, but had waited too long to bail and was now stuck. She thought it poetic that even Rizo's cat didn't want to have anything to do with his escapades. Everyone but Cordela gasped as Rizo seemed to slip and lose his grip as he neared the top. Cordela just shook her head. He was always so theatrical. He probably belonged on the stage over in the amphitheater more than he did climbing that tower. He climbed into one of the openings, then popped his head back out and waved nonchalantly at those he had left on the ground.

Cordela dismounted from Moon and went to examine the roadway. She initially found it odd that there were no signposts at the crossroads, but she realized that if everyone who would ever traverse it lived within a few hundred yards, signposts would be unnecessary.

Her attention was drawn back to the tower as Rizo was yelling something down to those on the ground. At first, she couldn't make out what it was. Then she realized that he was saying, "Should I ring this bell?" and she ran forward, swinging her arms, saying "No! Under no circumstances should you ring that bell!!"

"You think I should ring the bell?" Rizo's voice drifted down.

Cordela got all of them to chant in unison, "Come Down Now!" Rizo pretended not to understand for a moment, then finally grabbed Iko-Iko and started down, looking even at that distance very disappointed.

Cordela met him at the bottom. "Give your report, scout," she said in a flat voice.

Rizo heaved a sigh. "Sure, no one wants to hear about how I almost died, or wants to congratulate me on my athletic prowess." No one did. Cordela tapped her foot on the ground. "Ok, there are two villages to the west, one to the northwest and one to the southwest. The northerly one is about a dozen dwellings arranged in a circle. To the south is more like a village with branching streets, but still looks like just a bedroom community. The only one of the three villages that looks like it might have anything resembling commerce is the one to the east, which is a little bigger and has a building that just might be an inn."

Twenty One

WILLIE was scraping some old grease out of one of her saucepans. The noise made it harder for her to hear the sounds made by the musicians that Cordela was auditioning in the common room. Which was just fine with Willie. They were awful. She wasn't sure if the instruments or their voices were more out of tune. Willie thought she might recognize the song they were attempting to play, but they were slaughtering it so badly she wasn't really sure. She wondered how Cordela could listen so diplomatically, even appearing to appreciate what they were trying to pass off as music. She tried to think of something that might need her immediate attention out at the barn. Usually, she didn't like to leave the front of the Beaver Lodge unattended, in case prospective guests should arrive. But in this case, she was sure that the cacophony was probably keeping all current and future customers well away. She was beginning to regret allowing Cordela to hold her auditions here when, with a completely unnecessary and unwelcome flourish, they concluded their performance.

"Thank you, that was very audacious," Cordela said to the musicians. "If I select you for the event, I'll be sure to send word through the armory to you."

The musicians packed up their instruments, thanked Cordela for the opportunity, and went out into the street. Cordela came over to where Willie was hanging her saucepan to dry. "My ears will never be the same." She massaged their points gently.

"If they could have one time played the same note at the same time, it might have been tolerable. I hope the next group is better."

"They could hardly be worse."

"Well, while we're waiting for them you can go on with the story."

"Right. Where was I?"

"Rizo was about to get you into trouble."

"That doesn't narrow it down. Oh, I remember. We were in a place known as the Three Villages, which actually has three villages in it. Rizo had climbed their bell tower and was going to ring the bell, summoning a horde of unfriendly villagers to see who was ringing their bell."

"I hope you talked him out of it."

"Yes. Bowe turned out to be the most convincing. But even Rizo's antics were tame compared to what we encountered next ..."

Twenty Two

RIZO would have liked to explore the other villages, or see how they responded to the tower bell. He assumed the bell was used to summon the people for important business or decisions that affected the entire Three Villages. But Cordela, as usual, was Not Fun. It was Bowe that ultimately convinced him, though. As he put it, why would they want to sleep in a nice cozy inn when they could get run out of town and be forced to sleep on the hard ground with just a thin bedroll and thinner blanket against the cold, and possibly wake to a giant hedgehog turning you over to look for grubs underneath? In any case, Rizo thought, they might have some kind of market, and he still needed to replace the sandals that were dissolved by the ooze underneath Eridu. So, with much grumbling he acceded to their requests for just finding the inn and not stirring up trouble.

Rizo's assessment of the more commercial-looking one of the Three Villages being Triz was accurate, as he knew it would be. The Three Villages Inn was well maintained, and the keeper just wanted three gold pieces to put up them and their horses for the night. He didn't even make them sleep with the horses. Rizo wondered what he would have said if they had insisted on keeping the horses with them in the "people rooms." He decided not to press the point, since the keeper didn't seem to notice Iko-Iko hanging around at his feet, and he might have charged extra or banned him outright if he had. As indicated by Biggs the gardener, the inn was comfortable, but did not offer any food. There was a small market nearby, but it also offered little in the way of prepared food. They found a vendor who sold smoked fish. This was actually tasty, and they stocked up on kippers for future travels. And Rizo found a nice pair of leather strap loafers to replace his sandals.

They set out again early the next morning, and as the rising sun cleared the horizon they got their first glimpse of Mount

Ismara in the distance. The way the sun illuminated just the peak, it seemed to be levitating above the surrounding land like some magically endowed castle in the air. They were able to use the peak as a navigation aid, reorienting on it whenever they crested a hill.

Partway through the morning they began hearing the unmistakable sound of running water. A couple of rises later they looked down upon a rushing river that blocked their path.

"This river isn't on the map," Cordela announced after perusing it for a minute.

"It looks seasonal," said Valory.

"What does that mean?" Cordela asked.

So, thought Rizo, there *is* something Cordela doesn't know.

"It is made up of snow melt from the mountains," Valory explained. "The extra surge of moisture often forms rivers and streams this time of year. Within a few weeks, this will be down to a trickle, and by summer it will be bone dry."

"I don't think we want to wait three weeks," said Rizo.

"Maybe we can ford it, but that current looks pretty swift," Cordela observed.

"What does your horse think about it?" Rizo asked, only half serious.

"Hang on, I'll ask." Rizo tried not to look surprised. She took hold of her red malachite star-ankh and concentrated on a invocation. Then she began to snort and whinny, eliciting similar responses from Moon. Based on her facial expression and Moon's posture and tone, they seemed to be having an argument of some sort. Finally she said in human language, "The current is too deep and swift here to safely cross. We need to find another way around or over."

"Did she say anything else?"

Cordela sighed. "She also wants me to take her swimming more often."

Rizo couldn't suppress a chuckle.

"Launcelot seems to concur with Moon," Galahad offered, patting the neck of his destrier. If Launcelot, who was as large and strong a mount as Rizo had ever seen, was reluctant to ford this stream, then they really shouldn't attempt it.

"Well, Miss Mountain Maven," Rizo addressed Valory, "do you recommend upstream or downstream to find a usable ford?"

"Downstream the water is just going to get deeper as the land flattens out, although the current will also slow. We ought to have better luck upstream."

They followed the snow melt river upstream for a little over a mile. A series of boulders had been deposited there by the stream, providing adequate stepping points for crossing. The current was very fast here, but it splashed mostly around the rocks and the horses were able to find their footing easily.

"Lucky for us these boulders all landed flat side up in the river," Cordela yelled over the roar of the rapids.

"It isn't luck," Valory yelled back. "They were dumped here many years ago by a particularly large snow melt, and they've been weathered down by all the subsequent melts." She paused while her pinto navigated a trickier section of the rocks. "This is what I expected we would find by going upstream."

"No substitute for expertise," Markham said. Rizo couldn't miss the soft smile he delivered along with the compliment, or the quiet "Thanks" and wink from Valory in response. Rizo wondered if there was something more than friendship developing between them. So long as it didn't interfere with his goal, that was fine with him.

Once across the spring flood they were on their way back

toward Mount Ismara. Rizo was eager to reach the legendary magical city.

Twenty Three

THONORIS was back on front gate duty. Typically this was an easy assignment. Since Loerhold was really out of the way, few ever appeared at the gate. It had been a pleasant surprise the day before last when travelers had arrived, and had proven not to be attackers or others of ill intent. He was expecting his shift to be typically quiet. He was thus very surprised when the blonde-haired fellow arrived.

He was still more surprised, as the traveler made his way up the driveway, that his face seemed to be traced by red swollen lines. "Greetings, wayfarer," he called from behind the portcullis. "You look in need of assistance."

"Hail, Sir," the man responded. "I'm afraid I got in a fight with some stinging nettles while trying to dodge a low flying four-foot long dragonfly."

Thonoris laughed easily. "They never do watch where they're going. I always wonder why they are in such a hurry. You can tie your mount there. I'll call for a healer." He waved to Untim who was manning the pulleys today to raise the portcullis, and sent the runner boy — Timochee was it? — to fetch Morton, who had some healing skill but also knew how to deal with facial scarring. He'd always wanted to ask Morton how he came by that particular skill, but never seemed to get around to it.

The stranger sat quietly while Morton tended to the lacerations on his face. "What brings you to Loerhold today?" Thonoris probed as Morton was finishing.

"Actually, I am looking for someone. A half-elf lady by the name of Cordela Shent. Did she pass this way recently?"

Thonoris wasn't sure he wanted to answer right away. The

half-elf and her crew seemed friendly enough, and Master Samtor had extended his welcome to her and her fellows. If this stranger planned to do her ill, Thonoris would rather put him off her scent. However, before he could prevaricate or press the stranger for his motives, Morton blurted out, "Aye, she was here. And if yer planning to tussle with her, ye better be on yer game. She's one tough cookie."

"Thank you for that advice, sir," said the man, rising to his feet. "And for the salve."

"Anything else we might do for you?" Thonoris asked.

"Actually, I would be most grateful if you have a spare hand mirror you could part with. I'm happy to pay a fair price for it."

"Afraid not, sir," Thonoris shook his head. "We are far from craft markets here."

"Well, I thank you for the moment's respite from the road. I had best be on my way." He strode back to his mount, and headed back east the way he had come.

To Morton, Thonoris said, "I hope you are right about how tough that half-elf is. If that person catches her and has evil intent, she will need every ounce of resilience she has."

Twenty Four

"ANY other landmarks coming up?" Valory asked. Cordela, the unofficial keeper of the map, reined in Moon and withdrew the map case from her saddlebag and unrolled the map on Moon's neck. Rizo silently cursed that he and his pony were so short and craned his neck so he could see.

"There is a label 'Old Well' with a drawing of a building of some sort," she read. "It seems to be due south of Ismara. If we find it, we should be able to make a bee line to Ismara from there."

"How will we know we've found it?" Valory drew alongside Cordela and looked over her shoulder at the map.

"Well, according to the map it's the only thing in the area. Unless lots more has been built since the map was made, we should be pretty certain."

"Do we know how old the map is?" asked Rizo.

"I've been thinking about that," Cordela re-rolled the map and stowed it. "Loerhold is on the map, and based on the coat of arms I would guess that Samtor is probably its first Lord. He doesn't look extremely old, so even if he established his keep as a young man it couldn't be more than 30 or 40 years old. The map can't be any older than that."

"That's practically brand new," Rizo observed, "especially compared to some of our other sources."

"In any case," Cordela concluded, "not much time for lots of other structures to have been built up around this Old Well."

Markham and Valory had been riding a bit ahead of the others, and they were the first to spot the two-story structure isolated on a hill in the distance.

"Could be the building depicted on the map," Cordela allowed. "Let's head that way."

As they approached the building, Rizo could see that it was somewhat dilapidated and in need of repair. Several windows were missing or boarded up, a portion of the roof was missing, and faded red and blue paint hung in shreds from sections of the building not completely denuded of color already.

Still closer, Rizo could see that there was a welcoming committee standing in front of the building. There were about a dozen figures standing there. A few held nasty-looking pikes while the others wielded an assortment of clubs and swords.

"They look like halflings," he observed. "But there's something wrong with them." They looked dirty and wore rags. The men had beards, which no self-respecting halfling would ever be seen with. It generally didn't take much to stay clean-shaven either. Typically, running a razor over the chin every 10 to 12 days was enough to clear out any stubble or fuzz that had accumulated. For these halflings to be sporting beards of that volume meant that they hadn't engaged in any grooming activity for months or even years. It was extremely un-halfling-like.

"We can kill them, but save the horses. They'll be good eating," Rizo heard one of them call. This was also strange. Few halflings ever developed a taste for horse meat.

"Save me the little one!" cried the single female of the group. Her hair was knotted and unkempt, and she was as filthy as the others. Her bodice was ripped and hung open loosely in a manner very unbecoming of a halfling. "He'll get my special attention."

Rizo was distinctly not interested in receiving any of her 'special attention,' and was about to say so, when Cordela put up her hand and said, "Let's get out of here."

At that moment, the grubby halflings charged down the hill toward them. Even Rizo's pony easily outpaced the charging halflings, and they broke off pursuit at the bottom of the hill.

"What's wrong with them, Rizo?" asked Valory.

"I'd guess some kind of insanity," he replied.

"Maybe the Old Well is polluted."

"Well, we won't be able to use it as a navigation point," Valory said. "Anything else around?"

Cordela unpacked the map again, keeping a wary eye on the hill to be sure the halflings stayed put. "There is an area to the east of Ismara labelled 'Blasted Plain.' If we keep that on our right we'll know we didn't go too far to the east."

"Hmm. 'Blasted Plain.' " Valory mused. "I wonder who blasted it?"

"Let's ride," Cordela led off. They gave a wide berth to the hill of the Old Well. By now, the peak of Mt. Ismaros was a looming presence in front of them. As the sun made its way down the western sky, Rizo could see in the distance to their right an area of blackened earth creeping up the feet of the mountains to the east. He thought that it certainly met the description of a blasted plain.

They came within sight of Ismara with a few hours of daylight remaining. It looked very peaceful, nestled as it was up against the foot of the mountain. Beyond it to the west the afternoon sun reflected nearly blindingly from the lake. The city proper consisted of a narrow strip of buildings just below a rocky ridge, and farmsteads fanned out from the eastern and southern edges. A welcoming gate opened toward them on the southern side, and they headed toward it.

The road leading from the gate inward took them to a central square. Many market stalls drew shoppers making their end-of-day purchases. Cordela inquired about a place for travelers and was directed to an inn on the left. Rizo noted that the road continued to the north beyond the market square. "The monastery is supposed to be to the north of the city," he reminded Cordela. "That road seems to lead in the right direction."

"We'll check it out in good time," Cordela was amiable, "but first things first. Lodging, food, a stable for the horses."

Rizo nodded, and they set off toward the west in the direction of the inn. It was easy enough to find, but did not have a dedicated stable. "There is a very nice public stable across from the Arcade. Just make a left at Market Square," the innkeeper helpfully offered.

Cordela fished some coins out of her pouch. "Do you serve dinner?"

"No," the innkeeper replied. "Try the Arcade. They serve all day."

"Anything else of interest in town?" Rizo asked.

"Well, there's another market area down by the lake port. And plenty of craft shops along all the side streets. I can recommend some if you know what you want."

"Nice. And thanks," Rizo paused. "Do you know anything about the monks to the north of here?"

"Not much. Pretty mysterious. Not even sure exactly where they're from. They show up in town now and then. Always wear these blue and red outfits." The keeper took payment for lodging from Cordela. "I wouldn't try looking for them. If they want, they'll find you. Otherwise, good luck."

Back outside in front of the inn, Rizo said, "I'm going to check out the lakeside market. I'll catch up to you later."

"Fine, Rizo," Cordela said. "Just try to stay out of trouble. We're going to get something to eat at this 'Arcade' place after we stable the horses. You can meet us there."

Rizo loved getting the feel of a new town from ground level. He found that there was nothing better to get an idea of what made a city special than to move around, chat up a few locals, and just generally absorb the vibrations. He headed to the port, since the port was often a prime place to get the scuttlebutt on what was on top of people's minds. Iko-Iko seemed to have his own ideas about how to get to know the town and wandered off somewhere. Rizo was sure he would catch up to him later.

When he arrived at the lakeside, the conversations he heard were mostly related to the expected surge of barge traffic that would coincide with the high water levels in the river. The merchants at the port were very excited about the new goods that would be coming upriver, and anticipated reasonable rates for shipping things back down, since the barges — apparently the primary mode of shipping on the river — would be in port anyway.

Having gathered enough information to satisfy his curiosity, he began to make his way back toward the main square. He had gotten the idea that Ismara was a relatively wealthy town. That would certainly explain the phenomenon of few people ever leaving. And with the river to transport goods, there would be little reason even to travel to or from the city. So, few not already involved in river trade would even know about Ismara beyond tales and legends.

Rizo's mental processes gradually drifted to ways of relieving some of the town's inhabitants of their excess wealth. He concluded that just swiping it would be the simplest. It would give him an opportunity to work the rust off of his skills. To make things more interesting, he activated his invisibility ring. He spotted his mark, a merchant on his way from the port. He moved in carefully, dodging other traffic on the road. Sidling up to the gentleman, Rizo delicately reached for the coin bag that dangled from his belt. It was tied more securely than Rizo had anticipated, and he needed two hands to work the drawstring. As he was doing so, the coins gave out a little jingle, attracting the merchant's attention. Rizo dropped the bag instantly, but it was too late. The merchant called immediately for a constable. Rizo looked left and right for a convenient hiding place, but saw none. Where was Iko-Iko when he really needed him to provide a distraction? The next best bet was to get as far away as possible. He made his way as quietly as he could to a nearby alley.

The local police responded more quickly than Rizo anticipated. He could hear them calling to one another as they fanned out across the immediate area. They knew they were looking for some invisible assailant. If they had any invisibility detection magic, he would be cooked. He went as far down the alley as he could, until it dead-ended. Time to go vertical. He climbed up the three-level building and travelled to the east along rooftops. This part of the city seemed to be all cul-de-sacs extending off the main road, and a mostly solid line of buildings made up a spine backing all of them. He moved swiftly but stealthily along the spine until he found a side street that was empty. Down he went, flicking off the invisibility power as he landed. From there, he strolled as nonchalantly as he could back out to the main road, where he was accosted by one of the police officers.

"We're looking for an invisible pickpocket," the constable said to Rizo. "Have you seen any?"

"No, I haven't," replied Rizo, absolutely truthfully. "But if I do, I'll be sure to call you."

"Thank you sir. Have a fine day."

Rizo gave a slight bow and continued toward the market square. In the faltering daylight the merchants were busy securing their wares for the night, but they were nice enough to direct Rizo toward the Arcade where he was supposed to meet the others. "Hey now!" he called as he made his way there.

Twenty Five

GARYND DiMarco felt stymied. The disgusted look on his face said it all. His furrowed brow, hand on chin, and slumping shoulders all bespoke the foul mood he was in. If one followed his narrowed-eye gaze, one would see what had put him in such a disgusted state. He had been across this countryside several times, and seen at least a few maps, and in not one traversal or map had he ever seen a river running east to west through this part of the territory.

After pursuing them for many days, he was sure he was closing in on his quarry. He knew their destination, and they must have come through this region. He had a chance to catch them, but he could ill afford the delay that getting across this uncharted river would entail. He really wanted to catch them before they reached magical Ismara. There was no telling what kind of power Cordela Shent might acquire in that legendary city.

The half-elf cleric and her crew of Isis followers must have found a way across this body of water. But it certainly wasn't here, where the current was too fast and too deep. His mood changed from disgusted to pensive as he turned his energies and thoughts to the decision of whether to try going up or downstream, but an outside observer would not have noticed any difference. His hand even remained firmly on his chin. He knew he was already slightly to the east of Ismara. Upriver would take him even farther out of his way. So downstream and westward it was.

His abrupt shift from pensive to resolute would certainly have caught an observer by surprise, quite unlike the earlier transition. His hand went to the reins of his horse, his mouth shifted from a pout to a tight grimace, and his shoulders snapped into a firmly squared upright posture as he prodded his horse into a canter alongside the river.

About a mile downstream, Garynd encountered an orc who operated a ferry, basically a stabilized raft that he would pole across the river, which was a bit wider down here, and with slower moving current. Garynd's look of relief was genuine, if short-lived. The negotiations over how much Garynd would be paying for transport of himself and his horse were brief, and Garynd's twisted lips and grumbling would have indicated to anyone watching that Garynd felt he was paying too much.

As the ferryman poled the raft across the river, a crowd appeared to be gathering on the far bank. As the raft neared, Garynd could see that the slowly assembling welcoming party were all orcs, and the look of concern on Garynd's face indicated that he didn't think they looked too friendly. Shaking his head in expectation of an ill-advised ambush, he took out his cittern, a stringed instrument he was particularly adept at. He began strumming it, humming a jaunty tune along with the sound. As the ferryman tied up the raft at the north bank, Garynd began to add words to his tune. Initially, the orcs were still practically slavering to jump him and make off with his valuables, likely dumping his body in the river. But before they realized what he was doing, Garynd's song lyrics included suggestions that perhaps they really ought to leave the stranger alone, that he was a true friend, and that he would appreciate any help or assistance that they could offer. As Garynd expertly modulated his voice along with the strumming, the orcs gradually started to believe everything he was singing about. Their smirks and grimaces of greed and expected violence turned to grins and smiles of friendship. Three of the orcs held Garynd's horse while he mounted, and they all stood waving goodbye as he rode off as fast as he could. He would need to hurry, as this detour had cost him valuable hours in his pursuit.

Twenty Six

"IT'S getting late in the day," Cordela said as they emerged from the inn. "I'd like to see what the market has to offer before they close up."

"I can take care of seeing to the horses," Galahad offered.

"I'll help," Markham added. "They are a bit of a handful for one person to lead."

"Do you have enough coin to cover the fee?" Valory reached over to place her hand on Markham's elbow, just about where his greaves ended and his dark skin was exposed.

"Yes, I'm sure that Galahad and I can cover it between us."

Valory was smiling as she released her hold. Cordela said, "Thank you."

"Anything I should do?" asked Bowe.

"If you don't need anything at the market, we'll meet you outside of the Arcade, I guess. The innkeep said it was across the street from the stables."

As they walked amidst the stalls, Cordela could tell that Valory had something on her mind.

"What's all up in your armor today?"

Valory didn't pause her walking. "What do you think of Markham?" she asked.

"Clearly not as much as you do," Cordela tried not to sound too sarcastic.

"Is it that obvious?"

"Well, you two are trying to be subtle, just not succeeding. For example, I saw the way you were dancing at Loerhold."

"You were dancing with Galahad. You looked like you were having a good time."

"Yes, I was having fun dancing. You, on the other hand — "

"I felt like we were the only two people in the room." Her voice was wistful. "Maybe the universe."

"Exactly."

"But I don't know how it happened. It came on so suddenly ..."

"Really?" Cordela stopped and looked Valory in the eye. "It seems to me you have been growing closer for a while. You two have been seeing each other at the temple nearly every day. It wasn't just a coincidence that you both were having lunch at the Beaver Lodge when you invited yourself on this expedition."

"Oh, but that was an accident — I mean, I didn't think he would ..."

"Mmm hmm," Cordela lilted. "And as I recall, you were very much in favor of Markham coming along."

"Well, I mean he's a good friend. We've known him for nearly a year."

"And ... ?"

"And I didn't want to have to not see him for two weeks," Valory said, somewhat distantly.

"You just have to be honest with yourself," Cordela was firm. "Figure out what you want. Then go get it."

"What I want ..." said Valory thoughtfully. Then, more brightly, "First I need to think about what the Prince wants. I still need to find him a nice gift. I have that bracelet for the Princess."

"Yes," Cordela was fine with the change of subject. "Nothing here really seems to speak to me, though. Oh, those are cute." She was looking at a vendor who sold plush toy animals. "Oh look! A bugbear. Well, that's appropriate." She haggled with the shopkeeper a bit, finally dropping a whole gold piece on the doll.

"We just beat down a half dozen of those things and now you want to play with one?" Valory squinted at Cordela as though she was expecting to see someone else.

"Sure," Cordela gave the stuffed toy a hug. "I don't hate them. They just had something I needed and preferred to fight about it. Plus, he's adorable!"

"I'll grant you that. Is it for you or the Prince, though?"

"Maybe it's for the Princess. I'll decide later. See anything you want?"

"No. Let's go find the others."

"Can't let Markham be away for too long, can we?"

Valory punched Cordela in the shoulder and grimaced at her. Cordela grimaced back, only partly because her shoulder hurt. Then they both laughed.

"Maybe this road leads northward out of town," Cordela mused as they left the market area. "It might take us right to the monastery."

"Umm, I don't think so," Valory said. "It looks like a dead end."

As indeed it did. The street ran about a hundred yards or so beyond the square and terminated in a solid cliff. The ridge that the city was built up against was apparently very steep here. Unless they were up for some mountain climbing, there would be no reaching the monastery from here.

They found Markham, Galahad, and Bowe waiting outside a large building that was built right up against the cliff. Its entrance sported canvas awnings above wide, welcoming open doorways. From the well-lit interior spilled the sounds of music and revelry. Occasional cheers and the pounding of tables punctuating the hubbub indicated games in progress.

"That must be the Arcade," Cordela said. "Sounds like people are having fun in there. Let's see what kind of food they have."

The place was crowded, but not full. They found an unused round table sized for six and ordered some ale and fried root vegetables. The latter were highly recommended by their server. While they waited, Cordela watched a group nearby throwing daggers at a target on the wall, another playing a card game, and farther away some people were racing what looked like rat-sized horses for sport.

Cordela found the fried roots a bit oily, but they tasted fine and seemed to satisfy her fellows. The ale was good. They had just ordered another round when Rizo walked in. "Well, look what the cat dragged in," Cordela quipped, nodding at the feline perched on his shoulder.

"That smells good. Did you save me any?" he slid into the spare seat.

"Fresh is on the way, if you can wait that long. Learn anything at the port?"

"Some," he began. "Most of the shipping in and out is by barge, and barge traffic increases this time of year due to higher water levels on the river."

"Good to know, I suppose."

"Hey, are they throwing daggers over there?"

"They look like they're pretty good. I wouldn't mess with them," Cordela cautioned.

"Humph," Rizo dismissed her concerns and rose from his chair, placing Iko-Iko on the seat. "Hey gents! Got room in the rotation for one more?"

Most of the group backed off, leaving just one challenger for

Rizo, a medium-build man with jet black hair. "I'll take you on. Buy-in is 25 gold."

"I got that right here," Rizo fished his coins out of his shoulder pack.

They had a throw-off round to determine who was first, and Rizo won that round and so started the game off.

After several rounds of throwing, Rizo seemed to be doing well. At least, he was ahead in the scoring. After another round, the scores stood at Rizo 180, opponent 175. The fellow stopped Rizo before he could take his shot. "You know, you have to hit 200 on the nose to win, right?"

"Yeah."

"Want to go double? It's mighty close, don't you think?"

"I do think," Rizo said, smirking just a little. Cordela thought that she might be the only one in the Arcade that noticed. "Sure. Let's go double. 100 gold to the winner." They shook on the deal. Rizo made a big show of inspecting his knife, taking some deep breaths, and lining up the shot. Cordela just shook her head slightly and stroked Iko-Iko. Rizo finally threw his dagger. Right on the 20. Rizo collected his winnings and arrived back at their table just in time to dig into the fresh fried food. "Easiest hundred gold pieces ever. Hey, these are really good!"

"Better enjoy them quickly," Cordela advised. "Someone wants to talk to us." She had spotted coming straight towards them a man clad in a distinctive red and blue robe. He arrived at their table in short order.

"We have been expecting you," he said. "Follow me."

Twenty Seven

THE monk led them to the eastern end of the city, where the rise it was built against dipped to meet the gentle slope of the land south of the mountains. The walk was uphill, steeply in some places. Rizo grumbled that he didn't get to finish his fries.

"We have horses, if it might make this go more quickly," Cordela offered.

"The path to the monastery is narrow and treacherous," the monk replied. "Even the most sure-footed of mounts would not navigate the way."

"Do you have a *name*?" Cordela exhaled.

"I do. Perhaps I will share it with you, if you are worthy."

"I wonder what it takes to be worthy," Rizo muttered to himself.

"That you will find out soon enough," said the nameless monk.

It took over an hour, but eventually they came within sight of the Mortekap monastery. A few torches on tall poles illuminated the entrance, which was a large wooden gate in a stone wall that surrounded a taller stone structure that seemed to be built right into the side of the mountain. A stone outcropping above the structure seemed well-placed almost by intent to keep snowslides from burying the monastery. As they neared the gate, Rizo could make out a device painted on it in red and blue paint. A skull with an oversized round part — or perhaps it was meant to be a skull viewed from above — stared out at him. It was divided by a jagged bolt of lightning into a red and a blue half. The seam of the gate split the image along the lightning bolt. Their guide rapped on the gate three times.

The gate split at the seam and opened toward them, swung by two other monks. They followed their guide through to a narrow courtyard lined with wooden pilings lashed together with overlapping steel bands. The central structure of the monastery was ahead. The entryway was covered by a portico, below which an ornate door stood open. Another of the red and blue clad monks occupied the open doorway. She called out "Hey now." Iko-Iko leapt from Rizo's shoulder and bounded through the courtyard.

"Where do you think you're going?" Rizo called after his familiar, but the feline just kept heading toward the monk. Once he was inside, the monk closed the door. Instantly all the torches that had been illuminating the area were extinguished and the group was plunged into darkness.

"Time to whip out your bright shield, Cordela," Rizo said. Before she could do it, though, a bonfire roared into life before them. Rizo looked for the rest of his party, but all he saw was Cordela.

"Where did the others go?" Cordela said. Behind them was a solid wall of the iron-bound pilings with no sign of a door.

Before Rizo could even speculate out loud about what had happened to the others, a youth clothed in a manner similar to the monks, but all in blue, spoke from his place adjacent to the bonfire, "I'm gonna set your flag on fire." He held a flagpole taller than himself, with a solid blue flag unfurled hanging from it. He seemed to be speaking not to Cordela and Rizo, but to another youth, dressed similarly but entirely in red, across the bonfire from him. The red youth held a solid red flag on a pole.

"I'm gonna set your flag on fire," the red-robed young man said.

"I think it's some kind of test?" Cordela said softly to Rizo.

"Test of what, I wonder?" He approached the blue boy warily. The boy seemed to ignore him, and just repeated his earlier threat.

"I'm gonna set your flag on fire."

The red boy responded with his refrain, "I'm gonna set your flag on fire."

Rizo thought that the boys didn't look like they could keep their flags from being burnt. Or possibly they might need some help accomplishing their stated goals. In either case, he was going to 'help.' He grabbed the blue flagpole and wrested it from the youth's grip. It came loose easily.

"Yeah. That's it, Rizo," Cordela encouraged. She stepped around the bonfire and relieved the red boy of his red flag. Rizo moved with the blue flag to a point midway around the bonfire, where Cordela joined him shortly with the red flag.

"Now what?" Rizo asked.

"We burn both flags?" Cordela shrugged.

"No," Rizo had a flash of inspiration. "We make them each responsible for the other's flag." Rizo nodded, becoming more sure of his plan. "Go give your flag to Mister Blue over there. I'll give this one to Red. If they're serious about setting the flags on fire, it'll be easy and no one will stop them. But there will be no reason for the other one to take care of their flag, either."

"Yea," Cordela smiled. "Smart. I like it." She set off toward the blue boy, and Rizo went over to red. When they were both near their targets, Rizo nodded and they handed over the flags.

At first, the boys looked at each other, then at the flags they had been given. Blue started to say, "I'm gonna ..." but didn't finish the sentence. Red didn't get past "I'm ..." before falling silent.

An open door appeared in the wall of pilings behind the red boy. Their original guide was there. "You have passed the first test," he intoned. He retreated and disappeared within the dark opening, but left the door open.

"Shall we continue forward?" Rizo beckoned to Cordela.

"I guess it's what we're here for," Cordela patted the shoulder of the blue robed boy, and said, "Hang onto that flag, kid. You might need it," and joined Rizo on the threshold of the new door.

They stepped through together. Rizo wasn't surprised when the door closed silently behind them, and he sensed that Cordela wasn't either. They waited in the dark for the next test. Illumination came up slowly, barely perceptible at first. Eventually, Rizo could see that they were in a small room with an apparent exit across from where they had come in. Rizo moved to check if it was locked when a one foot square hole appeared in the left hand wall at the floor. Through the opening stepped what appeared to be a small pink bear with a purple bib on its neck. It was followed by another, this one orange with a green bib. More came out of the little door, in a variety of colors. Rizo looked at them in confusion.

Cordela knelt down and reached for one of them. "Aren't you adorable?" she cooed, and a yellow bear with its blue bib climbed up into Cordela's extended arms. Soon it was joined by a green bear and the orange bear. "Oh, you're so soft!"

Rizo wasn't sure what to think of the mysteriously animated plush bears, or whether Cordela's response was exactly appropriate. Then he felt a tapping on his leg. It was the pink bear, looking up at him with a hopeful expression. Rizo sighed, reached down and picked up the fuzzy animal. It was surprisingly soft and warm, like a real bear. But its movements and facial expressions were remarkably human, and to Rizo these 'bears' were clearly some kind of construct. This particular construct was nuzzling into Rizo's neck and purring softly.

"Ooh, I just want to take you home!" Cordela was saying. "You're so cuddly." Rizo pet the bear on his shoulder but could not discern the nature of this test.

The opposite door opened silently and their guide appeared there and said, "You have passed the second test. Follow me and I will lead you to what you seek." It was good news to Rizo, although he still puzzled over what the monks were testing for.

"Can I bring them with me?" Cordela lilted, stroking some blue fur and looking up at the monk hopefully.

"I'm afraid not," he answered. "The enchantment that animates them will not work outside this room."

"Oh well," Cordela pouted. "Goodbye, dear bears." She stood and moved toward the waiting monk.

Rizo lowered his pink bear gently to the floor and joined her. "Lead on."

The hallway beyond the door had stone walls, and Rizo realized that they were within the main building of the monastery and had been for some time. The monk led them at least fifty feet down the wide hall, then left into a narrower passage. On their right a door opened into a small vault which contained a stone pedestal carved with likenesses of the skull device from the front gate. The monk ushered them in. On the pedestal a thin book rested, opened to a hand-lettered page that read, "The Last Testament of Nasram al-Azhar."

"Simply knock on the door when you have completed examining the book," the monk intoned, and closed the door behind them. They were alone with the book.

Rizo stood by Cordela and examined the roughly penned manuscript.

Twenty Eight

THE Final Statement of Nasram al-Azhar

Soon my journeys will end. I write now to expiate my selfish deeds, and to warn those who would come after me. This monastery provides some comfort to my weary body and mind, but I know that no amount of rest or care can halt my inevitable decline or stave off the madness that even now claws at the edges of my consciousness. And I can know no peace knowing that my own greed and thirst for power have brought me to this circumstance. Yet the monks provide what respite they can. Soon I will place this manuscript into their loyal care, and I will set forth on the river to meet my doom. But first, my testament must be given.

I was a trusted servant of the Sultan of Susa, skilled in alchemy and magical arts, and for providing such service as I might to the Sultan I was rewarded with much luxury. I had several wives, a few that I loved, and ate sumptuously. O would that I have been satisfied with my lot! But alas, I lusted after greater knowledge, greater control of Magic Forces, greater power. Thus, I left the Sultan's domain. I said to my heart that I was merely desiring to improve my service, that I would return triumphantly to the Sultan and be rewarded for my increased value to him. But all the time I lied to myself. My goals were selfish. In time, my passion became all-consuming, and I let nothing deter me from acquisition of knowledge.

This insatiable drive brought me to Luxor, where I had the supreme misfortune of meeting the dreaded Nyarlathotep, the one man who could give me everything I sought — but the price, the price! Through him I learned secrets of Magic beyond belief, arcane combinations of ingredients most susceptible to enchantment, the ways of demons, elementals, and other unwordly creatures too horrible to describe. I happily agreed to his terms, but blinded as I was by power lust I did not see that the ultimate end would be to lose all my riches, all my wives, all those I loved or cared for. I was left alone, without any companions but my spells and those aweful denizens of the outer planes and the deep Earth.

It was then that I resolved to seek out the Magical Source, the wellspring of power by which magic enters the world. Ancient manuscripts described the fabled city of Ismara, whose residents rarely leave. Many claimed that the water of the lake nearby had magical properties, powers to heal, charm, strengthen, provide insight, and even to fly — although I am skeptical of those claims even now. Perhaps, I thought, the Magic Source was a literal as well as figurative wellspring.

After many months, during which I wandered the foothills of the Forlorn Mountains searching for the legendary city, I finally reached Ismara. There, I briefly felt a peace I had never known, and I understood why so many people are reluctant to leave. But in the end my power lust won out over other emotions, and I bade farewell to the gracious Ismaran friends I had made.

I found the mountain stream that feeds the lake soon enough. But finding the Magic Source was not as easy as following the stream upwards. For the Source hides itself well. All my years of study of the magic arts were put to the test, as the Source used every type of distraction, confusion, illusion, misdirection, attack, and barrier imaginable. Ultimately, this battle stretched my very sanity to the breaking point, resulting in the madness that I can only keep at bay through the ministrations of these kind monks. To those who would attempt to repeat my journey, be warned! For those of lesser magical skill will be killed, or may wander lost in the mountains for the rest of their lives. Death is preferable to this madness.

But though it cost me severely, I succeeded in approaching the great Magic Source. In a narrow canyon it appeared as a wondrous fountain. Its fine spray made rainbows appear in the sunlight, but brighter than any natural spectrum. The water flowed as if alive. Drinking, I was filled with the knowledge of all Magic. I realized I could capture its essence in a charm, and set to work immediately. I fashioned a very fine Ruby amulet, set in a platinum setting inscribed with runes of arcane power, and prepared for enchantment by all my past experience and the knowledge gained by consuming the water of the Source. I had no concept of time, but it must have taken weeks to fashion and enchant the amulet, during which I ate nothing and drank only the water of the Source. I believe it was this extended period without rest or nutrition that damaged my body irreparably.

This amulet contains within it the essence of the Magic Source. In the hands of any spell-caster, it will enhance any magic attempted, provided the magic user activates it first, with a phrase I learned from the monks of this monastery. They have vowed to keep it among their secret traditions, and will pass it down through generations. They will share it with those who they deem worthy, and will bind them with the same oath of secrecy.

Now, I will place this manuscript into the care of the monks, and I will set sail down the river in a small boat I have prepared. I surely will not survive to reach the ocean. I plan to give the amulet to someone kind that I meet along the way. If I am not insane by then, I might provide some hint of its origins or powers. But perhaps not. As I reflect upon the greed and selfishness that led to its creation, perhaps it would be best to let it be lost to the world. But then again, perhaps it will come into the possession of some worthy soul who can redeem me from my sins.

Thus ends the final statement of Nasram al-Azhar, The Great Magician, brought low by his own avarice.

Twenty Nine

CORDELA rapped on the door when they were finished reading. Rizo solemnly closed the book.

Two monks greeted them as the door opened. One was their guide from earlier, the other a woman they hadn't seen before. The woman addressed Cordela and Rizo. "Now that you have been tested, read the testament of al-Azhar, and understand the import of his amulet and his final wishes, you can decide if you are prepared to join us in our oath of secrecy and learn the phrase that unlocks the power in the amulet."

Cordela looked at Rizo. He did not hesitate. "I'm ready," he said firmly.

Cordela wasn't sure if she should join the oath. She probably didn't need to, since the amulet belonged to Rizo now. But, she might be called upon to activate it at some point. Also, Rizo might forget the phrase. So, she nodded her assent.

"This phrase of power, which you must not reveal to any other person, is used to activate the amulet before using any other magical effect. The phrase is this:

Jácomo Fi Na Nè."

Rizo was definitely going to need her help to remember that. She rolled the phrase over in her mind a few times. She wondered for a moment how the monks would know if she shared the information with anyone else, then considered that they somehow knew that she and Rizo were headed for the monastery, and why. And, they apparently knew that Iko-Iko answered to "Hey now." So it was probably not worth tempting fate and assuming that she was ever out from under the surveillance of these brothers and sisters of Mortekap.

"And now," their guide spoke again, "your friends await you. I am sure you will be as glad to see them as they are to see you." He led them back to the main hallway, and to where it ended in double doors. As he placed his hand on the handle to open them, a black shape moved lithely toward them from their right. "Ah. We missed you, Iko-Iko," he addressed the cat as he bounded up to his accustomed spot on Rizo's shoulder.

"You know him?" Cordela felt she might never be surprised again.

"He lived with us for many years," the monk explained. "About a month ago he mysteriously disappeared. I am pleased to see that he has found a good home." He opened the door and Cordela was immediately bombarded by sounds of conversation and clinking dinnerware.

"Cordela! Rizo!" Valory was the first to greet them from her place at a long table, between Bowe and Markham. "I'm so glad you're all right!"

Galahad rose in his place and set down his spoon. "Lady Cordela, Sir Rizo. It is good to see you again. The monks have proved very hospitable after a," he paused, "a somewhat difficult start. Please, sit." He moved so that he sat across from Bowe, leaving space for the newcomers.

"The fare is simple but satisfying," Markham shared.

"And you can tell us what happened to you," Valory took a drink. "If it's anything like what we experienced, I can't wait to hear it."

Rizo allowed Cordela to slide in next to Galahad, and sat on the end across from Markham. "I was concerned when we got separated," Cordela said as a monk brought her and Rizo some rice and beans and filled cups with a weak sweet wine.

"Us too," Valory said. "When the lights came back, it was just me and Markham. We were in a section of the courtyard with a small bonfire and a guy sitting on a chair like a throne. A monk was there, and introduced the man on the throne, saying: 'See that King dressed in green? He's not a man, he's a loving machine."

"How odd," Cordela observed. "What did you do?"

"Well," Valory related, "I said I didn't want to love a machine, and then I screamed 'What did you do with my friends?' and ran at the green king with my mace. Markham, who was really great," she smiled at him, "tried to hold me back, but I guess I was upset and confused, and wouldn't let him stop me."

"She *was* extremely upset," Markham agreed.

"So, anyway I didn't get far. The monk knocked me out in a matter of seconds. Markham tried to defend me, but ..."

"But the king took me down all too easily," Markham finished. "We woke up here just a little while ago."

"Yes, the monks apologized for having to subdue us, and asked if we were hungry," Valory added. "So here we are. I don't really understand what it was all about."

"It was a test of some sort," Cordela offered.

"I guess we failed," Valory shrugged.

"Well, righteous anger over your friends is a 'pass' in my book!" Cordela assured her.

"Thanks." She slumped a bit, then brightened. "What about you two? Did you get tested? How did you do?"

Cordela began telling their story. She let Rizo narrate how he dealt with the pyromaniac flag boys, then took over when the story got up to the stuffed bears. She briefly described the "diary" they were allowed to view and left out any mention of the secret phrase.

"Ohh, the bears sound adorable," Valory gushed. "But what was the test?"

Cordela shrugged. She had been wondering the same thing.

"You displayed considerable wisdom in how you addressed

the challenge of the flags," Galahad approved.

"In any case," Rizo summed up, "we got what we came for."

"That just leaves you and Bowe," Cordela said to Galahad. "How did you meet your challenges?"

"We were also presented with an imputed royal, this one resplendent in bright red clothing," Galahad delivered his story with frequent vocal flourishes. "The monk who attended him informed us thus: 'See that king dressed in red? Bet you five gold pieces he'll kill you dead.'

"Sizing up the situation as some sort of test of character, I responded, 'Bet you ten gold pieces he won't.' That seemed to stymie our interlocutor, and I had a mind to just let his mind churn while he worked out his next move. But I noticed out of the corner of my eye that Bowe here," he looked askance across the table, "was preparing one of his spells. I tried to warn him off, but the monk was faster than I, and had set upon the poor fellow before I could take any action."

"If the spell had worked, the monk would have done whatever I told him to," Bowe pleaded in his defense.

"Yes, IF you had been allowed to cast it, and IF the monk had not proven immune to your magic," Galahad was dismissive. "I should have let the monk have his way with you, but as I have pledged to serve, and you are Rizo's friend and ally, I attempted to intervene. Of course, I paid for my loyalty with a nice bruise on my skull."

"Well, I appreciate it," Rizo responded.

"We apparently value loyalty more than these monks do," Cordela added.

Their guide came to the head of the table. "I hope our simple food is satisfactory."

"I'm satisfactorized," Cordela chimed. The rest of her group gave affirmative nods.

The monk continued, "I also extend my apologies for any suffering or injuries you endured as a result of our examinations. If there is any assistance I am able to provide, I offer it wholeheartedly."

"How about your name?" Cordela said acerbically. "Earlier, you said we might know it if we prove 'worthy.' Well?"

"I am Prism," he said. "though you may find that less useful than you thought."

"Well, it's more useful than 'that monk' to help me remember you by. Besides, I always try to address people in their preferred way."

"You have much wisdom, Cordela Shent. It is only outshined by your loyalty to your friends."

"Perhaps one day we will consider each other friends, Prism."

He smiled, bowed slightly, and exited through a door in the back of the dining room.

Thirty

THE dinner crowd at the Beaver Lodge was hopping. Well, they were bouncing up and down in any case. That was thanks to the latest group of musicians that Cordela was auditioning. They were really good. Harmonious, on time, danceable. Several diners were unable to keep their seats and made the foyer into a makeshift dance floor. Many others were clapping in time. Willie even found herself swaying as she bussed the recently vacated tables. The performance was over too soon for most.

"That was spectacular," Cordela said, "best I've heard yet. I'll leave a message at the Wollier's Hall if we decide to hire you."

"Thank you," replied the bandleader. "Don't take too long to decide, though. Our schedule tends to fill up quickly. We're very much in demand."

"I can see — or hear — why. Thank you for coming."

Willie placed some dishes in the washbasin and went to sit next to Cordela. "They were really good. And they know how to work a crowd."

"I think they're the front-runners right now," Cordela smiled. "Now, where was I in my adventure tale?"

"You had just found out that Rizo's amulet was fabricated with power from the Source of All Magic. Unbelievable!"

"Yes. We're not sure if it's *all* magic, but it is obviously a powerful source."

"Did you try to find it?"

"No, we did something else equally foolish."

Before Willie could ask what, Rizo's wizard friend Bowe entered the Beaver Lodge and came straight to Cordela.

"Are you ready to go?" he asked.

"Absolutely. I'm sure Rizo is impatient to get on with his business. Let's go."

"Wait," Willie complained, "You're just going to leave me with that fireball? What could be as foolish?"

"Sorry, I'll have to finish later. Bye!"

"Hmph. Well, tell Rizo I said hi. See you soon."

It wouldn't be soon enough for Willie. She hated only hearing half a story.

Part II

Thirty One

"ON the one hand, it seems impolite to refuse the hospitality of these monks." Cordela was speaking to Valory outside the monastery in the crisp morning air. "On the other hand, we have rooms at an inn in Ismara that we already paid for. Should we just toss away that gold?"

"Well, since it's already morning, it seems that we already made the decision." Valory's eyes drifted skyward and she blew a hair off of her forehead.

"That doesn't mean I should be happy about it." Cordela was not letting the subject rest.

"Look, you got what you and Rizo travelled all this way for, right? Just put it down as expenses and move on." Valory clenched her fists impatiently.

Rizo tried not to laugh. He listened to the two of them from the front steps of the monastery for a few minutes. Ordinarily, he would walk away or cut in to end the pointless discussion. But they were waiting for the others and he had time.

"I should go back to that innkeeper and demand our money back, since we didn't actually stay there," Cordela was adamant.

"I think he won't be very sympathetic, since he couldn't very well rent the rooms to someone else when we didn't return."

"Are there really droves of tourists in Ismara beating down his door?"

Valory shrugged. She seemed about to say something, but at that moment Galahad emerged from the monastery.

"Lady Cordela, Sir Rizo," he began, "my oath of service to

you was for the duration of one quest. Since your quest has been successfully completed, I beg your leave to seek my own way."

Rizo rose to his feet and reached out. "No need to beg."

The larger man smiled and clasped the proffered hand. He turned to Cordela.

"We didn't really ask you to join us, so we have no hold upon you," she said. "I wish you success in whatever you do."

Galahad and Cordela hugged briefly. "May your goddess Isis continue to smile upon you."

"Sometimes I wish that was all she did," Cordela muttered.

"Where will you go next?" asked Rizo.

"I was very impressed with Lord Samtor and the loyalty he commands in his followers," Galahad said. "I plan to return there. I may serve him, if he will have me."

"Good luck!" Valory wished. "I am pleased to have fought alongside you."

"Farewell Lady Valory. I will not embrace you, for fear of arousing the jealousy of your suitor." He nodded as Markham appeared in the doorway. Valory blushed.

After all the leave-taking, Galahad set out on the path back to Ismara. By then, Bowe had joined them and they were ready to leave the monks behind. "Are we not going to Ismara with him?" Bowe asked.

"Cordela and Rizo have another idea," Valory said.

"It came to me at Loerhold," Cordela explained. "Remember that enormous dragon head mounted on the wall? He said he had faced off against it in these very mountains, and that there were still hundreds of them around."

"I'm not sure I like where this is heading" Bowe raised both hands in front of him.

Cordela was unhindered. "We need to get something for Prince Prothar as a wedding gift, and I thought to myself, 'That's got to be something he doesn't already have,' right?"

"So you want us to kill a dragon so the Prince can mount it on his castle wall?"

"Not exactly ..."

Rizo cut in. "I know from a prior career in large animal handling that dragons are particularly vain and suggestible creatures, and it is possible to subdue and train them with a proper show of force and the right incentives."

"You wish to capture and train a dragon for the Prince," Markham summarized in an even voice.

"What?" Valory glanced from Rizo to Cordela and back several times. "You didn't tell me that part of the plan!"

"We hadn't gotten to that yet," Cordela said without remorse.

"Hadn't gotten to the most insane part you mean?" She buried her shaking head in Markham's shoulder.

"Sounds like fun!" Bowe said brightly. "I'm in."

"Me too," said Markham.

Valory's head snapped up. "You've all been bitten by a scarab of insanity." Hands on her hips she concluded, "I guess I better come along to be a voice of reason."

"Great. Let's go," Rizo set off toward the back of the monastery. "I saw a path higher up into the mountains back here earlier this morning."

The mountain paths were clear of snow for some way, although from the dampness it was clear that they had been coated in white blankets until fairly recently, when the coverings had slunk off to join the seasonal runoff streams and the swollen river southward.

"It's probably late to ask this," Cordela inquired, "but any ideas where to look for dragons?"

"They'll likely make their lairs in the caves," he pointed to one in the mountainside across a narrow defile from the path they were on.

"Okay, that's a start," she puffed, "but I can see a number of those around. Do we just check all of them?"

"No, we can stop checking when we find a dragon," Rizo deadpanned. He waited long enough for Cordela to make an exasperated grunt, then continued, "Dragons will select the least accessible caves, since they can fly. But, they are very territorial and the weaker ones will have to make do with less desirable accommodations." He was enjoying being the resident expert for a change. "Weaker dragons, more accessible lairs, all adds up to easier for us to subdue and capture."

"How about that one?" Bowe pointed to a shadow just below the top of a nearby escarpment.

"Very high up," Rizo responded. "If there is a dragon there, it will probably be more than we can handle. Also, I'm not sure how we would get to it."

They trudged higher into the range. "That cave looks easy to access," Valory indicated a hole partway up the crag they were climbing.

"Not very dragon friendly," Rizo grabbed a rocky outcrop to keep himself from stumbling. "Too narrow. They like to spread their wings a bit."

Going onward, they saw some suitable caves that were empty and showed no signs of recent habitation. "Let's keep going. We'll find a dragon soon," Rizo encouraged his friends.

After several hours, they crested a rise and spotted a cave that Rizo confidently thought was exactly what they were looking for. Hard but not impossible to get to, with a wide entrance perfect for stretching the wings. He held a hand to his mouth and beckoned with the other to the group.

As they neared the cave mouth, they heard a screech and the rustling of wings. "So much for surprise," Rizo muttered.

"That didn't sound very dragon-like," Cordela said.

"It doesn't look very dragon-like either," Valory agreed. Three creatures emerged from the cave at once. They had feathered wings and feet that ended in sharp raptor-like talons, but their heads and naked upper torsos were humanoid, if rather ugly. They appeared to be either soiled or have very blotchy skin, and their hair was unkempt. They screeched again, showing mouths full of dangerous-looking fangs.

"Those are harpies," Rizo shouted.

"Sorry to bother you harpies," Cordela tried to placate the beasts. "We thought you were dragons! We'll just be on our way ..."

"I don't think they are just going to let us walk out of here," Valory observed. She charged forward with her mace raised and clipped one of the flying menaces. It turned and slashed at her with a talon, scratching her unprotected arm. Valory immediately went limp and sat down hard on the snow-covered ground.

"Watch out," called Rizo, "their claws have a charm effect if they scratch you."

Markham raced to intercept another harpy that was diving toward Valory. He deftly deflected the raking talons, but this one had a dagger in one of its humanoid hands and it found a chink in Markham's armor. Shrugging off the wound, he plunged his sword into the thing's chest, stopping it from reaching Valory.

"Don't hurt the nice birdy," Valory protested, clearly under the spell of the harpies. But she didn't rise to try to stop him.

Cordela had Tadlusa in hand and was trying to maneuver for a chance to whack another of the harpies, when a fourth one flew out of the cave and gripped her flail arm with its talons. Cordela crumpled to the ground and lay on her back with her shield facing upward. The bright light that still shone from it seemed to startle the harpies for a moment.

Rizo saw Cordela fall and was surprised. Her elven heritage ought to have been a defense against the charming effect of their talons. He realized that if anyone else succumbed they would be outnumbered. "Bowe, got any spells that could help here?"

"I can try putting them to sleep," the tall wizard shrugged.

"You haven't been having very good luck with that one. Maybe you're doing it wrong. Can't you use some force missiles?"

"Didn't you get a wand that can do that?"

"Cordela has it, and I don't know where she keeps it."

Bowe uttered the word of power and launched a handful of the magic missiles at the nearest harpy. It didn't fall, only screeched loudly and flew directly at Bowe. The other two monsters responded to the call and also converged on the source of the magic. "Now what, Rizo?"

"Duck!" Rizo advised, and drew his Freeze Wand, a gift from the wizard Lanthanum, from within his vest. "Tempestus Frigidatis," he said, invoking the power of the wand.

The creatures were instantly coated in a layer of ice and fell to the ground in a heap. To make sure they didn't rise again, Rizo gave each of them a poke with his dagger.

Markham slapped Valory on the cheek a few times to try to dispel the charming effect. She seemed to recover. "Can you stand, dearest?"

"I think so," she accepted Markham's assistance and slowly got up from the ground.

Rizo went to Cordela. "I can't believe you were affected by their charming," he said. "I thought you were supposed to be immune."

"That's right!" Cordela scooped up a handful of snow, smiling stupidly. "I'm a Myooon!" Giggling, she lobbed the snowball at Rizo.

He dodged just in time. Shaking his head, he slapped her a couple of times.

"Okay, okay, I'm back!" She put up a hand to block a third slap. "You don't have to enjoy slapping me quite so much."

Rizo's smile didn't waver. "You must be a really fun drunk."

"I'll have to make sure you never find out. Help me up," she extended a hand.

"Hey, those are harpies," Valory was still hanging on to Markham's shoulder. "Didn't you say the feathers are valuable, Rizo?"

"PIMNA will pay a premium for them," Rizo agreed.

"Let's save as many as we can, then," Valory said.

"You could help us collect them," Cordela huffed, "but you'd have to let go of Markham."

Thirty Two

CORDELA was cold, tired, and stiff. She wondered how she let Rizo talk her into this course of action that involved her sitting for hours buried in snow and waiting for something that probably wasn't going to happen.

They had concluded the encounter with the harpies not too much worse for the wear. Valory had used some magic healing to patch up Markham, and the charm effect left Cordela as rapidly as it had come on. But they had decided that they needed a new tactic, since some of the caves clearly had non-dragon residents. Investigating each one might prove too dangerous before they ever found what they were searching for.

"Maybe we can lure a dragon out into the open," Cordela had suggested, in hindsight rather naively.

"What attracts dragons?" Valory had asked.

"They love shiny things," Rizo had said. "That's why they always have treasure. They don't collect it to trade for things. They just like the sparkle."

"I have some jewelry we took from the bugbears," Cordela had mentioned. She was beginning to wish she hadn't.

"That'll be perfect," Rizo had smiled and had begun to explain how they could lay out the jewelry on top of the snow and hide themselves under it, leaping out to surprise any dragon that arrived to investigate the sparkly stuff.

They quickly had found a ravine that was mostly shadowed by the peaks around it and thus still had a healthy depth of snow. Here they had laid their ambush, carefully positioning the jewelry to catch the few rays of afternoon sun that shone into the ravine, and then burying themselves in the snow pack. That had been some hours ago. Now Cordela was cold, sleepy, and a bit cramped, and beginning to despair that any dragon was ever going to be interested in the gaudy jewelry. It was an embarrassing posture that Cordela definitely did not want to become part of her legend.

She was just about to move a bit to stretch her muscles when a shadow moved across the ravine, briefly blocking the weak sunlight that illuminated the snow. A moment later she heard the beating and rustling of great wings, and a truly magnificent white dragon alit right next to them. Its legs sank into the snow, but it nuzzled the jewelry playfully.

Cordela heard the two clicks from Rizo, their prearranged signal to set upon the dragon. He was up first. Cordela assumed this was because he would be less cramped since he was able to hide standing up, but she admitted to herself that it could just be that he was the one to give the signal. Markham was also up early, and pressed the attack immediately. Cordela noticed that he struck with the flat of his blade, minimizing actual injury to the dragon. Rizo hopped onto the great beast's back where he could choose his strike points very carefully to cause the most pain but the least actual damage. Cordela strained against her cramped muscles and leapt up to throttle the dragon at its neck, using her flail as a garotte. The dragon initially looked from side to side, unsure of what was even happening to it. Once it felt the attacks it began wildly thrashing. Cordela and Rizo had to hang on tightly and Valory had to dodge the tail. Eventually it tried to cover itself with its wings in some kind of defensive posture.

"Is this thing whimpering?" Cordela asked, easing up on its throat.

"We've done it," Rizo pronounced. "It will do what we want it to now, more or less."

"It's so pitiful," Cordela said. "There, there, we won't hurt you anymore," she cooed. She patted it on the nose and scratched it between its ears. "He's adorable. How can people be scared of such a creature?"

"Um, maybe the size?" Valory suggested.

"But look at that face!" Cordela gently pinched the dragon's cheeks. "Have you seen anything more friendly?"

"Those teeth look very far from friendly," Markham observed. "And he doesn't seem to appreciate you squeezing his jowls like that."

Cordela let go and smoothed the scales she had ruffled. "What should we call him?"

"I suggest something fierce and intimidating," Rizo said.

"How about Snowball?"

"Right. Very intimidating."

"I say we take him home."

"That's the idea," said Rizo. "Easier said than done. First, though, we need to go get the treasure from his lair."

"Do we really need the treasure?" asked Valory. "With the harpy feathers don't we have enough?"

"The treasure isn't for us," Rizo calmly explained. "It's to keep the dragon occupied and happy while we're transporting him halfway across the world."

The easiest way to get to Snowball's lair was to fly there, but Snowball was a medium-sized dragon and could only hold two smallish riders. Rizo and Cordela were the two smallest, and the others weren't sure they wanted to get that close, or trusted him enough to carry them. So they agreed to meet partway down the path from Mortekap to Ismara, far enough from the city that the townsfolk would be unlikely to recognize the arrival of a decent sized white dragon but close enough that they could easily venture into town to fetch needed supplies or arrange some sort of transport for their new acquisition. Then Cordela climbed onto Snowball's back and helped Rizo up.

"Can you use your spell to talk to Snowball?" he asked when

he was seated securely.

"It only works on normal animals, not wondrous beasts like dragons."

"Hmmm. Maybe he can understand simple language concepts?"

"Let's try. Home, Snowball!" The dragon raised his head and bellowed like a chorus of out of tune bugles, and with a heavy beat of his wings launched them into the air. Cordela exhilarated in the rush of cold mountain air and waved a quick goodbye to the three left on the ground.

The dragon's cave was nearby just below the summit of one of the smaller mountain peaks. Once there, Rizo and Cordela slid from Snowball's back and collected the various pieces of gold, jewelry, and silver servingware. Rizo was careful to show Snowball that they were taking everything with them, so he knew that he wasn't leaving any of it behind. It was getting dark by the time they finished.

"Will we be able to find the others in the dark?" Rizo expressed concern. Cordela wasn't worried.

"They'll have a fire. Besides, the dark will cover our approach so no one in Ismara panics."

Soon they were airborne once again, headed out of the mountains.

Thirty Three

RIZO was headed back to the lakeside port of Ismara. Markham and Valory had set a fire as expected, and they had no trouble finding them in the twilight. The problems started after that. Valory had started with the questions.

"Are you planning to just fly him all the way back to Palmyra?" she had asked.

"He can only carry two of us, and what would we do with the horses?" Cordela had explained.

"It's also too far to fly in one go," Rizo had added. "We would need to plan out waypoints that are 'dragon friendly' along the entire route. No, we need to find another way."

"Another way to move a 30 foot dragon 400 miles across heavily populated territory?"

Markham had put a calming hand on Valory's shoulder. "Let's hear if they have any ideas."

Rizo had nodded to Markham. "We'll have to ship him like any other large cargo."

"You said it should be easy to hire a barge downriver this time of year, right Rizo?" Cordela had asked.

"Right. I'll head there first thing in the morning. I already know my way around the port."

From there the discussion had turned to how they planned to feed Snowball. Since Rizo was arranging the shipping, they had put Cordela in charge of the food. So now Rizo pursued his part of the plan down the main road of Ismara toward the lakeside.

There were two main shipping houses at the port. He

selected between them by flipping a coin. He stepped into the large warehouse office and announced, "I need a barge downriver right away. What have you got?"

A stout man came forward from where he was counting some crates. "How much cargo?"

"One, er, package, about 30 feet by 10 feet by 10. Plus 5 passengers and horses."

"Terminus?"

"Pardon?"

"Are you going all the way down?"

"All the way?"

"To Ilium. That's the end of the river."

"Right. From there I can arrange sea transport, right?"

"Sure. You'll have to pay the dock workers there to transfer your cargo."

"I'm familiar with the ports of Ilium."

"What's the cargo?"

"Uh, livestock."

"Sounds like some pretty big livestock."

"Yep. How much, and when can I leave?"

"Let's see what I've got ready to go. Follow me."

As Rizo followed the man out of the warehouse, he thought to himself. Ilium might prove to be a problem. He had last left Ilium on, charitably put, not the best of terms. It was possible that Lorimer, the wealthy magnate that felt (erroneously) that Rizo owed him money, had forgotten about the affair. But it wasn't likely. It was also possible that the tycoon didn't still have a stranglehold on the city council. But that seemed even less likely. Rizo thought he might be all right as long as he kept a low profile.

The shipping agent led him out to the docks between barges in various stages of being loaded or unloaded. Checking with a small notebook he carried, he stopped at a mid-sized barge that seemed to be nearly empty. "This one big enough for you?"

Rizo estimated that Snowball would have some room to stretch out without knocking them or their horses into the water. "It'll do."

"Full river traversal, including service of our river pilot, 600 gold."

Ouch. They were going to have to sell off some of Snowball's treasure to cover that. "I really can't spend more than 500 to make this venture pay." He hoped the man would be willing to bargain.

"Can you do 550?"

Rizo made a show of thinking it over before agreeing. They shook hands on the deal, and the man scribbled in his notebook. Rizo gave the name "Dreego Boggin," one of his favorite pseudonyms.

The shipping agent introduced Rizo to the barge pilot and left. "So, Mister Boggin, is it?"

"You can call me Rizo."

"Hester," he identified himself. "What sort of 'livestock' are we transporting?"

"Can you keep a secret?" The man nodded. "It's a dragon."

Hester looked rather skeptical and also reluctant.

"He's very tame," Rizo tried to reassure him. "We'll have complete control over him at all times." Rizo hadn't had to lie like this in some time. He hoped he wasn't too out of practice. "This animal is being delivered by special order of the Prince of Kandahar. It is considered very important cargo."

Hester's eyebrows rose at the mention of the Prince, even though it was clear from his otherwise bewildered expression that he had no idea who he was, or even where Kandahar might be. He just nodded and said, "I'll be ready to leave in two hours. Think you can get your cargo here by then?"

"Should be no problem," Rizo replied.

Sale of a bejeweled goblet from Snowball's hoard yielded enough gold to cover the price of the barge and then some. After dropping off a down payment at the shipping office, Rizo returned to their camp just outside of Ismara. Markham and Bowe had fetched the horses from the stable, and Cordela had sent Valory into town to purchase some small livestock animal as food for Snowball. She had returned with a goat, and when Rizo arrived the goat and Snowball were staring at each other, seemingly sizing each other up. The goat seemed to have an unmerited confidence, perhaps encouraged by Snowball's hesitancy. It seemed that neither of them had ever seen an example of the other kind of creature. Abruptly, Snowball seemed to reach a conclusion about the nature of the animal in front of it, and the conclusion was: food. One second the goat was stamping the ground in front of the dragon belligerently, and the next it was just gone. The second after that Rizo heard Snowball swallowing.

"Okay, that's taken care of," Rizo announced his arrival. "I hope everyone else has eaten as well. We have an hour to get all of us plus Snowball down to the port."

"I think we're ready now," said Cordela. "Are we going to parade Snowball through the streets of Ismara, or do you have another plan?"

"I was hoping you could fly him in low over the lake to attract less attention," Rizo informed her.

"You want me to just sneak out of town without saying goodbye?"

Rizo silently glowered disapproval.

They decided that Cordela would do the flying, and Rizo, Bowe, Valory, and Markham would stand on the barge waving around some of Snowball's treasures to convince him to land there. Rizo instructed Hester to pull the barge partway out into the lake, to minimize any collateral damage if Snowball went off course. Hester, complied, but looked skeptical once more as he watched them waving jewelry around like madmen. However, he looked suitably impressed when the great beast swooped in and made a perfect gentle landing on his barge, hardly even rocking it as he settled down and furled his wings.

"Okay, then," Hester said, shaking off his astonishment, "we can get under way." He hoisted a yellow and a blue flag on the short flagpole on the barge.

"Signal flags?" Rizo inquired curiously.

"I just called for a tow," Hester explained. "We'll need it to get to the top of the river. Past there, the current will do the work for us."

A wide, open, flat-bottomed boat was rowed out to the barge by a team of six oarsmen. They tossed a rope to Hester, who lashed it to a cleat affixed to the edge of the barge deck. As the oarsmen leaned into their rowing to draw the barge away from the docks, Cordela went to the trailing edge of the barge.

"People of Ismara," she called in a voice intended to be heard throughout the city, but probably not loud enough to carry beyond the lakeside area. "I am world renowned Cordela Shent, Defender against Chaos and Savior of the World. I have traveled far to visit the city of Ismara. Know that the legend of this great city will grow even greater with my visit. Farewell, Ismara!"

"Was that absolutely necessary?" Valory questioned as Cordela stepped back from the edge of the barge.

"They deserve to know how close they were to greatness," Cordela answered without a hint of irony.

Rizo's eyes rolled, practically of their own volition. "Not too self aggrandizing today, hmm?" he said under his breath. So much for a quiet departure. More loudly, he said "How about this lake, though? It's so clear you can see the bottom."

"Biggs, the gardener at Loerhold, mentioned that. He said it was the clearest water you'll ever see."

The gardener fellow was right. Rizo could see the rocky bottom even though it was easily 100 feet down if not more. The scales of a particular kind of fish down there threw multicolored reflections across the rocks. They all watched the underwater tableau scroll by as they were rowed toward the lake outlet.

Thirty Four

CORDELA felt pretty good after informing the people of Ismara how close they had been to greatness and legend, regardless of Rizo's opinion on the matter. The towboat had left them at the head of the river, and the current of crystal clear water had soon picked up the barge and was carrying them southward.

As they made their way down the river, Cordela observed that there were two primary ways that barges made their way upstream. One used a well-maintained path along the east side of the river. Horses or mules trod the path bearing tow lines that dragged barges against the current while polers on the barge kept it from colliding with piers or other barges nearer to the shore. That way seemed somewhat slow, since barges often had to wait for other traffic to clear out, since the ropes would tangle or catch on anything taller than a horse. The other method was to hire a towboat with sixteen, twenty, or as many as thirty oarsmen to haul your barge upriver. This way seemed more reliable and potentially faster, but looked like very hard work. Cordela learned from Hester that he generally took whichever method was cheaper at the moment. The prices tended to fluctuate with supply and demand, and which one cost less could change from week to week.

Cordela consulted the sphinx's map to see if she could make out their location based on some landmarks. "Is that Person Hill over there?" she asked Hester.

"Yes," he said after following her finger to the gentle rise on the western side of the river. "The common knowledge is that it was named after a person named 'Person' who had something to do with it long ago." He shrugged. "No one seems to know who this 'Person' is or what he or she did to get a hill named for them."

"Hmm. How about this 'Old Dwarf Mine'? Is that still there?"

"Ha. I'm surprised that's even on the map. The dwarves abandoned it centuries ago."

"What's the 'Garsold's Ford' coming up? A convenient place to cross the river?"

"In most seasons," Hester explained. "This time of year, though, there will be a ferry service. The much higher water level makes even the Ford impassable. Other times of year, with normal to low water levels, people can wade or easily ride a horse or donkey across. Of course, during those times, barge or boat traffic has to pay for portage."

"Portage?" Cordela imagined someone dumping hot oatmeal into the river to make it easier for barges to slide over the shallows.

"Teams of men and mules that can haul your craft along the shore around the shallow water and deposit it on the other side. It's an added cost that many shippers prefer to avoid."

"Ah. That's why the people in Ismara were anticipating the increased traffic," Rizo chimed in. "This time of year, it's just easier to get to Ismara."

"Exactly. I myself don't usually bring my barge all the way to Ismara unless I've got a special order or delivery to make."

Cordela consulted hey map again. "Oh, Pistros! Is that where all the stone comes from?"

"It does. In fact, at any given time a substantial portion of the river traffic below Pistros is carrying Pistros Stone. It's really the most economical way to transport the stuff. Just float it down to Ilium and transship it from there to wherever you want. There are a couple of land routes, but they require specially built extra-strong carts, because of the weight."

"I see," Cordela appreciated that Hester was so willing to share his knowledge. He seemed to be quite comfortable with Snowball's presence by now. "I think we may want to stop in Pistros. Snowball will probably be hungry again, and we're almost out of kippers. Rizo's cat has been eating them all."

"I just shared mine with him," Rizo protested.

When they reached it the next day, Pistros certainly seemed to be a nexus of river traffic. Many barges would not sail any farther upriver, simply loading on what amount of stone they could hold and heading back down. Apparently there were hefty docking fees, and since they didn't have a lot to load or unload, Hester set flags to signal for a ferry to take them ashore.

The town of Pistros was built around a single large hill. This was the quarry where the precious and unique stone was mined. Next to the quarry were craft shops that made and repaired tools and pulleys used in the quarry. Beyond that were where the special reinforced carts were made and sold. After that produce and livestock were available. A medium sized market area sat right in front of the one guest house in town, The Hewn Stone. It seemed that most residents of Pistros resided in their shops, except for the quarrymen, who slept and ate in special barracks maintained for the purpose by the family that owned and operated the quarry.

The ferry cost them 3 gold for Cordela, Valory and Markham. They left Rizo and Bowe to mind Snowball, who was getting a bit frisky as his appetite returned. Cordela was a bit concerned about how much they were spending, given how much the barge had cost to hire, and she had no idea what it was going to cost to hire a ship to take him the rest of the way home. But they all needed provisions, and she couldn't carry them all herself.

In the livestock part of town, they bought eight more goats for Snowball, not really sure how big his appetite could get. Cordela put Valory and Markham in charge of four apiece, and told them to wait at the docks for her. She ventured into the market to get victuals for humans — and cats. She came away with some salted river fish, dried tuber chips, and some hard sourdough bread, along with several barrels of fresh water. She was going to have to rent a cart for those.

The shopkeeper gave her a marker and held her purchases until she could return with the cart. This spree dug into their gold account even deeper, and she was worrying over that when a voice called to her just as she was pushing her loaded cart out of the market.

"You dropped something there, dear."

The feminine voice was familiar, but Cordela couldn't quite place it. She checked the ground at her feet and spotted one of the wrapped sourdough loaves that had fallen out of the cart. She bent to retrieve it, and when she was upright she scanned the market for the nice woman who had called to her.

"Oh, it's you," said the voice. Cordela's vision locked onto the keeper of a small stall near the edge of the market. She looked familiar. Cordela approached.

"Do I know you?" Cordela asked.

"More or less. I sold you that red stone holy symbol you're wearing."

Cordela glanced down at her star-ankh, then back at the woman. "Yes, I remember you now. You should know that I wear it everywhere. It's one of my most prized possessions."

"I'm glad you treasure it so. And it's good to see you again. My name is Meeka, and the man trying to be unobtrusive back there," she waved toward the back of the stall, "is my husband Robert."

"Pleased to meet you — um, again. My high priestess was curious how you came by the star-ankh. She sent someone to find you, but you had already left Palmyra."

"Funny story about that," Meeka related. "We, Robert and I, were here doing our usual business in trinkets and whatnot, which is not such a great business much of the time, and up comes a sort of funny-looking older gentleman — and I mean older — and lays that symbol right on this counter here, and says we need to take it all the way down to Palmyra, and it'll be worth our while to do so. He seemed to know what he was on about, and dear Robert and I hadn't had a holiday in I don't know how long, so we took the hint, closed up our stall here, and galavanted down to Palmyra. Hadn't been there two days when you came along and bought the star-ankh for just enough to cover our round trip expenses. That done, we figured there was not much reason to stick around — Palmyra's not really the most exciting town, no offense intended — so we got right on the road back here to Pistros."

"That's quite a tale," Cordela nodded. "And this 'older gentleman,' did he mention his name? Have you seen him again?"

"Nope, didn't leave a name, and never showed here again."

"Lanthanum," Cordela said under her breath, shaking her head slowly. To Meeka she said, "Well, I need to get going. Some friends are waiting for me at the docks. Bye."

"Take care of that symbol!" Meeka called after her.

Cordela wasn't sure how Lanthanum knew she would be arriving in Palmyra when she did, and she really didn't know why he had such an interest in her. But it was borderline creepy.

Thirty Five

RIZO easily noticed the pick-up in traffic on the river below Pistros, going in both directions. He had mostly approved of Cordela's purchases, although he thought that eight goats might have been a little excessive. That, of course, was before Snowball had gobbled up four of them and washed them down with an entire barrel of water. And Iko-Iko had certainly approved of the salted fish. Rizo thought the tuber chips were okay, but the bread was a hit with everyone.

The next morning they were approaching Ilium, which Rizo knew to expect on the left bank of the river. Cordela asked their guide and barge pilot Hester about the marshy area on the right hand bank that they were passing.

"It's not named, nor heavily explored." Hester explained. "The rumors, legends, and stories tell of a banshee that eats the souls of those who venture there."

Rizo added, "Various tales tell of an unwanted wife or mistress that was left there to die and now knows only revenge."

"Okay, so avoid that area. Check," Cordela made a cancelling motion with her hand.

"Ilium should be visible soon on the right," Rizo informed her, in case she wanted to get her first look at the fabled city, the farthest eastern outpost of Greek civilization. As it happened, she was very interested, and craned her neck to try to see over the densely grown riverbank to the city beyond.

As Rizo expected, the first part of Ilium to be visible was the great statue of Apollo, recognizable even at this distance by the laurel wreath on the god's head, even though he faced toward the sea, away from their vantage point.

With Ilium so close, Rizo decided it was time to share his concerns with Cordela. "I need you to know that I'm sort of a persona non grata in Ilium." He thought that was a suitable opener.

"What do you mean?" Cordela looked askance at him. "What sort of trouble are you in?"

"Well, none of it was my fault, exactly." This might be harder than he anticipated. "You know I worked as a large animal handler, right? Well, I was apprenticed to the most well-regarded handler in Ilium. He had a contract for a black panther, which should have been easy."

"But it wasn't?"

"Well, the animal that he thought was a black panther was actually a displacer beast, which casts an image of itself a few feet from where it actually is. So it wasn't in the cage he thought it was in."

"And you didn't let him know?"

"Well, by the time I realized something was wrong, it was too late. There was not a lot I could do." Rizo rubbed the back of his neck. "Anyway, there was not much left of my master by the time the monster was through with him. But the rich magnate who had the contract, a guy named Lorimer, wanted his panther or his money back. I was in no position to provide either of those things, but Lorimer really insisted. So I got out of town."

"How long ago was that?"

"Thirteen years."

"Well, maybe he's forgotten you by now."

"Maybe."

"Wasn't there any judicial authority you could appeal to?"

"Not in Ilium. Lorimer pretty much has the entire city under his thumb. The only major player he doesn't control is the mint."

"Mint? Like the leafy herb?"

Rizo mused at the oddly specific holes in Cordela's knowledge. "Where they stamp coins. It is the only site in Ilium not dedicated to Apollo."

"Right," she nodded. "The Greeks place Hera in charge of money."

"So, I'll need to be careful. If Lorimer finds I'm back in town, he might not be too friendly. Luckily, I've got some contacts in town that can help put us in touch with people we need to see."

"Who do we need to see?"

"Well, in addition to arranging shipping for this beast," he jerked his thumb toward the napping dragon behind them, "we're also going to need a trainer."

"I think we've got him pretty well trained already," Cordela protested.

Rizo shook his head. "We're not planning to keep him. We need to make sure he'll obey the Prince or whoever he puts in charge of Snowball. Also, we've only done some basic flying. A true dragonrider might need to go into combat or who knows what. We'll need a real, experienced trainer to get him ready for that."

"I hadn't thought of that," Cordela agreed.

"Finally, the trainer will need some kind of signal for the training. So the dragon can have a sound to respond to."

"What do you have in mind?"

"What I've used in the past is some kind of whistle. Dragons can actually hear much higher pitched sounds than humans — or elves or halflings for that matter. We'll want a special whistle for the trainer to use. We will probably have to hire a silversmith to make it for us."

"Hmm. That's a lot to do."

Rizo nodded some more. "And you are going to have to do a lot of it yourself, since I can't really show my face all that much."

"How about your contacts?"

"Our first stop in Ilium is going to be at the house of Drax."

"Drax?"

"That's my contact."

Rizo had Hester anchor far out in the river, which was much wider here at its mouth. "If anyone asks, this is just a very lifelike marble dragon statue," Rizo informed everyone.

Cordela added, "It's the work of famed sculptor Jaliego Cuales, commissioned specially for the Prince of Kandahar."

"The statue just blinked," Valory uttered flatly.

"That's just how life-like Cuales' works are!" Cordela offered.

Rizo was pretty sure that no such sculptor had ever lived.

Hester flagged for a ferry to take them into town. "You'll want to ride Moon," Rizo told Cordela. "The river port is separated from the main part of town by a steep ridge."

"Are you riding in, too?" Cordela asked.

"I'll be riding with you. Invisibly. I don't want to advertise my presence."

Thirty Six

CAUSIUS was the stablemaster of the main public 'horse storage' in the city of Ismara. He had a good business based largely on his central location right near the main market and right across from The Arcade, and secondarily on his level of service, which was certainly adequate if not exemplary. At least, that was his standard level of service. There was always an option for customers to pay extra for "premium" service. The tall blonde haired fellow who came in had "premium customer" written all over him. Sure enough, he dropped some extra gold for the private stall, and Causius began to smile to himself. Then the questions began.

"Did a group of five or six leave their mounts here in the last few days?" "Was one of them a half-elf lady or a halfling gentleman?" "How many days were they planning to stay?" "Did they say where they were going?"

Causius lost patience quickly. "Hey, I just take care of horses. I don't ask people their business." In Causius' estimation, people who inquired so much into others' business were generally up to no good. He wanted nothing to do with such people, and he did his best to get this blonde fellow out of his stables as soon as possible.

Lieutenant Jukel of the Ismara constabulary had been issued a magic monocle just that morning. The previous evening, a merchant had reported that an invisible pickpocket had tried making off with his coin purse. The monocle supposedly could reveal things or people obscured with various magical effects, including invisibility. His assignment was to watch the streets for "anything magically suspicious." He was doing just that when he spotted something through his monocle that his unaided eye could not see. He alerted his squad with their practiced hand signals, and they converged on the location of the magical effect. At Jukel's signal, five constables leapt on the man-shaped field and wrestled it to the ground. Jukel approached with his sword drawn.

"Reveal yourself, wizard, or suffer the immediate penalty." Beneath his men there appeared a tall, blonde-haired man. He was armored, uncharacteristic of wizards. But he certainly had command of some magic. The constables secured his hands with a sturdy rope, and just for safety they placed a gag in his mouth to keep him from uttering any spells. "You are coming to the station house with us," he informed the prisoner.

Later, with the help of the Chief of Police, he questioned the man.

"My name is Garynd DiMarco, and I only arrived in Ismara this morning. There is absolutely no way I could be your invisible pickpocket."

"But you were prowling around the city invisible. Explain that."

"I'm looking for some people. I followed them here, but I don't know exactly why they are here. I thought I might overhear some talk about them and what they are doing if I eavesdropped invisibly on some of your townsfolk."

The fellow's explanation seemed plausible, but only barely. "You'll be staying here with us until we can check out your story. Get comfortable."

Causius was up early that morning, as he was on most days. He roused his one live-in stablehand and had him fetch water and fresh hay. He grabbed the shovel and got to work on the horse leavings. It was best to get those out of the stable first thing in the morning, before they started to stink. He was interrupted by the unexpected arrival of a police constable. He just had a few questions, he said. Somehow it didn't surprise him that the constable wanted to know about the blonde fellow from the day before. Causius just knew that the stranger was up to no good.

Lieutenant Jukel went to unlock the cage and manacles that secured the DiMarco fellow. "Best I can tell, your story checks out."

"So I'm free to go?" he asked, massaging his wrists.

Jukel nodded. "Just be careful how you use magic around here. You may be used to being the only magic user around, but things are different here in Ismara."

"Thanks for the advice," DiMarco said. Jukel escorted him out of the building, which was located adjacent to the port. As they exited the front door, Jukel heard a hubbub arising from the lakefront. DiMarco took off running toward its source. Curious, Jukel followed.

People at the docks seemed to be exercised about a barge currently making its way away from the docks. A woman on the barge was shouting. Jukel strained to hear as he jostled his way closer to the water. "Defender against Chaos ..." drifted across the harbor. "Savior of the World ..." People nearby were muttering "Shent," and "Cordela," and "dragon." Jukel tried to see what the barge carried, but couldn't quite make it out. It seemed like a large white dragon, but that seemed very unlikely. DiMarco was nearby, stomping angrily at the ground and uttering what Jukel assumed were vile curses in some language.

Thirty Seven

CORDELA felt a bit awkward riding Moon away from the Ilium river docks with an invisible halfling holding tight behind her and a black cat sitting nonchalantly in front of her. As she rode, Rizo explained in her ear how Ilium occupied a peninsula that was bisected by the river. Ilium was on the eastern side of the river, with separate ports on the river and the sea, the two separated by a ridge that was like a spine running down the length of the peninsula.

The road was well maintained, if steep, and wound back and forth as it ascended the escarpment.

"Good idea to bring a horse," Cordela said quietly. She didn't want people to think her insane or guess that she had an invisible halfling with her.

"Just remember to breathe when you get to the top of the rise," came the voice from behind her.

"It's that impressive?"

"Well, you be the judge."

She gasped as she crested the peak and looked down upon the city carved of dazzlingly white stone. The statue of Apollo dominated the scene. The iconic Greek god held in one hand a bow with arrows and in the other hand a lyre. Cordela thought this was extremely impractical, since it was not possible to use either without putting the other one down. But she wasn't in the mood to argue with a god. Below the statue a wider structure built in the classical Greek style was undoubtedly the temple of Apollo.

"What's the other large classical building beyond the temple?" she asked.

"That's the mint."

"The architecture mirrors the political rivalry."

"Got that right."

"I see a big oval in the other direction."

"That's the gymnasium. They hold Olympic games there every few years, and there are occasional smaller competitions."

"Interesting. I may have to check that out sometime.

"And I guess that's the seaport dead ahead," she saw piers jutting out into the water beyond the city, some cutting in right angles left or right before heading seaward again. Then they were headed downward once more. "We're coming into the city proper. I need you to steer me toward the place of this Drax."

"No problem. I'll tap your right elbow to go right and your left elbow to go left. If I tap you on the head, duck!"

Rizo steered her first to the right, then immediately left onto a broad boulevard lined in porticos. Halfway down, he led her to the right off the main thoroughfare into some winding alleyways between buildings, then finally around a hairpin turn where he instructed her, "Tie Moon here." They seemed to be in a low-traffic area, and Rizo dropped the invisibility as he fetched Iko-Iko from Moon's back. "Drax is ahead on the left. Just knock."

Cordela made sure Moon was secure, then went to the door that Rizo indicated and tapped it with the heel of her flail.

An elderly man's face appeared in a small square opening in the door that appeared just above Cordela's eye level. "Yes?"

"We are here to see Drax. Is he here?"

"Who are you?" the elderly man asked.

"I am Cordela, and I'm here with Rizo. I believe Drax is

acquainted with him."

"Just a moment." The square peep hole closed with a snap, and Cordela was left in the alley staring at Rizo, who just shrugged his shoulders.

A long minute later, she heard the sounds of the door latch opening, and the door slowly levered open. The same old man was there, but now he said, "Come in quickly, before you are seen out there."

"Is everyone in Ilium this friendly?" Cordela idly wondered out loud as she stepped from the relatively brightly lit street into the darker interior.

"In this case it's good advice," said Rizo cutting in front of her to get himself inside and hidden that much sooner.

The room inside was sort of barn-like, with a loft around three sides of it that could be reached via a ladder on her right. It was weakly lit by a few lanterns hung at intervals from the posts that supported the loft. The light grew even dimmer as their greeter closed the front door, shutting out the daylight.

"Well, this is certainly a surprise," said a new voice from up on the loft.

"Drax!" Rizo did a couple of slow claps. "It's been a while, hasn't it?"

"I'm a bit surprised you decided to show your face here in Ilium again. Then again, knowing your penchant for trouble, I'm more surprised that it took you so long." He strode over to the ladder and slid down in a single fluid motion. Cordela could see that he was rather stout, perhaps not any bigger than Rizo. He turned a knob on one of the lanterns, extending the wick to increase the illumination. With the increased light, Cordela saw clearly that Drax was actually a halfling. To the doorman he said, "Thank you, Frood. That will be all for now."

"Drax, I want you to meet my associate," Rizo gestured. "This is Cordela Shent. As you can probably see, she is a devotee of Isis. Cordela, this is Drax."

"Pleased to meet you, Drax," Cordela extended a hand.

"Charmed," Drax shook the proffered hand. "Is this your cat?"

"No, Iko-Iko goes with Rizo," she tilted her head in his direction.

"Really," Drax started. "Kind of pedestrian for you, no?"

"Iko-Iko is a very *special* cat," Rizo emphasized.

Drax shrugged. "What brings you back to Ilium?"

"Rizo hopes you can help us out with a couple of things," Cordela responded when Rizo hesitated.

"I've gotten into some hot water in the past by helping Rizo out," Drax looked at Rizo. "What is it this time? Need a diversion while you infiltrate someplace? Straight man for your latest hustle?"

"Cordela and I have a large animal we want to ship to Amorium."

"Not again, Rizo. That's what got you chased out of Ilium to begin with. What is it this time, gryphon? Giraffe? Giant porcupine?"

"It's a white dragon."

Drax slapped his forehead with the back of his hand. "Of course it is. You know they won't let it in, right?"

"Who won't?"

"Amorium. They have a strict ban on importing monsters. In fact, you'll have a hard time getting any captain to take your cargo if they know what it is. They don't want their ship impounded."

"That will complicate things. It won't be easy to keep the boy fed during the entire sea voyage without anyone noticing."

Drax just shook his head. "Where is this dragon now?"

"On a barge in the river."

"So, you also need to get it from the river to the sea without anyone noticing."

Cordela disregarded that little challenge for now. "We're also going to need to hire a trainer. Someone with dragon experience."

Drax tittered. "You two sure are made for each other. Anything else?"

"A whistle," Rizo said. "Preferably one that only dragons can hear. The trainer will need it."

Drax sighed. "Well, this is going to require planning and preparation. And for that, we're going to need dinner." He called up to the loft, "Lalla, we've got two more for dinner today."

A female halfling's head appeared over the edge of the loft. Her finer curls of hair drooped past her ears as she looked down upon them. "No warning as usual, hmmm? No problem, we've got plenty of broth. I'll just roll out a few extra dumplings. I hope I'll get a proper introduction to our g— Well if it isn't Rizo Malkin. Didn't expect to see you before a pink moon."

"Hi Lalla. I'll introduce you to my friend here when you come down."

"Looking forward to it!" She nodded toward Cordela and retreated from the loft.

"Shall I set table for four, Master?"

"Thank you, Frood."

After they were all seated, introductions were made, and dinner served, Drax brought the conversation to the matters at hand. "You're here from Palmyra, right? I'm guessing most of the currency you have on hand is Persian."

Cordela fished a few coins out of her pouch and looked at them. "I've never paid much attention to where the coins are from. Gold is gold pretty much everywhere." She scrutinized the coins more closely. "This one is Persian. This one is from Egypt. So what?"

"Most merchants here will only accept Greek minted coins. The first thing you'll have to do is get some local currency."

"Can I trade my other coins?"

Drax shook his head. "Anyone who would change the money for you is going to gouge you. Better if you've got something to sell."

"I've got some loose gemstones. How will those do?"

"Fine. I know a reputable gem dealer just around the corner who will give you a fair price. Next, your whistle."

"I'm thinking we need a silversmith for that," Rizo said.

"Probably. You want it to last." Drax thought for a moment. "There's a smith I've used in the past. I can't remember his name, but his workshop is near dock 4, across from an insurance house. If anyone in Ilium can make what you want, he can."

"How about shipping?" Cordela asked. "That's kind of the main thing, right?"

"Are Oblong & Sons still operating? They're pretty reliable," suggested Rizo.

"Yeah, they're likely to have a ship going where you want," Drax replied. "But they aren't going to touch your cargo."

"We'll work on that," Rizo said.

"Do we need enough local coin to cover the shipping, too?" Cordela asked. "That's likely to be a lot."

"No," Drax reassured her. "Since they do international shipping, they have plenty of ways to spend non-Greek currency. They are one of the few exceptions. That just leaves locating the trainer. I can put out some discreet feelers. Give me a couple of days, and I'll let you know what I come up with."

"Well, that was great soup, Lalla," Cordela finished up her second bowl. "Thank you both for dinner, the advice, and the help. I guess the only other thing we need right now is directions to this gem dealer."

Thirty Eight

WILLIE had been up early as usual. The Beaver Lodge Inn was getting more crowded every day. Traders were coming into town for the annual shearing festival, and they had to stay somewhere. Some who had other lodgings still visited the Beaver Lodge for meals, and Willie had been steadily increasing the size of the stew pot to accommodate them. Today she had just put on a second pot, to avoid running out. It was a bit of a risk, since she might end up with waste at the end of the day. But leaving customers hungry was a bigger risk.

When she saw the head of curly hair enter the inn, beyond the diners already seated at tables, she knew she needn't have worried about having extra stew.

"Hello, Rizo," she greeted the halfling, "welcome back to the Beaver Lodge. Here for dinner?"

"Just a snack, really," he grabbed a seat near the hearth. "I'm looking for that elf Ha'eilen. I need a whole bunch of that durable cloth he makes from the Palmyra wool."

"I think he's observing a shearing today," Willie scooped Rizo a bowl of hot stew and set it in front of him. "Why do you need so much material?"

"That is a long story. Got a spoon?"

"You know I love stories," she handed him a spoon. "Does it have anything to do with your recent journey with Cordela?"

Rizo blew on the stew. "How much has she told you already?"

"She was up to the two of you about to do something more foolish than trying to find the well-hidden Source of All Magic, before Bowe came and she had to leave."

"Right," Rizo ate a mouthful, "I guess you could say it was pretty foolish. Seems to be working out okay."

"What?"

"Capturing a dragon."

Willie took that as calmly as she could. She didn't want to let Rizo see her surprised. "And is that what you need the cloth for?"

"No, that's something else entirely."

"Well, tell me about the dragon first." Willie pulled up a chair. This was going to be good.

Thirty Nine

THE gem merchant was truly around the corner from Drax's place. Out his front door, past the hitching post where Moon waited quietly, and back around the hairpin turn brought Cordela and Rizo right to his shop. The door was unlocked, and Cordela held it open for Rizo before following him in. The interior was lit by afternoon daylight coming in through barred windows that faced the street. A pedestal on the left had a novice's guide to gemstone quality — color, cut, clarity, and weight — with some examples affixed firmly to the surface. A high counter filled the wall opposite the door. There was not much else to see. Some bells on the door had announced their arrival, and a voice from behind the counter had said, "Just a moment," so they waited patiently.

Eventually, a smallish head appeared above the counter. It had little hair, and the sharply pointed ears seemed to pull the entire face back from the nose. Cordela recognized him as a gnome. He must have been standing on a high stool or other support, as the counter was easily half again as tall as an average gnome. "What can I do for you?"

"We're here to see Porthos. Drax sent us," Cordela announced.

"I am Porthos. So nice of young Drax to send business my way. So you need some gemstones?"

"Just the opposite, actually," Cordela stepped toward the counter. "We have gemstones, and we need some local currency."

"I see," said Porthos. "Set what you have on the counter here. I'll go fetch my loupes, scales, and testing materials so I can give you an accurate appraisal." He disappeared below the counter, and Cordela could hear him climbing down from his perch now that she was close enough. She placed a small bag of 8 gems on the counter. She looked at Rizo and shrugged.

"Gnomes tend to really know their stuff when it comes to gems," Rizo offered. "He'll give us a fair price."

Porthos returned shortly with a wooden hard-sided tray, basically a drawer, holding magnifying lenses, a balance, and some other blocks that Cordela didn't recognize. He weighed each stone, inspected it closely through one or more lenses, and several he rubbed against a block or two. Seeing Cordela's puzzled expression, he explained, "Have to check the hardness sometimes to positively identify the stone. A harder stone will always scratch a softer one."

"I see," Cordela replied. She smiled at Rizo, guessing that his assessment was probably valid and that Porthos knew what he was doing. Rizo smiled back.

"For this collection, I'll offer you 55 gold Hera," he finally said. "That's a bit more than I would usually pay, but since Drax sent you I'll help you out a bit."

"That should be enough for our immediate needs, right Rizo?"

"Yes, and sounds fair. Most of those stones are pretty small," Rizo replied.

"Actually, the small ones are of much higher quality," Porthos informed them. He disappeared again below the counter, and momentarily re-emerged with a leather sack, from which he counted out 55 gold pieces. These he handed to Cordela. "Send Drax my greetings, won't you?"

"We will. It was a pleasure doing business with you," Cordela stashed the coins in her interior pouch.

"Enjoy your time in Ilium."

Back in the street, Cordela waited a moment for Rizo to get his bearings, then followed him partway back toward Drax. Then he veered to the left down an alley behind the building that housed Porthos' shop, then quickly to the right. They emerged abruptly at the waterfront, which was bustling with activity. Cordela had to dodge a fish cart and cage full of ducks and almost lost Rizo in the crush.

Cordela looked for numbers on the piers that extended hundreds of feet into the water.

"There. Dock 4," Rizo said.

"Where? Is there a sign that you're seeing?

"Right in front of you."

Cordela looked straight ahead. She saw a post that had a large triangle on it. Large triangle. Triangle. "Oh. Delta. Greek. 4."

"I knew you'd get it eventually. Now we need to find this silversmith."

Cordela looked away from the water at the significant two-story wood and stone facades that lined the waterfront. She saw a sign in a second floor window, "Aegis Assurance."

"Didn't Drax say it was across from an insurance broker?" she asked.

Rizo nodded, followed her gaze upward. "Good eyes, as always." Cordela reached the stair up to the second floor first, but stood aside and let Rizo by.

"You have a better idea about this whistle than I do," she explained, then followed him up. She found that she didn't mind deferring to Rizo. She had been doing so a lot recently. He found the entrance to Aegis Assurance on the left at the top of the stairs, and to the right was a small shop with a modest sign that read "Hyracolos Silversmith."

Rizo strolled in with his usual blend of nonchalance and chained aggressiveness. A man, presumably Hyracolos, looked up from his workbench. "Greetings, fellow. Picking up or dropping off?"

"I need something special," Rizo said. "I'm looking for some kind of whistle that can produce a sound too high for normal human hearing."

"For animal training?" Cordela hadn't expected that the smith would be used to such requests.

"Exactly," Rizo replied with a smile.

"I have one ready now. Here, you can take a look." Hyracolos rose and went to a display shelf on his wall. He took out a silver cylinder about as long as Cordela's index finger and handed it to Rizo. Rizo sounded the whistle.

Cordela's ears could just barely make out the very high tone. Rizo must have had good high pitched hearing as well, as he appeared to be analyzing it and thinking it over. It was also possible that it was all an act, and he actually couldn't hear anything. But after his show of listening or pretending to listen, he said, "This should do nicely.

"It's for a gift. Do you think we can get it engraved?"

"It should not be an issue," Hyracolos took the whistle back from Rizo. "You'll have to come back for it, though. I'm in the middle of another project at the moment."

"Can you have it ready for us by tomorrow? And how much is it?"

"Easy by tomorrow. With the engraving, 40 gold. I'll need you to write how you want it engraved."

The whistle wasn't very big, and they had to economize on the wording. After some debate, they agreed on "Prothar and Namané, from friends Rizo and Cordela." They counted out 20 gold as a deposit and handed it over.

"Will there be anything else?" Hyracolos inquired. He seemed a bit eager to get back to his work, but Cordela was not ready to let him go just yet.

"How much do you want for that bracelet on the stand over there?" The brightly faceted piece of jewelry had caught her eye.

"I'll take 8 for it. It's been sitting there for quite a while."

"I'll take it." Rizo looked disapprovingly her way. "As the rest of the gift. Something with the bride in mind."

"I think I see what you're thinking," Rizo's expression changed. "We've got the coin, might as well."

"What next?" Rizo asked as they descended the stairs from the silversmith.

"Well, how far is it to the gymnasium from here?"

"If I recall, it's just a few blocks that way, at the end of the waterfront boulevard."

"Can we see it? I'm really curious."

"Sure. There is probably not much going on there."

"That's okay. Let's go!"

Cordela was very excited. She had read of great Olympic competitions of the past, and even if this arena didn't compare to the legendary ones in Athens or Corinth, she still wanted to have a look.

The waterfront road ended in a large plaza, beyond which the gymnasium occupied the entire area between the mid-peninsula ridge and the sea. Sloped banks of earth grown with well-kept grass formed the stadium where spectators could stand on either side of a large oval race track. The long axis of the track as well as the stadia ran parallel to the coast away from Cordela's vantage point in the plaza. At the far end of the oval another statue of Apollo watched over the field of competition, this time holding a discus in one hand and more appropriately nothing in the other. Beyond the statue was a smaller version of the temple, probably for pre-competition offerings. The cauldron was unlit at the moment. The track was occupied by a single runner, and a javelin thrower practiced on the green in the center of the oval. Cordela took it in for a few glorious minutes, while Iko-Iko chased a bird. Eventually she nodded to Rizo that they could go.

"I think there's a shorter way back to Drax's from here." Rizo led Cordela across the plaza to a street that led off in an inland direction. The short street abruptly ended on a diagonal approach to a corner. "Left or right?" Cordela asked with a shrug.

"Right is north, back toward Drax." He led the way down that street. He seemed to have guessed correctly until the street made a right turn and came to a dead end.

"Back the way we came, I guess," Cordela sighed. "We passed some interesting shops on the way. Care to have a closer look?"

They stopped at a store that sold nothing but hats and similar headware. "We need something to wear to the wedding, right?" Cordela said.

"What do you think of this one?" Rizo was showing off a parti-colored hat with bells.

"Very silly," Cordela scoffed. "Perfect for you."

Rizo frowned and replaced it on the rack. Cordela tried on a sequined narrow brimmed hat. "Very sparkly and showy," Rizo advised. "Not you at all."

They found a pair of similar if not quite matching leather toppers with brass clasps on their silk bands. They both looked very good in them. But the price exceeded the amount of local currency they had left, by a lot. Cordela felt some sadness as those hats also went back on the shelf. "We should probably get going. I'm not sure how late the ferry service runs here."

"They usually operate until sunset, but that is coming up. Let's go."

Three rough looking fellows were waiting just outside the store. One held a dagger and the other two had heavy clubs.

"So Malkin," the biggest one spoke, "you decided to show your face again. Lorimer will pay up handsomely when we deliver you to him — dead or alive!"

Forty

CORDELA quickly ducked back into the hat shop. With her peripheral vision, she saw Rizo vanish. "Probably should have been using that ring all day," she said to herself. None of Lorimer's thugs seemed to be following her right away, but just in case this seemed like a good time to try out a new spell that she had recently been granted by her goddess. It was supposed to make her appear as something of no concern to potential enemies. If she did anything to attack them, it would break the spell, but as long as she stayed passive it should prevent them from even noticing her.

"Where did he go?" one of the brutes outside was saying.

"I don't know, but there's his cat," another replied. "Get the cat, that'll bring the half-mug out into the open."

Oh, no, Iko-Iko! Cordela needed to take care of the familiar so that Rizo could do what he needed invisibly. "Hey now!" she called. Iko-Iko responded quickly, slipping away from the goon that tried to grab him. "Get up here," Cordela patted a shelf. She could see one of their attackers heading into the shop after Iko-Iko. The cat cooperated by leaping up onto the display shelf that Cordela was tapping. She dropped an oversized headdress on him. "You stay hidden here, Iko-Iko." Then she grabbed another hat that was rimmed in black fur. She put it on the floor near the thug that had entered the store, moving it with her hand to attract his attention. Once he noticed, she pulled the hat back behind a display rack, and moved away from Iko-Iko's hiding place.

The man followed, saying, "Here, kitty." Cordela kept the fur-edged hat just at the edge of where he could see, leading him farther to the back of the store and away from Rizo and the cat. Ultimately she ran out of concealment, and put the hat on her head, where she assumed the spell would cause him to just ignore it along with the rest of her.

"Hey," the brute accosted the shopkeeper. "Where did that cat go?"

"Cat, sir? I don't think there was a cat in here."

"I just saw one."

Cordela left the guy scratching his head and trying to explain to the shopkeeper how he had followed a cat through the store, and went to check on Rizo from inside the store entrance. She saw that one of the other two thugs was already on the ground, a scarlet puddle slowly forming under him. The other was looking frantically around and swatting his weapon at the air. Then he grunted and clutched at a bloody wound that had appeared in his side. He cursed Rizo in a way that offended even Cordela before he dropped to the ground next to his buddy. The third goon came out of the store, saw the bloody mess that had become of his associates, and ran away, back in the direction of the gymnasium.

Cordela retrieved Iko-Iko from under the headdress, doffed the furry cap, and stepped back out into the street. "Seems like they remember you," she said to the seemingly empty air.

Rizo materialized out of it a moment later. "I'll have to be more careful from now on. Let's get back to Drax rapidly."

Rizo stayed invisible most of the way, popping in once or twice when Cordela lost the way, and once again to let Drax know they were heading back to the barge, and would return tomorrow. Moon seemed happy to be moving again as she carried her three passengers back to the ferry landing.

The others were glad to see Cordela, and Rizo too once they actually could see him. "How has Snowball been?" Cordela asked, even though she could tell that they were eager to hear about the progress she and Rizo had made in town.

"Well, he's been sleeping most of the time," Valory gave the update, "so he hasn't been any trouble. And it was easier to convince some nosy onlookers that he was just a really well-executed carving, as you and Rizo suggested." Her expression fell. "But he seems not well. The sun today was really hot, and there's no respite from it out here on the river. I know I got a tad burnt. It can't possibly be good for a beast used to the frozen north."

"Do you think he might die?"

"Do I look like a dragon medic?" Valory's voice had a hard edge. "Using magic I can cure wounds. This is completely different."

"It sounds like whatever we do, we had better do it quickly," Rizo observed. "If we don't move this dragon soon, it might not matter."

Cordela thought a moment. "We still need to arrange for shipping. It's too dangerous for Rizo to do. I'll have to take care of that."

"I'll come with you," Valory patted Cordela on the shoulder. "But, if you didn't arrange shipping, what did you do all day?"

Cordela and Rizo took turns describing dinner with Drax, the silversmith, and the attack by Lorimer's goons, while they all enjoyed a simple supper of salted fish and the last of the sourdough bread rolls.

The next morning dawned clear and bright again, and Cordela's mind was occupied with how to get Snowball into someplace at the very least less sunlit and preferably cold. Valory was readying her stallion for the ride into town. Cordela made sure Rizo was awake. "Are you coming into town today?" she asked.

"Yes, but I'll try to stay out of view." Rizo's tone was typically laconic. "Drax said he was going to try to find us a trainer. If he's found any candidates, I'll want to interview them."

"All right. You can ride behind me like yesterday."

Cordela asked Hester to flag down a ferry for them and their horses, and busied herself preparing Moon for the ride into town. She glanced at Valory to see how ready she was, and saw Markham embrace her just before she climbed onto her stallion. Cordela caught the tenderness, and the way they looked into each other's eyes for just a moment. Then Iko-Iko leaned his two front paws on Valory's horse, meowing loudly. Cordela boosted him up to sit in front of Valory. When the ferry arrived, Cordela tipped the ferryman a bit extra to make up for the invisible halfling that he wasn't charging them for. Then they were headed back into Ilium and to the house of Drax.

When they arrived, Drax was out. But he had left instructions with Frood to let them in. Cordela introduced Valory to Frood and Lalla.

"Rizo, do you know where this shipping agent's office is that you and Drax mentioned yesterday?" Cordela asked.

"Oblong & Sons. I assume they haven't moved. Their office ought to be right across from dock 9."

"Nine," Cordela translated. "Zeta, eta, theta — iota. Got it. First floor?"

"Should be."

"Okay. Valory and I will meet you back here for dinner." She grabbed his head to make sure he was looking at her. "Try to stay out of trouble!"

Cordela judged from her experience the day before that the Ilium waterfront was a bit more navigable on foot than horseback, so she and Valory left their mounts tied outside Drax's "hole" and walked to the seaport. Cordela easily retraced her steps, leading Valory through the winding street that met the port boulevard just above dock 4, or "delta" as Cordela now recognized it. To her left, she saw "epsilon." Assuming that the piers were arranged in some semblance of order, she led them in that direction.

Cordela was impressed at the variety of ships moored at the Ilium port. There were wide, flat, oared galleys, tall dual-masted cogges, fast corvettes that could be powered by oar or sail, and small launches from ships that stayed at anchor in the nearby harbor, sheltered from strong winds by the same ridge that separated Ilium's sea and river ports.

Eventually Cordela spotted the Greek 'iota' rune, a single vertical bar with short horizontal caps on top and bottom. Across from it, on the large three-story oceanfront building, was a sign lettered in both high Greek and the region's vernacular script, "Oblong & Sons."

"I guess this is the place," Valory was nearly yelling above all the seaport noise.

Cordela leaned in so she wouldn't have to shout. "Let's go."

The noise ended abruptly as they stepped into the office and Valory closed the door behind. A man and a woman each sat at a desk piled high with ledgers and sheets of paper. "Good morning," the woman said without looking up from what she was writing. She seemed to be copying from a wrinkled piece of paper into the ledger open in front of her.

"Hello," Cordela began. "I need passage to Amorium, for five people, five horses, and, er, cargo."

"How much cargo?"

Cordela quailed. How much did a dragon weigh?

"Um," Cordela finally guessed "About a thousand pounds?"

"Hmmm. How is your cargo contained?"

Cordela wasn't prepared for all these questions. She took a deep breath. "Probably, one large crate, maybe 30 feet by 15, by ..." She wondered if Snowball would be okay not picking up his head for a week or more. "... by 15."

"Let me see," the woman took another ledger off of her stack and looked at it for a minute. "I have a ship leaving tomorrow for Amorium. That one will be 400 gold pieces for the passengers, 1400 for your cargo."

Cordela quailed. They would have to convert almost all

their treasure to cover that. Rizo might have to pawn his new magic ring. "Anything else?" She held onto a thin hope.

"Thyros, have you got anything?"

The man at the other desk, who had not even acknowledged the visitors' presence, opened one of his ledgers. "A ship from Miletos is due two or three days from now. Our turnaround time will be eight days or so. So perhaps it will head back to Miletos in two weeks. But if you can wait, you can save. Passengers 200, cargo 1000."

Deflated, Cordela held up a finger, "Give us a moment."

Two weeks? By then Snowball would be dead. But could they afford the earlier voyage? Really, Rizo should be taking care of this. He would handle the situation, just as he had been since they arrived in Ilium. Blast him for always getting himself into trouble. As usual, Cordela needs to solve everything. She held her head high to boost the confidence she didn't quite feel. And found herself looking right at Valory.

She whispered to her friend, "We can't wait. But the ship tomorrow is really pricey. And where are we going to find a crate? Not to mention getting our 'cargo' into it. I'm not sure what to do."

Valory's voice was soft and gentle. "Calm down, friend. First things first. We need to get moving, that's priority. We'll raise the money. Then we can work on the other problems one at a time."

Cordela clasped Valory's shoulder tightly. "Thank you." Valory smiled, and Cordela released her. Turning back to the woman at the desk, Cordela said, "Please book us for Amorium, leaving tomorrow. Can we pay you in the morning?"

"The office opens a few minutes past sunrise. Your ship is the Rowan Grouse, moored at dock 10. She sails at midday. Be sure your cargo is ready to lade two hours before. I'll need your signature on a couple of documents."

Cordela began to breathe easier. She was capable, but she didn't have to do it all herself. She had friends she could rely on. They would solve their problems together.

Forty One

RIZO Malkin was a bored halfling.

After being waylaid by the goons outside the hat shop, he judged it too risky to be seen anywhere in the city, and while certain things were fun to do while invisible, they weren't all that useful for him or his companions just now. He tried napping, which shouldn't have been a lot of effort, since the barge was not exactly a comfortable locale for sleeping. But despite his concerted exertion, he was unable to doze.

Instead, he thought over the fight outside the hat shop. He had almost instinctively activated the invisibility effect of his ring. He was rather pleased at himself for mastering its use in such a short time. He had known that his sudden disappearance would not confuse the attackers for long, so he dodged and weaved while still being as stealthy as possible. He had also to maintain an awareness of the entire situation, so he knew as soon as Cordela had ducked back inside the shop, followed by one of the thugs. That left just two for him to take down. He had recalled his personal dictum not to stick his dagger into anyone unless they were really asking for it. He had concluded that these two were indeed asking for it, loudly and clearly. To his benefit, they were still both investigating the space that he had been occupying just a few seconds before, and he had little trouble getting around behind both of them.

At that point, he had to make an executive decision. He could take stabs at both of them, probably not taking either out of the fight. They might not give him such an easy shot at both of their backsides again. Or, he could be very thorough with one of them, making the other that much easier to outflank. That sounded like a much better option. But that still left him with a quandary — which one to take out first? The smaller of the two brandished a dagger, certainly the more potentially lethal weapon. But the larger fellow with the club had greater reach, and a lucky swing might cause Rizo some major problems.

So, the larger of the pair got to experience Rizo's special technique firsthand before his buddy. Rizo replayed in his mind how he had expertly spotted the seam in the man's hard leather jerkin and angled his blade just enough to penetrate a couple of vital organs. Rizo's target slumped with a thud that was satisfying to Rizo and startling for the other goon.

Before the remaining attacker triangulated where the knife that felled his partner must have come from, Rizo had nimbly danced away. The dagger-wielding thug was now totally alert, swiveling his head to and fro to try to pick up any sound Rizo made. Rizo, in response, grew more cautious, waiting for an opportunity. He knew he couldn't wait too long, because the third goon might get to Cordela or Iko-Iko. Losing patience, he feinted left noisily, then more quietly moved right. His opponent fell for the trick, and Rizo had a clear shot at his unprotected left side. He went down in an instant.

When the third man emerged from the shop, Rizo stayed silent and invisible while the thug got the message that whatever reward Lorimer was offering wasn't worth ending up like his two associates. He returned to normal when Cordela walked out with his cat.

That had been exhilarating, but he knew that the next bunch of hooligans Lorimer sent might not be so easy to deal with. On their way back to Drax's place after the fight, he told Cordela that he wanted to go right to the source and take Lorimer down. Her opinion was that they had enough to do just getting Snowball out of Ilium without him dying or them being arrested for illegal animal smuggling, and they didn't have time for personal vendettas. Rizo begrudgingly agreed. He would have to settle his score with Lorimer another time, and for now try to stay out of the sight of any more of his goons. He just had to hope that Cordela and Valory could handle the shipping arrangements on their own. Meanwhile, he could try again to get some sleep.

He had barely dozed off when the gentle rap on the door heralded their return. Frood saw them in.

"How did it go? Do we have a ship?"

Valory smiled, but Cordela's expression was more guarded. "Yes, we can leave tomorrow," she sat in one of the dining chairs near Rizo. "But it's going to cost us. And," she tucked a few loose hairs into her bun, "she sails to Amorium. So somehow we need to crate up that dragon, and convince the captain that the crate holds 'produce' or 'textiles' or something legal."

Valory placed her hand on Cordela's shoulder. "We'll deal with those issues soon. For now, you need to rest, and maybe have some dinner."

"Dinner. Great idea," Rizo rose from his seat and climbed partway up the ladder to the loft. "Lalla! Are you serving dinner, or should we get it at the market?"

"You, sir, are not going anywhere," the halfling's voice drifted down from above, "for dinner or any other reason. I'll have victuals ready for all of you in a few minutes."

"Well, you know I prefer your cooking to the ogre fodder they serve at the docks," Rizo slid back down. "So, we'll be dining in. Have a seat, Valory."

Rizo was holding the chair for Valory when the sound of a key in the front door lock drew all of their attentions, and Drax let himself in. "Things are heating up out there," he announced as he approached the table. "Lorimer is furious about what you did to his men yesterday. He's got half the city out looking for you."

"I figured it would be prudent to lay low today," Rizo replied.

"You may need to get out of the city altogether. I'm not sure my place is going to be safe for long. It's only a matter of time before they come looking here."

As Drax spoke those words, there were three loud thumps on the door. Drax looked wide-eyed at Rizo. Rizo looked at

Cordela. Cordela looked at Valory.

"See who it is, Frood," said Drax in a monotonic voice. Rizo held his breath. Cordela and Valory seemed to be doing the same. Frood had a brief conversation with someone outside, via the small sliding window opening in the door. He came to the table and addressed Drax.

"A man and a woman, apparently followers of Poseidon, are asking after the Lady Cordela," he gestured in her direction. The group let out their collective breath, and they all looked toward Cordela. Her eyes were open wide enough for Rizo to see a considerable amount of white. He wasn't sure if surprise or confusion dominated her expression.

"Were you expecting someone?" Drax asked.

"No one knows I'm here." She shrugged, looked at Valory, then Rizo. "I'm a bit curious, though. Maybe they are admirers who have heard of me."

Rizo planted his face in one hand.

"Show them in, please, Frood," Drax requested.

A minute later he was back, followed by two well-armored people. Rizo could tell they were adherents of Poseidon by the blue-green clothing that showed out from under their armor, the trident carried by the very tall woman, and the fins that decorated the helmet of the slightly shorter man. "Sintros, and Athera, clerics of the Temple of Poseidon in Amorium," Frood announced them formally, "here to speak with the Lady Cordela. This is Drax, the master of this house."

Rizo thought he recognized the pair. The mention of Amorium jogged his memory. He was pretty sure they had met when he and Cordela had visited the Temple of Poseidon and witnessed an oracle. Cordela seemed to have an even better recollection.

"I remember you," she said, rising from her seat. "You were at the Rabbit Cave with us."

The woman, Athera, responded, "Yes. I am pleased you remember us. You were responsible for a sizable force that day, and you could be forgiven if you didn't recognize us. We noticed you at the docks this morning and followed you."

"But what are you doing here in Ilium?"

"The necromancer Tillingast had been corresponding with a wizard near here about awakening Kronos. It was part of their plan for Chaos taking over the world. We were tasked by our leaders to investigate."

"And you've been here ever since?"

Athera's answer was cut off as Lalla called down from above, "Two more for dinner?"

"We were just about to sit down to dine," Drax said to Sintros and Athera. "Would you join us?"

"Yes, that is very gracious," Sintros replied. "Thank you."

"And you can report on what you discovered about this wizard," Cordela suggested.

Rizo helped Frood carry two more chairs from a closet at the back of the room to the table, still shaking his head that the unexpected guests turned out to actually be admirers just looking to say hello. Lalla sent down a tureen of stew, plates of noodles with steamed vegetables, and a roast bird of some kind before joining everyone at the table. Rizo thoroughly enjoyed all of the dinner, and helped himself to extra noodles and slipped a chunk of roast to Iko-Iko under the table as he listened to Sintros and Athera describe their surveillance of the wizard.

"We've been observing him for many weeks," Athera said between spoonfuls of stew. "His daily routine generally involves puttering around his garden, or doing the occasional repair to his modest house on the outskirts of the city."

"Are you able to tell if he is trying to summon or awaken Kronos?" Cordela sharply cut her off.

"I've hardly seen him even use minor magic," Athera complained. "If he didn't have a reputation around Ilium, I wouldn't believe he's any sort of wizard."

"If he is trying to wake Kronos, he doesn't seem to be in any sort of hurry," Sintros offered.

"What does he do all day?" Valory asked.

"Best we can tell," Athera shrugged, "he reads. And writes sometimes."

"What does he write?" This was Cordela.

Sintros half-smiled. "According to the courier that visits his house periodically to pick up the manuscripts," he paused. Rizo was not sure what he expected, but it certainly wasn't what Sintros ultimately said — "Adventure novels."

Cordela squinted quizzically at Sintros, then Athera, and finally Valory. She unwrinkled her face and continued, "Did you notice anything suspicious going on at this house?"

Athera sighed. "Just that the fellow that delivers food every week seems to bring more than the wizard could eat by himself and stay that skinny."

"Hmm. Have you tried talking to him?"

"Our instructions were to be discreet," Sintros offered.

"Well, I don't have any such instructions," Cordela had the tone of voice that Rizo associated with her being determined, which often presaged getting him into trouble. "So I think it's time we paid a visit to our wizard friend." Definitely trouble. At least it kept things interesting. "Can you take us there?"

"When do you want to go?"

"Right after dinner."

Interesting or not, Rizo was happy that the answer wasn't "Right now." Lalla always made some delicious noodles.

Forty Two

AS you may have guessed by now, dear reader, this is the point of the story where yours truly becomes involved. I was just finishing up a reread of *Polemos Draconis*, considered by most to be the most complete, if not entirely accurate, chronicle of the Dragon Wars. My attention was distracted by a shadow falling across my front window.

I saw a woman peering through the window, her hands placed against the pane as a shade against the midday sun, trying to discern what, if anything, was going on inside. Her features looked vaguely elven, with thin outwardly sloping eyebrows and smoothly graceful lips and nose. I soon saw another face at my other window, or rather half a face. Judging by the dark curly hair, and that I could only see the top half, I assumed he was probably a halfling. I was fairly sure that neither of them could see me, since I had placed illusions of an empty room on both windows. But I let them study the empty room while I stayed back and tried to gauge their intentions. Behind the woman I saw the pair of Poseidon worshippers that had been watching me on and off for the past several weeks, but had not been sufficiently bold enough to actually approach me. These two seemed to have more gumption, and I was intrigued.

I could see them conversing a bit, but could not quite make out what they were saying. They ventured back to the Poseidon pair and talked some more, then returned for another round of peeking into the windows. Eventually, weary of that game and curious about the reason for their interest, I called out so they could hear, "You know, you could just try knocking at the door."

They were startled, but only hesitated a moment before taking my advice. "Yes, just a moment," I called out, acting the part of a feeble oldster who takes an inordinate amount of time getting up. Opening the door, I could see that the woman was half-elven, and clad in impressive-looking mail formed of many metal disks woven together. Her mousy brown hair was tied smartly in a bun. Behind her was another woman, taller, with black hair held back with a bronze clip. She fingered a mace that hung at her side and her eyes were narrowed beneath her dark eyebrows in what I took to be suspicion. The halfling wore a jerkin and leggings of hardened leather, and had a leather sash diagonally across his chest which held a number of knives seemingly balanced for throwing. The other two remained at a distance. "Good afternoon," I said with as much cheer as I could muster.

"Um," the woman said. She looked first at the other woman, then at the halfling. "Um."

"Yes, you said that before," I smiled and waited for more. When nothing more was forthcoming after a moment, I tried prompting her. "You are?"

She shook her head briefly. "I am Cordela Shent. This is Rizo," she indicated the halfling, "and this is Valory."

"I am pleased to meet you. You may call me Klepsis."

"Um," she said once more, and I was concerned that the conversation was going to be intolerably tedious. But she quickly regained her composure and went on. "I don't mean to be too blunt about this, but are you trying to awaken the Titan Kronos?"

Now, dear reader, you might think that this is not a question that one gets often, particularly from strangers who arrive at one's door unannounced and uninvited. And you would be right. And, certainly, one might be forgiven if one were taken off-guard and had no sufficient reply for such a question. However, I endeavor to always have some cogent answer to all reasonable questions, and this one was no exception. "Do you think that is something I ought to be doing?"

"My friends and I saw some correspondence between you and a necromancer named Tillingast, in which you seemed to be claiming to be doing just that. So, are you?"

So that's what this was about. "Ah, yes, Tillingast, that fool. I pretended to play along with his silly games for a time, in the vain hope that I might get back the amulet he stole from me. You didn't happen to see it, did you? Large ruby set in platinum, with arcane glyphs carved around the rim?" Cordela and Rizo glanced at each other. "Well, no matter. I assume Tillingast is no longer of concern?"

"He has been dealt with," Cordela stated, "after his 'silly games' caused major disruptions and forced thousands out of their homes."

"Perhaps you should come in," I took a welcoming step back, "and I can allay any residual concerns you have. Your Poseidon friends are also invited."

With all of my unexpected guests comfortably seated, I magically lit up a fire in the hearth and put on a kettle with an herb tea infusion. Cordela introduced the two Poseidon followers.

"Athera? Now that's a suggestive name," I said, returning to my seat.

"My father is a devotee of the goddess Hera and vowed that his daughter would be named in her honor," the tall woman who had thankfully left her large trident outside explained, "while my mother served Athena, and had made a similar vow. My name served as a way to satisfy both oaths, and keep their respective divinities happy."

"It suits you well, with your goddess-like stature." She smiled at the compliment. "And, of course, you serve Poseidon."

"Neutral territory," Athera said.

"Valory's name has an interesting origin as well," Cordela injected into the pause in conversation.

"Ugh. Don't embarrass me," Valory complained.

"Nonsense, young lady," I assured her. "Whatever the story is, I'm sure it reflects well upon you and how you carry the name — even if it is only by contrast. Do tell!"

"Well," she began timidly, "I was named for my grandfather Valorius. He was apparently a hero of the Dragon Wars."

"*General* Valorius?" I leaned forward in my seat. "He was t*he* hero of the Dragon Wars. I was just reading about him when you arrived," I gestured to the book, still on my side table where I had placed it. "Without him, the battle of Carad Vinos might have gone very badly for the allies."

"I've never heard the full story," the Lady Valory sat up with great interest. "What does your history book say?"

"To summarize, since the author of this book is a bit too prolix for my taste," I began, "the allies gained advanced intelligence that the Dragon army would attempt to join up with the White Dragon forces in the Forlorn Mountains. If they were successful, the combined fire and frost attack would have been unstoppable. So the allies laid a trap for them in a vineyard just to the south of the mountains — Carad Vinos, 'Field of Vines.' Since the dragons had adopted the tactic of leading with a barrage of fire breath, the allies enchanted the field to multiply the fire and redound it back on the dragons. But to lure the dragons into the trap, they needed bait — an entire division of the allied army. Most of the army did not know of the plan, but the leaders, particularly General Valorius, did. He had to demonstrate forthright leadership and maintain discipline, even knowing that his army, many of whom were lifelong friends, were doomed."

"Wow," Valory gushed, "he really was a hero. I wonder why my family never tells that story?"

"You should really be proud of your name," Cordela laid a hand on the taller woman's shoulder.

"Indeed she should," I responded. "The area was renamed Carad Tostas, 'Blasted Plain.' It still bears the scars."

"We passed such an area on our way to Ismara," Rizo recalled.

"Certainly you would have done. The very one, still black and desolate.

"But now, you should tell the tale of the late, lamentable Tillingast, his schemes, and how he met his end."

Cordela and Rizo took turns relating their adventure, from their first meeting with the necromancer to the final unwinding of his plans. But you can read all about that in Book 1 of this series, *Water Against Chaos*, available from purveyors of fine books across the physical planes of existence.

When they concluded, I opined, "Perhaps it was unwise of me to be so encouraging to that poor fellow. Ultimately, however, it seems that he needed little encouragement — or assistance."

"It seems," said Cordela, "that we have little to be concerned about regarding your activities. You have provided adequate accounting of yourself. And been a most gracious host."

"There is one curious matter," Sintros spoke up for the first time. "We noticed that your regular deliveries include more food than you appear capable of eating yourself."

"Ah, that is easily explained," I said, rising nimbly from my seat. "Follow me if you wish to learn." I led my visitors through my house to the back door, through which the attached garden shed is accessible. "This is where I keep my menagerie. Remember, these are all wild beasts, so watch your fingers."

It always amuses me when people get their first look at my collection of miniature monsters. Particularly the adventuring types, who have previously encountered full-sized versions of many of the beasts. This group was no exception. I smiled as I absorbed the shocked gasps, the "ooh"s and the "aah"s, and the soft cooing over the more adorable specimens.

"Is that a miniature Catoblepas?" Cordela asked.

"Yes, it is," I replied. "Don't look too closely. It's gaze no longer has the power to kill, but it can still give you an awful headache."

"So, you use a form of diminution magic?" Rizo asked analytically.

"My own version of the spell," I was feeling professorial, and also showing off a bit. "The common version only lasts a short time, but I have discovered a way to make the effect permanent."

"Are you thinking what I'm thinking, Rizo?" Cordela asked the halfling as she stroked my gryphon's beak.

"Maybe," he answered without looking away from me. "Is there any kind of creature you haven't been able to reduce?" His expression didn't change, but I sensed that he was very busy calculating behind those brown eyes.

"None that I've found," I shared. "Is there something in particular you had in mind?"

"How about a dragon?"

That actually surprised me. I think my eyebrows may have risen just a tad. Perhaps just one. "I've always wanted to try. They usually won't sit still for the procedure."

"I think we can handle that part. Will you do it for us?"

I didn't want to appear too eager at this point. Knowing that these adventurers managed to capture a dragon alive raised my appraisal of them. And I was ready to jump at the chance to work my enchantment on it. But I hesitated just a moment to see if I had any advantage on the exchange. Cordela provided me an opening.

"We can't really pay you, though," she said. "And time is short. He needs to be shrunk by tomorrow morning."

I made a show of stroking my beard in thought. "As to payment, if you'll grant me publishing rights to the tale you shared earlier, and an option on however your adventure with this dragon turns out, we can call it even."

"Right, you're a writer," Cordela laughed. "That sounds fair. How about the urgency?"

"I suggest we head to where you have this dragon secreted immediately," I intoned.

Forty Three

CORDELA had described the location of their dragon, and Klepsis had suggested that they ride downriver with a nearby fisherman that he was acquainted with. Unfortunately, the tiny fishing skiff would not accommodate their mounts, so Cordela sent Valory with Sintros and Athera to convey the horses back down to the river docks where they could be safely ferried back to the barge. Cordela and Rizo accompanied Klepsis.

Rizo found that he trusted the old man. Oh, he immediately saw through his "harmless little me" manner. But besides that, Rizo sensed a genuine relaxedness that indicated that he was unlikely to be scheming the world's downfall. Rizo hoped it was his normally reliable judgement of character, and not just some influence charm that the mage had cast on him.

Along the way, Klepsis regaled them with a synopsis of his (claimed) semi-autobiographical work, Dragonslayer: A Young Wizard's Tale. It was apparently the story of a young wizard's apprentice, who takes up his master's quest to rid a distant village of the vile dragon who preyed on their children, after the older wizard is viciously murdered. Along the way he meets many challenges, chief among them the blacksmith's daughter. Naturally, Klepsis did not finish the tale, advising instead that they would have to "buy the book" if they really wanted to know what happened.

Rizo knew that powerful mages could fetch a high price for their service. He wondered how book publishing could possibly be as remunerative. Perhaps he had discovered some magical way to produce thousands of copies of a work at a time.

They arrived back at the barge in the late afternoon. Snowball was if anything looking even worse than he had been when they left that morning. Cordela introduced Klepsis to Markham and Bowe.

"Is Valory all right?" Markham expressed concern.

"She'll be here soon with the horses."

"And to what do we owe the pleasure of the company of Klepsis?" Bowe asked.

Rizo spoke up. "We hope he can help us solve our shipping problem."

Klepsis nodded to Bowe and Markham, then turned to the dragon. "So, this is our subject. He looks rather poorly, doesn't he?"

"He isn't used to sitting in the sun all day," Cordela said.

"Hmm. At least he won't squirm during the procedure. But do you have a plan to keep him cold afterward? It would be a shame to expend powerful magic just to have the subject die shortly thereafter."

Rizo had actually given the matter some thought. "I have some frost magic. That should chill him for a while."

"Excellent. I'll begin my preparations."

Preparations included setting out several jars of foul-smelling unguents, a blue silk ribbon, some small semiprecious gemstones, and an unusual instrument that looked like a steel rod with lenses affixed in a column to one side of it. Rizo looked over the wizard's shoulder as he placed the instrument up to one eye, and saw that it produced a very small image of what it was pointed at, much like an inverse telescope.

While he was setting up, Valory arrived with their mounts. "Since we are headed to Amorium, Athera and Sintros wrote a missive to their high priest for us to deliver."

"I think we can handle that," Cordela replied. "It was fortuitous that they found us in Ilium."

"Isis certainly guided them," Valory nodded, then added, "That is, if this magic works. Does he really need all that claptrap?"

"I assume," Cordela shrugged.

"Well, it looks like you got him here just in time. I don't think that dragon is going to last another day under this sun."

Klepsis waved his arms to demand silence from everyone, and began a low chant. Rizo recognized some of the words as part of a regular shrinking spell that most wizards learn early in their training. It was just the inverse of the spell he had used to make Markham the size of a bugbear. But Klepsis wove it between other spells used to imbue ordinary objects with magic, and elements that were beyond Rizo's experience and knowledge. The unguents he used to paint sigils on the deck of the barge surrounding Snowball, placing the gemstones at focal points of the design. The chant gradually increased in volume, and rose and fell in pitch. The pattern made some sense to Rizo, but as much as he tried he could not anticipate it, and the underlying arcane logic eluded him. Klepsis completed the painted design, and the tempo of his chant accelerated. He stared through his instrument intently. The stains on the deck began to glow a pearlescent white, and Klepsis held on a single note of his chant for a few seconds. An intense flash blinded Rizo for a moment, and when his eyesight cleared the sigils and the gemstones were gone. Rizo initially thought that the dragon had vanished as well, but then he saw that Snowball was still there, asleep on the barge, but reduced to the size of Iko-Iko. Or perhaps even smaller.

"Nice work, Klepsis," Rizo congratulated the older magic user.

"That took a bit longer than I'm used to," he replied, "but I would say the results are quite satisfactory."

"Ooh," said Valory, "He's adorable!"

"We need to get him somewhere cold," Rizo reminded everyone. He walked to the stack of provisions that Hester, the barge master, was leaning against. He quickly found one of the empty water barrels, rolled it toward the sleeping dragon, and pried the lid off. "He ought to fit in here, don't you think?"

Cordela nodded, and bent down to scoop up the tiny dragon. He awoke and squirmed weakly, but Cordela held him firmly and cooed softly to calm the beast.

Rizo set the open barrel upright and withdrew his frost wand from his vest. He aimed the wand into the barrel and muttered the control word. The interior surface of the barrel instantly was covered with a thick coating of ice crystals. He waved to Cordela to set Snowball down in the icy container. Rizo replaced the lid. "That ought to perk him up."

"How long will it stay cold in there?" Cordela asked.

"I don't know," Rizo shrugged. "Long enough, I hope. I think that was the last charge on this wand. Unless Klepsis can recharge it?" He proffered the stick to the older wizard.

"Hmm. Fine craftsmanship," he admired the magic item. "Looks like the work of Lanthanum." He handed it back to Rizo. "Afraid you'll have to return it to him for refills."

"Well, I would say you have done enough to aid us. We won't keep you any longer."

"I thank you for the opportunity to practice. And watch your local booksellers for the *Adventures of Cordela and Rizo*."

"Don't you mean Rizo and Cordela?"

"Of course. If I could just trouble you for the price of a ferry ride, I'll be off."

Forty Four

IT was not all that unusual to see a single-person craft navigating the waters of the Kaystros River. So, few paid any heed to the small skiff that bore Garynd DiMarco southward. If they had, they might have noticed the gloomy eyes and frowning chin that reflected Garynd's feelings of disgust and frustration that ate away at his insides. He had failed to catch Cordela Shent at Ismara, where she had acquired unknown but doubtless very powerful magic, and also of all things a very large dragon. All due to the misunderstanding that had landed him in a prison overnight. And to add insult to injury, he had overpaid for this very boat since none had been willing to rent it to him for a one-way trip. He hoped he could sell it for a decent price downriver, but meanwhile he was the reluctant owner of this barely river-worthy rowboat.

He would have been in a marginally better mood if he had the luxury of lazily drifting with the current. But that would not have made up the time he lost while boat shopping, and he could not afford to lose the trail of Miss Shent. So he needed to provide some of his own propulsion. Unfortunately, due to the biomechanics of rowing, he had to keep his back to the direction of travel for the best efficiency. That meant that it was difficult to watch where he was going, and the heavy level of traffic on the river required his constant awareness to dodge all of the much larger barges and other shipping vehicles. His progress was not as rapid as he desired, which contributed that much more to his grumpiness.

The traffic grew even worse as he approached Pistros. As all of the transport barges jockeyed for position to dock there to load on the valuable Pistros stone, Garynd was hard pressed to keep from being crushed between them. As his attention was focused on collision avoidance, he did not notice the barge with the large dragon napping on it until he was well past that part of the river. Garynd emitted an Icelandic curse. Rowing back upriver was out of the question. Not only did Garynd not wish to tangle with all the traffic he had just spent the last 30 minutes dodging, but the current was too swift and he was too exhausted from the dodging to fight it. However, having finally overtaken Cordela, he could now seek a suitable spot to lay in an ambush. Just above Ilium he located the perfect area. It was a shallow marshy place on the west side of the river. The shallow water would make for an easy anchorage, and the tall reeds that grew there would offer him an adequate view of the river while concealing him from the eyes of those traveling on it. All he had to do was wait for Cordela's barge to float into view.

As Garynd waited it began to grow dark, but this did not concern him at all. Lights from a cottage on the east side of the river offered backlighting to limn the silhouette of any barges that floated into view, even if they had none of their own lights. He retrieved some dry rations from his pack and stretched his legs across the benches of the tiny rowboat. His mood had finally begun to improve when he froze mid-chew as a low keening sound drifted through the reeds. He had only heard such a sound once in his life, and it was almost the last sound he ever heard.

It was the wail of a banshee.

The last time he had heard it, he and the band of ruffians he was loosely attached to at the time were on their way to deliver an artifact they had been hired to lift from the home of a local noble. The job had gone well, and the cheap duplicate they had left in place of the heirloom was close enough that the theft wouldn't be discovered for a while, long enough for them to collect their pay and be gone. The night sky was overcast, leaving the area dark and perfect for stealth. The shortest route to their drop point for the artifact was across a moor overgrown with bracken that offered plenty of cover. It seemed a natural shortcut to take, and they had ignored the local legends of haunting spirits that roamed the moor.

It was the last mistake most of them would ever make.

They first heard the keening as though from a great distance, and they ignored it, assuming it the call of a dog or other harmless wildlife that would likely give their large group a wide berth. Then as a momentary rift in the overcast allowed the starlight to illuminate a patch of sand in front of them, they saw the banshee. Spectral, bony, dressed in threadbare raiment, it extended its arms toward them, reaching and grasping. Then it wailed again.

Of the band of ten, only Garynd and one other survived. The other never spoke again, leaving Garynd the sole person to tell the tale, but only after spending a full week recovering under the ministrations of a skilled healer.

But he would never forget the sound, and here it was again, half a world and many years away from that forsaken moor. This time, though, Garynd had two defenses. One was experience. The other was his cittern. He reached for it under the seat of the skiff, extracted it from its protective leather envelope, checked that the strings were intact. He looked up to see the glimmering form of the banshee floating toward him over the marsh. Garynd thought that she might have been beautiful in life. Somehow this delicate, once fair woman had been abandoned in the marsh. Such was the manner in which these vengeful spirits came to haunt a place. Garynd began to play, just as the banshee wailed again.

As he had learned, and hoped was true, the music shielded Garynd from the worst effects of the keening. Still he felt the scream reaching out hungrily for his soul, full of longing and vengeance. And still the banshee approached. Garynd realized that as long as he kept playing, both his hands were occupied so that he could not fend off the spirit, whether with a sword or anything else. But if he took his hands off the instrument, the wailing would kill him instantly. He tried singing some suggestions to the banshee, but they had no effect. His only option was to abandon the rowboat and try to outrun the touch of the corrupt spirit.

The banshee pursued Garynd for the rest of the night, with only the rays of dawn driving it away. Garynd was relieved, but also muddy, tired, hungry, and, he realized, completely lost. He at least had the rising sun for bearing, and was able to navigate back to the river. He arrived just in time to watch Cordela float by on her barge with her dragon, impotent to do anything more. It was hours later when Garynd found his little skiff and was finally able to resume his pursuit.

Forty Five

THE following morning, the interior of the barrel was still quite frosty. Rizo took that as a good sign and went about making sure that everything was efficiently packed for loading onto the ship. Cordela was trying to coordinate what everyone needed to do before they could sail.

"Bowe, Markham," she had been trying to get the attention of both of them at once for a minute or two. "You two need to get all of our packs and bags, plus the barrel, plus our horses to the ship two hours before midday so they have time to load it."

"Two whole hours just to load a few bags and horses?" Bowe asked absent mindedly.

"Well, they were expecting a very large crate, so if we don't give them the full time it will probably be all right. Are you listening?"

"Sure. I got it. We'll give them two hours just in case. Now how did that chant go again?"

Cordela's left hand went to her head as if to pull out her hair, but instead it just fiddled with the crossbow bolt that pinned her bun in place. "Markham, are you paying attention? The ship will be at dock ten. It's called the Rowan Grouse."

"That name doesn't inspire confidence," Markham shook his head. "But we'll be there, with all the cargo and animals."

"I'll help Markham," Valory said. "And Bowe," she added as an afterthought.

"No!" Cordela's grip on the crossbow tightened. "You need to head to the shipping office and let them know we only need passage for five people plus mounts."

"Six people," Rizo corrected.

"Six?"

"Assuming Drax has managed to find us a trainer. We'll want to take them with us right?"

"Right. That's our job, Rizo. Thanks for reminding me." Releasing the bolt, she turned back to Valory. "You'll have to renegotiate the fare, and pay them." She grabbed a sack from the crate that Rizo was packing. "Here. This is about a thousand gold pieces. That should cover it." She fished a handful of coins from the bag, then handed Valory the bag.

"I don't want you wandering around Ilium alone with that much gold on you," Markham's normally dark and even voice was plaintive with concern.

"Don't worry dear," Valory responded. "I can take care of myself!"

Cordela handed the loose coins to Hester the barge pilot. "Thank you for waiting the extra days for us to make our arrangements. I hope you haven't lost much trade on our account."

"It was no problem," he smiled and accepted the gratuity. "Besides, where else would I have had the opportunity to observe a dragon up close for so long? Good luck getting it home, and I hope the Prince appreciates his gift."

"Thanks. Can you flag us a ferry? I think we're ready to go."

When the ferry deposited them at the Ilium river port, they all helped to unload the cargo from the small flatboat. Rizo had Cordela block him from the sight of casual passersby so he could put up his invisibility shield. Then Cordela went to arrange for a transport cart to the seaport for the cargo, and into the city for Valory and herself. Cordela didn't want Valory to delay her visit to the shipping office any more, so they didn't stay to help Markham and Bowe load their cart.

Rizo silently hopped into the wagon next to Cordela, who somehow already had Iko-Iko on her lap. "Why the rush?" he whispered to her.

"I'm afraid if we don't pay up the shippers will sell our spots to someone else."

Rizo wasn't so concerned about that, but he wasn't going to complain about not cutting it close. Besides, he thought they had something else to do in Ilium before they set sail. He couldn't remember what it was, though.

The wagon dropped them off at the head of the main East-West thoroughfare. They parted ways there with Valory, after Cordela gave her a brief hug. "See you at dock 10," Valory said and was off toward the offices of Oblong & Sons.

Rizo and Cordela turned to the south toward the home of Drax. As they approached, Iko-Iko became skittish, staying close to Rizo's feet. "Something's wrong," he alerted Cordela.

"It looks like his front door is open," Cordela said. A bit closer she added, "It's actually off of its hinges."

They both drew weapons. Cordela carefully swung the door open and waved Rizo inside.

Drax's house was dark. The lamps that usually hung on the loft supports were not lit, and Rizo wasn't even sure they were still hanging in their usual spots. He tried to move quietly, but the floor was littered with shards of broken dishes from the overturned table. He listened for any sound from elsewhere in the house, but heard none. He was pretty sure he was the only one inside, but he let Cordela, still waiting outside, wonder what was going on for a bit longer. He dispelled his invisibility, and waited another beat. Finally he said, loud enough for her to hear, "What a mess."

Cordela followed Iko-Iko through the door and illuminated the interior with her still glowing shield. "What happened in here?"

"Either Lorimer's lackeys, or maybe his paid-for officers in the Ilium police force, finally figured out that Drax has been helping us."

"Do you think Drax might have been captured?"

"Maybe not," Rizo made for the ladder up to the loft. "I think we can get an idea, though. Point your shield up here for a second."

Cordela followed him up. He led her back to the kitchen.

"What exactly are we looking for up here?" Cordela sounded impatient as Rizo examined the pots that hung on a circular rack above a work table.

"I'm noticing that everything is put away and in order," Rizo gestured around. Then he went to the hearth. "And here is the clincher. The stove is cold."

"And what does that tell us?"

"That Lalla had plenty of time to make sure her kitchen was taken care of before she left."

"So she had advanced warning about whoever busted in!"

"Exactly." Rizo appreciated that Cordela usually caught on quickly. It was a welcome change from some of his prior associates. "I'm guessing that Drax got wind that they were getting visitors, and got everyone out beforehand. So there's a good chance that he's also safe somewhere."

"Well, that's a relief," Cordela said. "But where do we find him?"

"I think I know just where to look," Rizo was cagey, just in case there were any spies eavesdropping. "Let's go."

Rizo led Cordela through the nearby streets while checking to be sure they weren't followed. Or, it would be more accurate to say, since he had resumed his vanishing act, that he led Iko-Iko through the streets, and Iko-Iko led Cordela. At their destination, he used the shadows of the building's entryway to reappear.

"The Thirsty Turtle?" Cordela read the sign hanging at the entrance as she followed the cat inside. "A pub?"

"It used to be our favorite hangout," Rizo explained. "And it was always a safe place to meet if the temperature got a little too warm elsewhere in the city."

"You think he'll be here?"

"I would almost guarantee it." He moved farther into the dimly lit drinking room with Cordela close in tow. There were not many customers. Rizo wondered about the few present, drinking even before dinnertime. Night workers, perhaps. They ignored the newcomers, at least. Rizo made for the bar.

"What can I get you?" the bartender asked without looking up from the cask he was tapping.

"I'm looking for Drax."

"Oh, it's you," the barkeep finally noticed. "Come with me, and keep quiet."

The barkeep led Rizo and Cordela down a hallway adjacent to the bar. It led to a storeroom stacked high with barrels and crates. "Wait here," the barkeep instructed them, and left the way they had come in.

Cordela had on a confused and questioning look, so Rizo provided some explanation.

"Drax is probably watching us from a safe spot. He's being very careful."

"You bet I am," came the familiar voice, followed soon by the rest of Drax from behind a stack of crates. "You have got me in a world of trouble."

"He's very good at that," Cordela agreed.

"Sorry about your place," Rizo offered. "I hope you got out in time."

"Sure," Drax smiled, "I heard they were planning to visit, so I sent Lalla to stay with her sister and kept to places they would be unlikely to look for me."

"Glad to hear it." Rizo clapped the other halfling on the shoulder. "We ship out in a few hours. That ought to take the heat off of you soon enough. We came to say bye and thanks. But I was also hoping you had managed to locate a trainer for us."

"As a matter of fact I have." Drax waved back toward the stack of crates, and a tall man came from behind the crates and bowed slightly. He had olive toned skin, curly hair that may once have been dark but was now streaked with gray, and an aquiline nose. Drax made the introductions. "This is Forescythe. He is the only one I have heard of east of Athens with experience with dragons."

"Cordela. Pleased to meet you." They grasped hands briefly.

"I'm Rizo. I've actually heard of you. You have a very good reputation. I thought you did mostly land mounts — great cats, giant boars, that sort of thing."

"Heh, I've heard a bit about you as well," the trainer laughed. "The mounts are more common, easier and more reliable work. But I've done quite a few dragons. Mostly black, some green. I hear you've got a white?"

Rizo nodded.

"Should be no problem."

"You'll do fine. How much do you want for the job?"

"Drax tells me you'll need me to travel. That puts my fee at 2000 gold, plus travel expenses."

"I was expecting more like 1000," Rizo shook his head.

"I don't train a dog for that little. Anything else, or am I wasting my time?"

"1600. Plus return passage included."

"1800, plus I get to keep the first molting."

"Deal. Be ready to go an hour before midday today. Dock

10."

"I'll need something to signal commands to the beast as well."

Right. That's what Rizo had been forgetting all day. The whistle. He and Cordela would have to go by the silversmith before heading to the ship. "We've got that already taken care of." He glanced at Cordela, who nodded.

"An hour before midday?" Drax interrupted. "That's pretty soon. You had better go get your affairs in order, Forescythe."

To Rizo and Cordela the curly haired man said, "See you shortly." He excused himself.

"Thank you for all your help," Cordela said to Drax. "We're really sorry about all the trouble."

"I'm rather used to it with Rizo," he clapped his fellow halfling on the shoulder. "But he's gotten me out of more than a few scrapes, so I'm glad I can return the favor. Did you make all the arrangements for shipping your 'cargo' yet?"

"Yes, we found a, um, creative solution to that problem. Remind me to tell you about it someday."

Drax laughed and shook his head. "I can't wait. Good luck, Rizo."

"It was nice to meet you," Cordela waved a farewell.

"Likewise. And don't let this guy get on your nerves. He can be the most annoying troll ever, but I would rather have him watching my back than anyone else."

Forty Six

BY now Cordela had gotten used to talking to someone she couldn't see. But for now, she could just talk to Iko-Iko. Usually he was pretty squirmy, but at the moment he was content to let her hold him. She had insisted on doing so to Rizo, since she didn't want to lose him in the bustle of the seaport and have to hunt him down, possibly missing their ship. Rizo had assured her that his empathic link to the cat would make that very unlikely, but Cordela wasn't hearing it. So as they walked in the direction of dock 4 — delta, Cordela reminded herself — she pretended to speak to Iko-Iko as he gently purred in her arms.

"I don't think we're going to have that much coin left, even after Valory renegotiates our passage," she cooed into the cat's ear.

"I'm sure we can convince him to take payment in treasure," said the voice of the invisible Rizo in reply.

"I hope so. We can't very well gift the Prince an untrained dragon, can we?" Her voice lilted to keep up her pretense.

"We might end up gifting him a trained miniature dragon if we don't find a way to return him to full size," the air responded.

"We'll ask Lanthanum for help with that while we're in Amorium, won't we kitty?"

"You know he can understand you, right?"

"I'm pretty sure he understands me better than you do. But he doesn't seem to care as long as I keep scritching his ears." She gave said ears a ruffle.

"Here is the silversmith," the Rizo voice trailed off up the stairs to the second floor shop. Cordela followed, still stroking the soft fur. At the landing, she waited for Rizo to go inside.

"Ahem," said Rizo's voice.

"Are you going in?"

"I don't want anyone seeing the door opening on its own."

Cordela grunted and set down a disappointed-looking Iko-Iko on the landing. She pushed the door, but it didn't budge. She knocked, then listened at the door. There was no sign of the silversmith. She banged louder. Still no response.

A woman's head emerged from the insurance office at the other side of the landing. "Looking for the silversmith?" she said. Judging by the elongated ears, she was probably some kind of elf, with dark hair and thin eyebrows.

"Is he open today?" Cordela hoped the answer was 'yes' or they weren't getting their whistle.

"Hyracolos just stepped out for a moment," the insurance elf informed her. "He ought to be back soon."

Cordela inhaled a relief breath. "Thank you. I'll just wait here then."

After the woman had drawn her head back inside the insurance office and closed the door, Rizo's voice complained, "He had better get back soon. We don't have much time."

Cordela sat at the top step idly twirling her flail. She wasn't sure what Rizo was doing, but when she periodically checked to see that he was still there, he always was, either on the stairs near her or on the landing. Finally, Hyracolos returned carrying a basket of scrap metal and assorted pieces of candelabra and serving utensils.

"Ah, you are here. Sorry I was out. I was expecting you yesterday. Your item is ready. Is your halfling friend about?"

229

"Yes, he's close by," she told the smith as he unlocked the door to his shop. "I'll wait here for him to catch up, and then join you inside." She smiled in a way that she hoped didn't look unnaturally forced. Rizo did some stomping on the stairs to emulate himself arriving from the street, then reappeared in front of Cordela on the landing. "Let's hurry up and finish our business here."

The engraving on the whistle was finely executed, and Cordela agreed that the Prince would be very pleased. As Rizo counted out the remaining gold they owed on the work, Hyracolos placed the whistle in a varnished oak box lined with velvet, and Cordela asked him, "Do you happen to know the time?"

The smith waved toward a glass dome on his counter. It held a miniature sundial, elegantly fashioned in silver. Its gnomon cast a shadow on its face as if it were illuminated by bright sunlight.

"Very nice enchantment," she complimented. Then she noticed the time. "Hey Rizo. It's nearly midday. We need to go."

"Nineteen, twenty. That should settle us up." Rizo grabbed the box with a flourish. "Let's go."

"Thank you, Hyracolos," Cordela called out as she followed Rizo out of the shop.

"Pleasure doing business with you. Best of luck."

At the bottom of the steps, Cordela called out, "Hey, now!" and Iko-Iko emerged from behind the steps and bounded into her arms.

She headed for dock ten.

She got to about halfway between docks 6 and 7 when she found her way blocked by three officers of the Ilium police force.

"Hold it right there," one of them said, "we've been looking for you for quite a while now."

"Looking for me? Why?"

"Not you," the policeman said. "The halfling."

Cordela followed the officer's gaze to her left, and saw Rizo there, securing the whistle box in his belt.

"Why aren't you invisible?" she said quietly through her clenched teeth.

"I thought I was," he muttered.

"Ugh. We don't have time for this." At her words, Iko-Iko leapt from her arms and landed on the face of the policeman nearest Rizo. Cordela used her now free hands to sling her shield and flail from their clasps. The officers to her right were focused on Rizo and were unprepared for her onslaught. She brought her shield up under the chin of one of them. She heard and felt the crunch as his jaw dislocated. The second policeman recovered more quickly and advanced on Cordela with his sword drawn. Cordela deftly caught the sword on Tadlusa's chains and whipped it out of his hand. In her peripheral vision, Rizo was taking advantage of Iko-Iko's distraction to bring the third adversary down. As her foe dove for his sword, Cordela pounded the back of his exposed head to drop him.

"Now we're really late," Rizo quipped. "We better run like Hermes."

As they scurried northward toward where the Rowan Grouse awaited them, Cordela said, "Those weren't just more of Lorimer's goons."

"No," panted Rizo, "things have gotten serious."

"What sort of trouble are we in now?"

"I hope the Rowan Grouse is ready to sail when we get there."

No one else got in their way. Valory was waiting for them near the pier with Forescythe and another woman. "There you are! I was beginning to wonder if you were going to make it in time."

"We had to stop by the silversmith for our dragon whistle. And we stopped for a brief, um, conversation."

"I assume you know these two people?"

"This is our dragon trainer. But I'm not sure who you are," Cordela addressed the woman.

"Allow me to introduce my assistant, Herodia," Forescythe spoke for her.

"Pleased to meet you," Cordela said. "But I don't think we booked passage for you."

Valory confirmed this with a shake of her head.

"I'll catch up later," Herodia's voice was melodic, but Cordela imagined that it could project far in a pinch.

"Herodia will secure my fee for me. I presume you have it?"

"Valory, how much coin is left from paying for our passage?"

"Not much. The extra person was almost as much as the cargo space we didn't need."

"I guess they assume they don't need to feed cargo."

"Can we pay you in treasure?" Rizo cut in. "What have we got, Valory? We need 1600 gold pieces worth."

"Our agreement was for 1800," Forescythe was plaintive.

"Making sure you are paying attention." Rizo drew a silver chalice and a jewel-embedded necklace from the sack that Valory produced from beneath her cloak. "These two are worth close to 2000 together."

"Why are you standing on the dock with a sack full of treasure, Valory?" Cordela squinted at her friend.

Valory shrugged. "I figured we would have to pay the trainer somehow."

"Good thinking." Once again, her friend showed her that she didn't need to do everything herself.

Forescythe and his assistant examined the articles and conversed in low tones during this. "I value the goblet at least 1000. The necklace is harder to value, since neither of us is a gem expert. We will have to have it appraised."

"Can Herodia do it?" Rizo asked. "We already paid for your trip, so you might as well come along and enjoy the cruise. Keep the necklace either way, it will at least cover your return trip."

Forescythe spoke to his assistant quietly again. "The proposal is acceptable. Herodia will send a message with the appraisal value. If it is sufficient, you will have a trainer for your beast."

"Great," said Cordela, nervously eyeing some uniformed fighters approaching dock 9. "Then let's get aboard, shall we? I'm sure the captain wants to get moving."

At the top of the gangway, they were met by an extremely large bald man who wore no shirt but had large hoop earrings in both ears. Valory introduced him as Bonshpiel the ship's boatswain — although adopting the nautical style, she pronounced it "bosun."

"Is this the last of your party?" Bonshpiel asked Valory.

"Yes, we're all aboard, now."

"Welcome aboard the Rowan Grouse. I'll show you your quarters later. Meanwhile, have a seat by the mainmast. The captain will address everyone soon." Then, to various crew members he called, "Raise up the gangway! Throw the lines! Ready the sail!"

Cordela hadn't realized how quickly her heart was beating until the gangway closed behind her and she took a deep breath.

Forty Seven

THE Beaver Lodge was getting pretty full. Even during the post-dinner lull many tables were still full. Willie was having a hard time keeping up with cleaning the dishes, preparing supper, and making sure the rooms were straight. The seasonal help her father had brought in helped, but Willie as usual found that in order to make sure things were done to the level of quality that guests of the Beaver Lodge were used to, she had to do much of it herself.

She had just added a kettle to the hearth so that she would have enough hot water for dishwashing when Rizo strolled back in carrying a large paper-wrapped package. He sat himself and the package down at the table nearest her washbasin.

She had to wait for the water to heat, so she took a moment to sit with him.

"Is that your cloth from Ha'Eilen there?"

"Oh, no. I'm having him deliver that directly to where I need it. It would be much too big for me to carry it."

What could Rizo be doing that required more material than he could lift? Willie guessed she was just going to have to get the full story, bit by bit. "So, you were telling me about Ilium. You had just narrowly escaped being arrested and missing your ship."

"Well, we made it to the dock on time. That was when this adventure really got started."

"You mean traipsing all over the northern territories with a gigantic dragon wasn't adventure enough?"

"Well, let me tell you..."

Part III

Forty Eight

RIZO stood near the mainmast with Cordela and the others, as instructed. Toward the bow from them there was a large rectangular box that extended all the way to the foremast. Atop it sat an inverted rowboat. Aft of where he stood was a space with hatches in the floor, beyond which was a large superstructure that occupied the entire rear of the ship. Ladders provided access to the deck on its roof. As he waited he watched a tall, lanky man with a man-bun and hoop earrings shepherding some crew to a nearby area. He seemed to have a position of authority on the ship, and the crew obeyed him alacritously. Any hesitation, and a scowl from Mister Man-bun was all it took to get them in line. "Is that the captain?" Rizo whispered to Cordela. She shrugged.

"He's the first mate," Valory said. "We haven't seen the captain yet."

"Is that unusual?" Rizo wondered aloud.

"It's mighty rare to see the cap'n before we're underway," said a nearby crewman. The man was average height, with a full build and very close-cropped reddish hair.

"So, not your first cruise, I take it?" Rizo extended a hand to the fellow. "I'm Rizo."

The man laughed silently, and did not return the gesture. "Pequod," he said, before a stern look from the first mate silenced him.

As the man Pequod had suggested, they were well out into the offing before Man-Bun strode along the row of crew he had assembled with one arm raised, and announced, "Captain Aylson will address the crew and passengers. Give the Captain your full attention."

A door in the aft superstructure opened and out stepped a

woman in a lavender blazer over a purple bodice, with a matching tri-corner hat. Her tight coils of hair bounced on her shoulders, and the sheathed saber at her hip stood out against her dark leather pants. She was not tall, perhaps the same height as Cordela, but Rizo sensed that she was not one to tussle with.

"Greetings. I am Captain Kenna Aylson. Welcome aboard the Rowan Grouse, or welcome back if ye've sailed with us before."

Rizo couldn't quite place her accent. Definitely not local.

"Ar winds should be fav'rable, an' we ought to reach ar destination of Amorium in seven ta ten days. Mistar Finnlar here will be yer first mate." She indicated Man-bun. "Fer yer own safety and that of everyone on board, ye will follow his instructions immediately an' without question. He is my representative and is fully authorized to make any necessary decisions on me behalf.

"Since we have some passengers aboard, I'll take a moment to review the safety features of this vessel. There are no safety features on this vessel. Just watch yerself, an' stay out the way of the crew. You've got 15 minutes to get to the mess when Cook rings the dinner bell or no slop fer ye, an' ye best be at yer shift an' ready ta work on time. Mistar Bonshpiel here handles the duty roster. That'll be all."

After her welcome speech, Captain Aylson approached Rizo and his fellows. "Yer horses and luggage are in the starboard hold. You are expected to care for, feed, and clean up after them. We arn't runnin' a stable here. Ye may be called upon to pitch in with rowing, fighting, or other work. Also, make sure he knows to stay well back from the rails," she waved at Iko-Iko, "an' don't let him bother the crew." Her countenance relaxed then a bit. "With that understood, I'd like to invite you all to sup at my table this evening."

Cordela was quicker to answer than Rizo, "We would be delighted and honored."

"Great. Just meet right here at sunset. Finnlar will show you in. Now, please excuse me. I need ta see that the crew has settled in."

The Captain headed abow, and Rizo was about to follow out of curiosity, when Pequod placed his meaty hand on Rizo's chest.

"If ye could hold there a minute, I've a proposition fer yer consideration." The way he said "proposition" triggered Rizo's deal-making reflex. Cordela and Valory also stood by. Probably waiting to see what fresh trouble Rizo was getting himself into.

"This is my twelfth cruise with Cap' Kenna. Done pretty much every job on this ship. But for this trip, Ole Bonshpiel has assigned me tarring the beam. You, sir, would be much better suited for that task. I'm offerin' ta take care-a yer horses, an' e'en clean up after 'em, if you'll tar the beam fer me."

Rizo wasn't sure what it might mean to "tar the beam," but he knew he didn't much like shoveling horse dung. Of course, he would be sharing that job with his four fellows. But avoiding it altogether sounded even better. He looked at Cordela.

"Make the deal, Rizo. Whatever you need to do for Pequod here, we'll help you out. Meanwhile, we won't have to worry about the animals."

"All right, mister Pequod," Rizo was still tentative. "I'm not sure what I'm getting myself into, but if you care for our mounts for the entire cruise, I'll tar this beam for you."

"It's much appreciated, mister Rizo. I aim to make sure ye don't regret it."

"Pequod! Cook needs you to watch his stew pot." Bonshpiel interrupted just as their agreement was concluded.

"Aye, Bonshpiel. On me way." He waved to Rizo and disappeared down a nearby hatch.

"I can show ye yer quarters now, if ye like," offered the large bosun.

"Thank you, that would be great," Cordela responded. Bonshpiel led them forward, past the large box. Near the bow was another large superstructure, not as impressive as the one aft, but with similar doors. Ladders provided access to the top of it, and Rizo could see Markham and Bowe up there talking with some crewmen. Bonshpiel led them to the door on the right — starboard, Rizo reminded himself.

"Here ye are. It'll be a bit cozy with the six o'ye, but I reckon you'll manage. Ye seem like hardy type folk, nay?"

"It should be fine." Cordela seemed like anything would be just dandy, so thrilled was she to be on her first sea voyage.

Rizo looked inside the small cabin. A low bench along the far wall was the only seat. Latching cabinets underneath provided a bit of storage. Hammocks hung two high along three walls would suffice for sleeping accommodation. A small washbasin completed the appointment.

"If ye need anything, just ask me or Finnlar."

"We will," Rizo replied before Cordela could try to stop him. She huffed.

"Thank you, Mister Bonshpiel," Cordela was polite and sweet.

"Just 'Bonshpiel' is fine," the big man said. "Cap' Kenna's always so formal with the introductions. I'll check on ye later."

As the bosun left to see to his duties, Rizo turned to Cordela. "What are your plans for the afternoon?"

"Well, I'm going to walk around and see the ship. I've never been asea before, and I'm very curious."

"And we need to make sure Markham, Bowe, and Forescythe know where to find our cabin," added Valory. "What about you?"

"I plan to test out one of these hammocks," Rizo smiled. "Make sure I'm up in time for supper."

The gentle rock of the Rowan Grouse made it one the best naps of Rizo's life.

Forty Nine

CORDELA and Valory found Markham on the forecastle, above their cabin. She took pride in knowing a few nautical terms from her reading, like "forecastle." Markham seemed to be getting some lessons in how to use a large piece of armament that was fastened to the deck on a pivot.

"It's called a ballista," Markham was explaining to Valory. "It's basically just a big crossbow. The heavy bolts sink a bit more, so you have to compensate for that while aiming." He was turning a crank to bring the cup down into firing position. "It does help to have a second person to assist with loading. And it's affixed to the deck, so there is some limit to what you can shoot at. Leeman here has been walking me through the finer points."

The crewman that Markham was referring to nodded her head, "He's a natural. Picked it up right away. And I've never seen anyone who can spin that crank as fast."

Valory wore her "Of course, Markham is awesome" look. But Cordela was impressed as well. "I noticed they have a catapult as well. Do you plan to train on that also?"

Markham laughed. "I think the exact term for that piece of artillery is 'mangonel.' No, the projectiles from that thing have to arc a lot more. You need to know a lot of math to use it properly."

"Well, when you're done you may want to find our cabin before supper. It's right below here."

"I'll show him," Valory offered. "You said you wanted to look around the ship."

Cordela smiled. "Okay, um, thanks. Careful not to wake Rizo."

"That guy can sleep through anything."

"Uh huh. I don't think he even needs to sleep that much. He just likes it." She shrugged, waved to Valory and Markham, and went on her way.

Cordela watched the crew work the sails as the Rowan Grouse tacked with a shifting wind. They called brief instructions to each other to coordinate the almost elegant dance, while Finnlar up on the aft deck called directions to the tiller, who must have been on a lower deck, as Cordela couldn't see him.

Later, Cordela found Forescythe and Bowe sitting on the main deck. Bowe looked a little green.

"The sea not agreeing with you?"

He just shook his head.

"Hmm. I'm not sure I have a spell for seasickness. But let me try something." She chanted an elvish rhyme from her childhood, and ran her hands from the top of Bowe's head down to his shoulders. It wasn't magical at all, but she was pretty sure Bowe didn't know that. "Better?"

"A bit." He nodded. "Thanks."

She described how to find their cabin, warned the two of them that Rizo might still be asleep there, and wished Bowe to feel better, before heading on her way.

As she made her way around the deck, she noticed that the crew seemed to spend an inordinate amount of time scrubbing the deck with these long handled mops. She asked crewman Leeman about it.

"It's for safety. When the oil drips on the deck it can get awfully slippery"

"Oil?" Cordela didn't follow at all.

"Aye. We always keep the rope lines well-oiled so they're easier to pull through the eyes and stays. Also keeps them from fraying so they last."

"But the oil drips, and lands on the deck," Cordela finally caught on.

"So, we have to swab it," Leeman finished.

"Cap' Kenna runs a tight ship," Leeman's fellow swabber cut in. "'Tain't always so. I was on one ship where a fella slid right under the gunnel rail, right into the drink. That Cap'n didn't even think much of it, just laughed. The first mate went an' fished 'im out."

"Sounds like that captain didn't have much concern for his crew," Cordela observed.

"So true, that," the man nodded. "I don't mind the extra work when I know Cap' Kenna has me back."

When they were done swabbing, they taught Cordela a seagoing song that they called a "shanty." Its rhythm was very different from the marching and traveling songs she knew. It was much more suited to the gentle rolling of a ship on the waves. This one featured lyrics about a "lassie" from a far-off port known as Liverpool. After going through it a couple of times, Cordela thought she had the words down. The sun was low in the sky, nearly time for her to head down to meet "Cap' Kenna" for supper.

Fifty

RIZO Malkin was an annoyed halfling. He was annoyed because he was awakened from his nap some time before he felt he was through with it. It wasn't the arrival of Valory showing Markham their cabin. They were quiet and discreet. It wasn't the sound of footsteps on the deck above. That was background ship noise that Rizo easily filtered out. It wasn't the sound of sea shanties drifting down from the upper decks. That was pleasantly soothing and lulled Rizo deeper into his slumber. No, what awakened him was Iko-Iko sitting on his chest and meowing into his face. Apparently, the cat was hungry.

Rizo flopped out of the hammock, dumping Iko-Iko unceremoniously on the floor. He splashed some water on his face and stepped through the cabin door out onto the deck. Bowe was there, looking a little unsteady on his feet.

"Still haven't got your sea legs, huh?" Rizo gently chided him.

"Just still feeling a bit queasy," the wizard replied. "Cordela's spell helped a lot, but the flutters aren't gone yet."

"What spell did she use?" Rizo didn't know of any anti-seasick magic.

"I don't know," Bowe shrugged. "Just basic curing, I guess."

"Uh-huh." Rizo nodded, but was skeptical. "Say, you didn't happen to notice where the galley is, did you?"

"I haven't noticed much of anything except things rocking back and forth. But I think I heard it was down one deck."

"Thanks. Maybe you want to lie down for a few minutes? Our cabin is right there."

"Thanks. I think I will." Bowe lurched in that direction.

Rizo looked around for a hatch or some other way to get to the lower decks. He saw what he was looking for adjacent to the front mast. Smells that Rizo would best term "interesting" emanated from the open hatch. A rope ladder invited him to pursue the odors, and Iko-Iko's incessant mewing provided additional impetus.

The ladder dropped him in a somewhat triangular shaped hold that obviously filled the bow. It was mostly full of ceramic jugs, of the type used to store and transport wine or olive oil. Through an open door to the aft he saw tables arranged across the short axis of the ship. Probably the mess hall. Rizo headed there, Iko-Iko in tow. The aromas grew stronger. To his left — that would be starboard now — a large window opened to the kitchen area — galley, he hastily corrected himself — beyond. The window had a wide sill like a counter or the bar of a tavern. The arrangement reminded Rizo of a certain kobold lunchroom he had visited some time ago.

"Supper eez not yet ready. Wait for bell, come back zhen," the burly cook said from behind a large stock pot.

"I'm looking for something for my cat."

The cook peered from behind the pot. His mustache twitched like a fish caught in a net. "You are not crew?"

"No, passenger. I'm Rizo, and this is Iko-Iko."

"A fine name for proud animal. I am Chef Prudhomme. What would ze chat like for supper?"

"Well, he is quite fond of kippers."

"Hmm. I haf no kippers. But I do have plenty salted fish. I keep in case I run out of fresh ongradients. See if he likes."

Iko-Iko tore into the salt fish like the fierce predator he assumed he was.

"And anysing for you, monseur?"

"No thank you. I'm supposed to be having supper with the Captain this evening."

"Ah, oui! I have prepared something extra especiale for you. Bon Appetit!"

"Thank you." Rizo led the now satisfied Iko-Iko aft. The Captain had said that their cargo was in the starboard hold, and since the hold in the bow was in the middle — he guessed that would be 'amidships' — the side holds must be at the other end of the ship. As he headed aft, to port he saw what appeared to be crew quarters. A few crew were dozing there, perhaps resting before an evening shift on duty. Past the main mast he could see where the hatches outside the Captain's quarters opened to the deck above. Another in the floor led to a third deck below this one. Far to aft he could see the tiller with the helmsman boredly leaning on the lever. Just before that a door to starboard led to the hold he sought.

The animals had provender, and their area was immaculate. Clearly Pequod had been, at least initially, true to his side of the deal. Next, Rizo found the barrel containing their miniaturized white dragon. Prying off the lid, he was surprised to find the interior still very icy. Rizo guessed that the dragon had been using its frost breath to adjust its environment. That was good, since Rizo's wand of frost was empty. Snowball looked up at him with what looked like a question in his eyes. Rizo expected that the question was probably "when do I get some food?" As he refastened the lid he resolved to ask Chef Prudhomme if he had any raw meat.

The remainder of their cargo, including what treasure they had left after paying for their passage, was secure. He thought about setting a trap for anyone on the crew less than trustworthy, but he would need some extra materials to pull that off. It would have to wait.

The chef rang the supper bell. Rizo thought he had better head up to meet the rest of his party. As he exited the hold, he saw another crewman come to relieve the helmsman on the tiller so he could eat. The sailor shot right past Rizo on his way to the mess. Either the fellow was extremely hungry, or Chef Prudhomme's slop was worth rushing for. Rizo found a rope ladder dangling from one of the hatches to the deck above and climbed while Iko-Iko clung to his hip. When he emerged into the main deck, the cat immediately ran off. "Stay out of the water," Rizo advised.

Cordela was already waiting on deck. "There you are. I stopped by the cabin like you asked, but you were already up."

"Iko-Iko was hungry," he explained.

"You didn't happen to check on our cargo while you were down there, did you?"

"In fact, I did. Pequod seems intent on keeping his part of our deal."

"And our *other* cargo?" She leaned closer and squinted one eye.

"Will need some tending."

Cordela nodded, just as Bowe arrived.

"You're looking much better," Cordela observed.

"At Rizo's suggestion, I had a lie-down in the cabin for a bit," replied the lanky wizard.

"It did you a world of good."

Rizo was about to comment that his remedy was more effective than Cordela's "spell", but was prevented by the arrival of Markham and Valory.

"Looks like we're all here," Valory said.

"We're missing Forescythe," Cordela reminded her.

"I hope supper is soon. I'm hungry."

"Apparently, the chef has prepared something extra special," Rizo offered.

Finnlar descended from the aft deck with Forescythe in tow. "The Captain will see you now. Right this way."

He showed them through the door from which the Captain had emerged earlier. The cabin had a high ceiling, where a chandelier held many lit candies that illuminated the room brightly. A large table and chairs filled most of the room. A staircase to port led upward, to what Rizo assumed was the Captain's private quarters. The table was already set for seven.

"The Captain will sit at the head," Finnlar intoned. "Sit anywhere else you like." With that, he left the cabin.

Rizo took the place to the left of the Captain. This was a habit developed over many years, assuming that most people were right-handed. Cordela either hadn't developed such a habit, or else trusted the Captain, as she took the seat to her right. Valory and Markham filled the seats to Cordela's left and Forescythe sat to Rizo's right. That left the end for Bowe, nearest the door.

They sat silently looking at each other for several long minutes before the Captain finally appeared at the top of the stairs. "I hope yer hungry. Cook tells me he outdid himself with supper for tonight."

"That's the report I heard as well," Rizo tracked her as she descended to her place at the table. He noted with satisfaction that she wore her sword on her left hip.

"Then you've already met our 'Chef' Prudhomme."

"My cat was hungry. Chef broke out some salted fish that satisfied him."

"Well, we will be getting fresher fare. The food is always better at the beginning of a cruise." Before she sat, she pulled on a chain that dangled on the wall behind her seat. Rizo heard the muffled tinkling of a bell just outside the cabin. "I assume by now that you know me as Captain Aylson. Might I have the pleasure of your names?"

They had barely finished the introductions when a pair of

crewmen carried in full platters and set them on the table. There was a salad of mixed lettuce and radishes with tart berries, steamed broccoli with nut slivers in a rich buttery sauce, braised beef with mushrooms, and a spicy squash. A third crewman brought one of the ceramic vessels that Rizo had seen in the hold and decanted wine into everyone's goblet.

Rizo tried every dish. He enjoyed everything but the squash, although Markham said it reminded him of his home in Tamilnadu.

"And where is home for you?" Rizo asked the Captain.

"The Grouse and I both hail from Glasgow," she said with some pride. Rizo now knew where to place her accent.

"I have not heard of Glasgow," Cordela said.

"It is about as far away as Tamilnadu, but in the opposite direction. Are ye all heading out from Ilium, or back to somewhere else?"

Cordela answered. "We are all from Palmyra, except Forescythe here, who lives in Ilium. We are heading back to Palmyra by way of Amorium."

"What brought you out to Ilium?"

"We were pretty far north, and came into possession of something, um, valuable, but too large to carry over land. Our solution was shipping downriver, and then by sea."

"But you didn't load anything bigger than a horse."

"Right," Cordela paused to chew, but the way she glanced at Valory told Rizo it wasn't the only reason. "We found an eager buyer in Ilium, and it made more sense to take the money. So, here we are."

"And you, Forescythe, joined them in Ilium?"

"Yes, I am offering some consulting services that require my presence."

"I see," the Captain seemed to accept the explanations. "I pegged ye for adventuring types as soon as I laid eyes on ye. Reminded me of me self in me younger days. Did a fair bit of adventuring of me own back then."

Rizo cut in. "How did you change to the sailing life?"

"I been asea practically me whole life. Who says ye can only find adventure on land, aye?"

Everyone at the table laughed at that. Then Rizo went on. "So you haven't been serving on merchant ships always?"

"Were you a pirate?" Valory blurted out.

"In those days, we preferred the term 'Freebooter.' " The Captain feigned hurt.

"Sounds fun," said Cordela. "Why did you leave it?"

"Well, at a certain point me nautical skills were enough to get me a high share on a merchant ship, and that paid better." The Captain sighed. "Also, high seas piracy ain't as fun or as glamorous as it might appear. And now I've got me own ship, and my prior reputation means that the scofflaws think twice afore messing with Kenna Aylson!"

"I've noticed that the crew all seem to call you Cap' Kenna," Cordela asked. "That would seem to soften your reputation somewhat."

"Ah, well. The Rowan Grouse's not that big a ship. There's only so much formality one can enforce. So long as the crew respect me and Finnlar, and work efficiently, they can call me what they like."

"Well, they do seem to respect you a great deal," Cordela shared. "My judgment is that they would do just about anything for you."

"The real question," Rizo asked before the Captain could respond, or even blush, "is what should *we* call you?"

"I suppose Cap' Kenna will do just fine," she said with a

chuckle.

Fifty One

SUPPER, and the ensuing conversation and wine tasting, had gone late into the night, and most of Rizo's traveling companions were still slumbering when Rizo quietly exited his hammock and went out on deck. As a test, he tried activating his invisibility. To his delight, it had recharged overnight. Not one to waste a magical effect, Rizo did some clandestine surveillance around the ship. When Cap' Kenna emerged from her quarters for her morning survey of the crew, he slipped behind her through the open door. Once inside he headed up the stairs.

The Captain's private bunk was functional and utilitarian. Besides the bed alcove there was a small wardrobe, a locked chest, and a small writing desk and bookshelf. Most of the books were old ship's logs, manuals on weather forecasting, or navigation guides. However, Rizo was amused to see a copy of *Dragonslayer* by R. A. Klepsis on her shelf. The chest was double-locked and booby trapped, so Rizo left it alone. Once he was back on deck, he found a hidden spot to reappear in. By then, Cordela, Valory, and Markham were awake and out of their cabin.

"Not used to seeing you out of your armor," Rizo approached them.

"Well, the likelihood of combat seems low, so I thought I'd let my skin feel the sea breeze for a change," Cordela replied.

"But I see you still saw fit to wear your flail."

"Well, can't be too careless. You're out early. Up to no good, I assume?"

Rizo stuck out his lower lip. "Just having a look around. What did you think of our Captain last night?"

Valory's brows lifted as she replied quickly. "She seems like a very capable and trustworthy individual, with a considerable amount of personal authority and charisma. Someone I wouldn't mind following, or fighting alongside of."

"She is definitely a formidable woman," Markham added.

Rizo nodded. "I'll warrant she can hold her own in a fight, all right. But something tells me she's got some devious skills as well."

"I guess it takes a thief to recognize one," Cordela said sardonically. "Did you find any breakfast while you were out making a nuisance of yourself?"

Rizo flashed his most annoying smile. He wasn't going to be baited. "Nope. Let's check the mess."

When they got below deck, they saw that Forescythe and Iko-Iko were already there enjoying a meal. Rizo introduced his friends to Chef Prudhomme.

"Bonjour! I hope you liked supper with ze Captain!"

"It was delicious," said Valory to general nods of agreement all around. "You seem to have found something for Rizo's cat as well."

"He is very picky," the Chef looked stern. "I do not sink I can keep him happy for long."

"He'll have to make do with what you can provide," Rizo furrowed his brows at his animal.

"What have you got for us this morning?" asked Cordela.

"Toasted bread, and batter fried tubers." He tossed four dishes on the counter.

"Mmm," Cordela reached for hers immediately. "Smells good."

"If you say so," Rizo muttered under his breath. But he took his portion. "Have to make do," he smiled at Iko-Iko and followed Cordela to a spot near Forescythe. Soon Bowe joined them as well. He seemed to be over his seasickness.

On their way out of the mess after eating, Cordela grabbed a stool that seemed not to be in use. "I feel like relaxing on deck," she explained.

On the main deck, she set her stool near the port rail and closed her eyes. Valory stood nearby leaning on the rail. Markham went up to the bow upper deck to do some calisthenics. Iko-Iko decided to climb the rigging, and Rizo watched nervously from below, following him around to starboard. The cat was nonchalant and sure-footed as he made his way out onto a spar. Rizo was finally relaxing a bit when he heard a scream.

He darted back around the large box amidship just in time to see Valory hoisted nearly off her feet by a giant tentacle that snaked over the rail back into the water.

Cordela was trying to leap from her stool to assist Valory, but had another tentacle wrapped around her ankle. He glanced back over his shoulder. "You stay there where it's safe, Iko-Iko." Then he let fly a handful of magic force missiles aimed at the tentacle around Valory, and dashed to Cordela's side.

"Let go you stupid squid," she said as she pounded the thing with her flail.

"Hold still, I'll try to stab it," Rizo was trying to grab the tentacle to keep it still.

"Just hit it farther up!"

Rizo stabbed and wrestled the tentacle off of Cordela's ankle — only to have it immediately wrap him up in its clenching grip.

He saw an enormous conical bulk rise up out of the ocean. Its wet skin glistened, and fins or vanes along the sides of it quivered grotesquely. A beak snapped hungrily in anticipation of a meal.

"That's a big squid," Cordela observed needlessly, and attacked the tentacle that enfolded Rizo.

Rizo yelled, "Go help Valory! I'm fine."

"You are not — " she was cut off by a loud "ka-Thunk" that came from behind her. A ballista bolt flew over their heads and glanced off the sea creature's thick hide.

"A little lower, Markham!" Cordela called to forward. Then she leapt to where Valory was nearly over the rail and into the water.

Rizo's dagger arm was pinned to his side, so he was actually in a bit more trouble than he had let on. He used all the escape skills he had, but barely got his arm free. He slashed at the appendage, but it seemed not to mind. He began to see spots as the air was slowly squeezed out of him. Just before he lost vision he saw Bonshpiel arise from the nearest hatch, an enormous scimitar in each hand. He felt the tentacle tremble as the big man hacked at it. All at once it relaxed, and Rizo gulped air.

His vision returned just in time for him to see another tentacle snaking its way from the water toward Bonshpiel.

"Behind you," he coughed out weakly. The warning was late, but Rizo saw Cap' Kenna step over him, longsword glinting. She dispatched the new tentacle with a couple of thrusts. Looking back toward Valory and Cordela, it looked like the Captain had already dealt with that one as well. More arose from the sea, the creature undaunted until a second "ka-Thunk" sounded, sending a bolt into one of the squid's oversized eyes.

"Nice shot, Markham!" Cordela called out. The sea monster thrashed, raising foam tinged with pink. Then it vanished beneath the waves, trailing dark streams behind it.

"Are ye all right, Rizo?"

He coughed, and nodded. "Thanks, Cap."

"Mistar Finnlar, what's our status?" she called up to her first mate, still on the aft deck.

"All crew present and accounted for," he called back. "Minimal damage."

"Passengers?"

"I haven't seen the tall wizard."

"You mean me?" said Bowe, peeking out from the starboard hatch.

"All present and accounted for, Captain," Finnlar concluded. A large sea bird landed next to him on the deck. The lanky mate reached down and drew something from a pouch attached to the bird's leg. Rizo stood up for a better look. It appeared to be a small scrolled piece of paper or parchment. Finnlar unrolled it, read for a minute, then beckoned to someone behind him that was out of Rizo's line of sight. "It's for you," he said.

Forescythe came forward and took the message, stared at it intently. He looked down at Rizo. "The appraisal on the necklace values it as sufficient to cover my fee. I'm yours for the duration."

"Excellent," Cordela replied from behind Rizo.

"Let's get back on our way, Mistar Finnlar." The first mate began barking orders to the crew, directing them to set the sails to get the Rowan Grouse back on course to Amorium. Rizo turned to check on Valory. Cordela was helping her stand.

"The ocean can really take your breath away, huh?" he quipped.

"In my case, it also swept me off my feet," she replied weakly.

"I thought that was Markham's duty," Cordela winked. Valory's already ruddy face turned a shade darker red.

"Will she be all right?" Rizo looked at Cordela.

"She had a bruised rib. I fixed it, but she'll be sore for a while. How about you? The monster had a decent grip on you there."

"I'll be fine. Our friend Stonefoot hugs tighter than that thing."

"I'm glad ta hear that," came a heavily accented voice from behind him. It sounded like crewman Pequod.

"Because you are always so concerned with my welfare?" Rizo turned.

Pequod laughed. "If yer in such fine fettle, now is a perfect time ta tar the beam, per our deal."

Rizo frowned. "A deal is a deal, I suppose. What do I do?"

"Come wit me. I'll show ye."

As the red-headed sailor led him to the hatch below deck, he whistled for Iko-Iko to follow.

Pequod headed to the bow hold and retrieved a bucket and brush from behind a stack of casks. From a crate he withdrew a block of something sticky and placed it in the bucket. "We'll ask cook to put it near the stove for a few minutes to melt the tar, and then I'll take you below to show you the area you'll need to cover."

While they waited for the tar to melt, Pequod explained to Rizo the importance of regularly waterproofing the inside of the hull.

"Wouldn't it be even better to do the outside of the hull?" Rizo asked.

"Aye. How good a swimmer are ye?"

Pequod guffawed at his own joke, and Rizo chuckled. "I guess you need to put the ship in drydock for that."

"Aye." He stood. "Tar must be softened by now."

It was, and Pequod guided Rizo down the aft hatch near the

starboard hold. The bottom deck was a single cargo compartment, but was nearly empty.

"Ye'll haf ta move a few things to cover the whole hull, but the Grouse is fairly light this cruise. Jest get a good slathering o' that tar over tha entire floor, up ta where it hits tha ceiling there and there." He indicated the fore and aft ends of the hold, where Rizo could see that the floor of the hold, which was the keel of the Rowan Grouse, sloped upwards to meet the bottom of the deck above. "Ye know where ta find more tar when ye need it. Jest make sure ye don't miss a spot." With a wave, he was gone back up the hatch.

"Well, Iko-Iko, I guess I'd better get started." He began initially aft, working his way just to where the hatch, and his only way out, opened to the deck above. The tar smelled awful, and the hold was cramped. He had to admit, though, that he was much better suited than the hefty Pequod to fitting into the small spaces where the floor met the deck above. Iko-Iko grew bored quickly and wandered off.

Rizo wouldn't say he was enjoying this task, but he compared it with his potential future of sitting in one place with his nose securely stuck in some dusty book or scroll. At least with this job, he got to move around a bit. And it certainly took advantage of his natural talents — even though it was really just his small size. On the other hand, there was gain in building more research abilities. After all, it was a stack of old books that had led to unlocking the mystery of his amulet. But it really wasn't for him. Unfortunately, tarring the beam probably wasn't going to make him the fortune he sought. He thought he could cope with the sailing life, though. The sea and waves really agreed with him. And Cap' Kenna seemed to do all right in the income bucket. But how did one break into being a sailor? He wasn't really interested in starting over at the bottom.

He did not get a chance to contemplate the answer to that question, as Iko-Iko returned just then. Rizo felt the cat's presence behind him and looked over his shoulder. Iko-Iko had a large rat clamped in his jaws. He placed it down next to Rizo with a self-satisfied meow and dashed off again. Rizo put the dead rodent in a pocket. Maybe Snowball would appreciate it. He needed to go upstairs and refill his bucket anyhow. He would drop Iko-Iko's gift into the dragon's barrel while he waited for the tar to melt.

Fifty Two

GARYND DiMarco had been fairly well covered in mud by the time he made his way back to his small skiff. He had also frayed the strings of his instrument, and was nearly dead on his feet from being awake the entire night evading the marsh spirit. He nearly sailed right past the docks and out to sea while unintentionally dozing at the oars.

Initially, the innkeeper didn't want to rent to Garynd due to the putrid smell that accompanied him. But, as had been Garynd's experience many times before, gold overcame all objections. There was not much left of Garynd's first day in Ilium after he had washed up, and by the residual glow of sunset he could see that the barge with the enormous dragon was still anchored off the river dock. He assumed that the Shent woman would not be leaving Ilium without her prize catch. The rumors around the docks, that it was an incredibly lifelike statue, brought an ironic smile to Garynd's lips.

His plan for his second day in Ilium was to trail Cordela wherever she went and wait for an opportunity to detain her. Unfortunately, he was stopped first by a priest of Apollo, who recognized him as a performer and insisted that he grace their stage that afternoon. Wishing that Apollo would have stuck to archery and mathematics and skipped music, he spent all morning scouring the city for his preferred type of strings. After his performance, he asked around and found that Cordela had apparently left the city on horseback.

Uttering the vilest Norse curses he knew, he slunk back to his inn, only to notice that the half-elf's barge was still parked mid-river.

The following morning he tried again. Cordela and that halfling seemed to be around the seaport doing some business, but he lost them in the crowd for nearly an hour before spotting them again.

They seemed to be involved in some commotion near one of the piers. He pushed through the crowd to reach them, but the crowd seemed to be pushing the opposite direction, trying to get away from the fracas. When he finally emerged to the clear area, all he saw there were three unconscious police constables. He was scanning to see which way Cordela had gone when some more, conscious, constables arrived.

"You are under arrest for assaulting an officer of the law," said one of them, binding his arms behind his back.

His protests that he hadn't attacked the policemen were not heeded, at least not until several hours later, when the constables woke up and did not identify him as their assailant. By then, Cordela Shent had already set sail, and Garynd had lost her trail.

Fifty Three

CORDELA stood in the Temple of Isis in Luxor. It was unlit, and mostly as she remembered. The large statue of the goddess and the Phoenix was not there. One of the frescoes seemed to be partially plastered over — or perhaps was still unfinished. She turned toward the entrance, and there stood Isis as she normally appeared to Cordela — garnet robe, gold collar, headband of gold with a gull's head emerging from her forehead.

"A storm is coming from the east," she intoned, beckoning.

Cordela grasped her offered hand, and felt a fierce, cold wind whip through her. Then she was above a dark sea, still holding the hand of Isis.

"Wadj-wer will guide you." Cordela heard the words clearly despite the crashing wind. A light appeared beneath the surface of the sea below. "Recover the artifact." Isis smiled at Cordela. Then she let her go.

Cordela was sucked away, tumbling out of control. She inhaled abruptly, but could not draw breath against the pressure of the wind. She stabilized, face down over the water. The waves rushed by as she was blown ever faster.

"Be brave. Be true."

She was flying low over the surface of the sea now, the wave tops growing steadily nearer. Ahead she saw a sailing ship. It rapidly enlarged as she approached. She could not avoid the collision. She threw her arms in front of her face and braced.

Cordela awoke panting.

She carefully slid out of her hammock, to avoid waking Valory below. Looking around the cabin, she was not surprised to see that Rizo was already out. She quickly tied up her hair and pinned it with the crossbow bolt she always used, buckled on her belt with her flail Tadlusa, and silently exited to the main deck.

The sky was already brightening, but the activity aboard the Rowan Grouse that Cordela had grown accustomed to was notably lacking. She heard some voices to aft and went to investigate. She found Rizo there throwing darts with some crewmen.

"Good morning," she greeted.

"Mornin', Lady," said one of the crew.

"Shouldn't you be trimming the sails or something?"

"Fer what wind?" Several others chuckled or shook their heads. Cordela then realized that the quiet aboard the Grouse was not just the lack of bustle. She was becalmed.

"Good point," she agreed. "Well, I hope Rizo here isn't taking too much of your money."

"Actually, Yewman and Trotter here are pretty good. I was just about to bow out before they really clean my lock."

"Care to see what Cook has for breakfast?"

"Sure."

They each got a biscuit with a pat of the ship's dwindling supply of fresh butter and sat near the back of the mess.

"How was it 'tarring the beam'?" Cordela asked.

"I'd say it was not too bad, all told." Rizo nibbled his biscuit. "It was really just applying a fresh coat of waterproofing to the inside of the hull. As Pequod thought, my small stature made hitting some of the less accessible corners much easier. The smell was pungent, but I got used to it."

"What did Iko-Iko do while you were busy?"

"He hunted down every rat on the Rowan Grouse. I assume that's why he's not here for his salted fish this morning."

"He ate a whole shipload of rats?" Cordela nearly spit out her biscuit.

"Well, he shared a few with me..."

Cordela lost her biscuit.

"Which I passed along to Snowball," he whispered.

"What did he think of them?" Cordela wiped butter and crumbs off of her tunic.

"He was very appreciative."

"Good. I was wondering how we were going to feed him." Cordela downed the last bit of biscuit before she had an opportunity to lose it. "So what happens with us not having any wind? Do we just wait here until some decides to show up?"

Rizo shrugged, just as Bonshpiel slid down one of the aft hatches nearby and shouted, "All hands on deck! All hands on deck!" He crossed to the crew quarters and rapped the hilt of one of his scimitars against the door frame. "All hands!"

Grumbling, the crew filed out and made their way up the various hatches.

"I reckon we should follow," Cordela cocked her head.

"My guess is that we'll get an answer to your question."

Cordela and Rizo were the last people to arrive. The crew already stood, sat, or crouched within earshot of where Cap' Kenna already stood on the afterdeck. The usual rough banter was absent as everyone waited in rapt silence.

"As ye can see," Cap' Kenna began, "the winds have abandoned us. I was hopeful that this was a short, temporary lull, but it seems to be one of the doldrums that happen now and again this time of year.

"We will therefore break out the oars and row to the north, where we might pick up a fav'rable wind coming off the coast. Those are me orders. Mistar Finnlar, make it so."

"Right, you heard the Captain," bellowed Finnlar, "break out the oars. Halifax, you're in charge o' setting the benches."

Cordela watched with interest as several crewmen pried open the large box amidship and began withdrawing large oars from it.

"So that's what they keep in there," Rizo echoed Cordela's thoughts. They watched the crew insert the oars into locks in the gunwale that Cordela hadn't even noticed before.

Bonshpiel approached the two of them. "We could sure use some extra backs into the rowing."

"We're happy to help," Cordela replied. "I'll rouse the rest of our party."

"I'd like to help, but I would probably just be a hindrance," said Rizo.

Bonshpiel looked down at him. "I've got a special job fer ye. Come with me."

Cordela found the others already awake in the cabin. She explained to them the situation.

"If I'm rowing, I probably shouldn't wear armor," Valory said. "I just hope there are no more giant squids today."

Markham was detailed to row with one of the larger crewmen. Bowe and Forescythe were assigned to the same bench together, to switch off with two other teams. Bonshpiel had given Rizo a drum and sat him atop the forecastle, where he kept a steady beat to help coordinate the rowing. Cordela and Valory were also paired. Cordela used the opportunity to tell Valory about her dream.

"Storm from the east," Valory was thoughtful. "That could be anything. Disease, wild animals, foreign invasion. But 'find the artifact'? That seems like a pretty specific instruction. Much more direct than typical for Isis."

"Right," Cordela allowed her frustration to show in her voice. "But what artifact? And where am I supposed to look for it?"

"Who is Wadj-wer? The one that's supposed to help?"

"The name sounds familiar, but I'm not sure where I heard it. Someone from Egyptian myth, probably."

"Well, anyhow it's a quest, direct from the goddess herself."

"I wonder why it is so important?"

"Probably just saving the world again." Valory tried to smile, but it turned into a grimace from the strain of rowing.

"Why does it need saving so much?" Cordela chuffed. "You would think it would eventually figure out how to take care of itself. Oh, well. Maybe I'll gain more recognition from it this time around."

"I guess it just needs some help now and then," Valory reflected. "And I think many people step up to provide it. You don't have to do it all yourself."

Valory was right. Cordela had her friends to help. Even Rizo, in his better moments. Also, lots of other people she didn't even know did their part to protect the innocents who were just trying to get along, and to defend against all sorts of evil. And some did so with no recognition at all. People like Karela of Loerhold. If Cordela's part was to fetch this artifact for Isis, she could probably handle that without complaining. Much.

They had been rowing for a bit over three hours when wind from the northwest arrived and filled their sails. Great cheers went up all over the ship, and crewmen not presently at the oars leapt into action to trim the sails and get them back on course and on their way to Amorium. Valory helped Cordela unlock their oar from the gunwale so that a crewman could collect it and return it to the box. Cap' Kenna found them waiting with the oar.

"Thank ye fer pitching in," her smile seemed genuine.

"Well, you did warn us when we came aboard that we might be put to work," Cordela tried to match the Captain's mood. "Your instinct about getting wind off the coast served us very well. It's no wonder your crew is so loyal."

"Well, maybe not for long," Cap' Kenna's countenance dropped. "Nearer the coast we are much more likely to encounter pirates. There may be fighting ahead. You might want to don your armor."

Despite Cap' Kenna's dire warning, the rest of that day passed uneventfully, and they seemed to be making good speed toward Amorium, perhaps even better than they had been before. Cordela tried to get the others in her party to learn some sea shanties, but Valory was the only one that even humored her, and even she seemed like she preferred to do something else. What that something else was, Cordela could only guess that it had something to do with Markham. Rizo was nowhere to be seen, and Cordela wondered if he was playing with his ring of invisibility. She called for Iko-Iko and asked him where Rizo was hiding, but the cat either didn't know, or didn't care.

When Cordela awoke the following morning, she could not figure out why her shoulders and upper arms were so sore. Then she remembered all the rowing she had done the day before. She tried stretching her muscles, which helped a bit. She still struggled to get armor on her torso. After breakfast she asked the others if they were feeling the same. Valory, Bowe, and Forescythe agreed that the exercise had been a bit more than they were used to, but Markham shrugged. Cordela considered adopting his calisthenics regime. Rizo, of course, was feeling just fine except for the calluses on his hands from beating the drum.

"Hostile flag!" called a lookout from atop the mainmast.

Finnlar sounded his whistle. "Arm for battle! Load the artillery! Stow the sails. Fire abatement!"

"Why are they dropping the sails?" Valory asked. "Can't we try to outrun them?"

Cordela craned her neck to try to get a good look at the approaching vessel. "That looks like a fast galley. Built for speed. Even with the most favorable winds, I doubt we could evade them."

"I think they furl the sails so they aren't a big target for fire," Markham offered.

Cordela drew her flail. "Ready for a fight?"

Rizo had his dagger out already. "Bring 'em on!"

Markham went to man one of the ballistae, just as Cap' Kenna came by. "Looks like we'll be putting you to work again. As I feared, pirates prowl these waters frequently, and some have found us."

"I guess this pirate hasn't heard of your reputation," Cordela chided.

"This fellow is called Krazen. He's one of the more ruthless ones. The key to surviving will be to try to keep his men from boarding. The battle will be at our gunnels. Good luck." The Captain alit to the aft deck where she could keep a good view of the battle. Cordela brought Valory to starboard to prepare for the attack.

"What do you think I should do?" Bowe asked.

"Get to somewhere high up, so you can see what's going on." Cordela advised. "If you see an opportunity to help out with a spell, go for it!"

The galley drew up alongside the Rowan Grouse. As Cap' Kenna had expected, they threw rope ladders across the narrow gap and began their boarding attempt. Cordela heard the loud "ka-Thunk" of ballista fire, but the attacking pirates were much smaller targets than the giant squid, and it had little effect. The first men were almost to Cordela's position at the end of one of the rope ladders. She made her way out onto the narrow bridge and swung Tadlusa at the nearest pirate, connecting with his skull. Stunned, the man lost his grip on the ladder and plummeted into the ocean. Cordela advanced on to the next assailant. This one, having seen his crewmate's fate, was ready with a drawn saber. He parried Cordela's first swing, and she caught his return strike on her shield. Her second blow caught him in the chest, winding him. She adjusted for a finishing slam, but he caught it on his saber tip. The maneuver cost him his balance, though, and he dropped between the rungs of the rope ladder, his saber tangled with Cordela's flail chains. She was yanked downward along with the pirate. She pitched forward right through the same gap. She swung her shield desperately trying to snag the rope and break her fall, but it just slid across the rung. Now she was twisted and stretched, and began to tumble downward toward the water. Tadlusa's chain disengaged from the other combatant's saber, but it was too late for that to matter. She had a moment to take a breath before she plunged into the water. Cordela's armor weighed on her, and she sank quickly. She struggled with all her strength to get back to the surface. She couldn't end here, she had a mission for Isis to complete. Who was going to save the world with her at the bottom of the ocean? And no bard was going to tell her legend if it ended like this. Her chest ached and her vision clouded. The surface just got farther and farther away. The dark sea closed around her, illuminated faintly by her still glowing shield.

Fifty Four

RIZO Malkin was a halfling with a plan. Like most of his plans, it wasn't very detailed. But he deemed it a good plan, a judgment even he bestowed on very few of his plans. Instead of waiting for the pirates to try to board, he thought, why not take the fight to them? Step one of the plan was to get over to the enemy ship. Step two he would work on once he was there.

Rizo headed for the mangonel. "Have you got a range to that target yet?" he asked the artilleryman.

"Aye."

"Get me over there." Without waiting for a response, Rizo vaulted into the cup.

"Fire!" he shouted.

As the catch released, Rizo felt more acceleration then he was expecting. Tumbling a bit, he had to twist in the air to find a landing spot on the enemy ship. The movement seemed very natural to him. Perhaps his connection with Iko-Iko was providing some additional benefit. As he stabilized his flight, he activated his ring of invisibility with a thought. Looking down, Rizo thought he might overshoot, and even if he didn't he was going to have a hard landing. When he was definitely over the pirate galley, he cast a spell that made him light as a feather. He gently wafted to the deck and landed silently.

Safely down, Rizo headed for the nearest grappling ladder. His dagger sliced cleanly through one of the stays, and the ladder immediately listed to that side, spilling a few pirates into the water.

"Hey, one of them's here, and he's invisible!" called another

R. A. Klepsis

pirate from nearby. He and two other men rapidly converged on Rizo's location. Rizo had to leave the other ladder stay to prepare for whatever they were planning. One threw dust in Rizo's direction. The fine powder stuck to him and he realized that invisible or not, they would be able to find him. He dismissed the now useless invisibility effect, and faced the enemies, now between him and the still swaying rope ladder. Their eyes glinted with malice as they closed on Rizo. No, Rizo thought, their eyes weren't glinting, they were glazed. Then all six eyes rolled up into six eyelids, and the attackers crumpled to the deck in a pile.

"That's odd," thought Rizo. "Did I do that?" Then, through the space previously occupied by the pirates, Rizo saw across the gap between the two ships to where Bowe, in the rigging of the Rowan Grouse, was doing an elated dance, celebrating that his sleeping spell had finally been effective.

"There! Get him!" Rizo heard from his left. There, the pirate captain stood on the aft bridge of the long galley overlooking the battle. Rizo hastily updated his objectives and headed straight for the captain. A narrow stairway near the gunwale provided access to the command bridge. It was unguarded, but the captain had a couple of lackeys with him on the bridge. As he ran, Rizo mentally ticked through his remaining spells. Not many were of any use against a crowd. He could create a spray of fire from his fingertips, but he'd have to be close to the target to use it — and he'd have to convince them all to stand in a small area. He could create a cloud of foul-smelling vapor, but that usually didn't do much besides being an eye irritant. It was his best option, though. "Time to see if this amulet works," he thought. Reaching into his inner pocket, he touched the Amulet of al-Azhar and whispered, "Jacomo Fi-na-ne." Then, a bit louder, "Nimbo noxio!" Instantly, the bridge was shrouded in a greenish gas. Rizo dashed up the stairs hoping for the best.

Emerging onto the bridge deck he quickly surveyed the effects of his spell. The captain's two henchmen were unconscious, and the captain was on his knees retching. The stinking cloud quickly dissipated in the ocean breeze and the residual vapors did not bother Rizo. He efficiently trussed the captain with a nearby rope and was about to

274

congratulate himself when he realized that the three thugs that Bowe had put to sleep had revived and were mounting the stairs to where he stood.

Casting his gaze about the bridge deck, he spotted a lantern hanging near a map stand. He tossed the lantern into the path of the oncoming pirates, spilling oil across the deck. Now he made use of his flaming fingers spell to ignite the oil. Two of the pirates were badly burned and were out of the fight, and the third hung back, deterred by the flames.

Smugly, Rizo approached the captain to apprehend him, but started back in alarm as he drew his sword to confront Rizo. The fire had also burned the ropes that Rizo had used to bind the captain.

The halfling had nowhere to run. The fire he had started completely blocked access to one stairway, and a second one currently had more pirates ascending it. Rizo evaded or blocked the captain's sword thrusts, but he wasn't able to duck within the larger man's guard to do any damage. He also couldn't let his guard down long enough to cast a spell. He was running out of time. More men were heading toward the bridge and would be there in seconds. Rizo considered leaping into the water to escape, but he wasn't even sure he could make it that far.

The ship rocked violently, throwing Rizo and the pirate captain to the deck, and spilling the approaching men back down the stairs. The captain braced against hitting his head on the deck with both arms, dropping his sword in the process. Rizo recovered first, sweeping up the sword and circling around behind the kneeling captain. Sword at his throat, Rizo commanded, "Order your men to back off!"

The pirate captain didn't answer, instead staring slack-mouthed at the space between the two ocean vessels. Rizo followed his gaze and saw the reason why the ship had listed so suddenly. An enormous bubble was rising out of the ocean, forcing its way up between the ships, shredding the grappling ladders and throwing waves of water aside.

"Just what does she think she's doing now?" Rizo exclaimed.

For there, standing like a goddess of victory in the center of the giant transparent sphere was Cordela Shent.

Fifty Five

CORDELA had never known darkness so deep. Even the normally bright emanation from her shield barely penetrated the black. The water was icy cold, yet her chest burned like the fire of the sun. Down, down she sank, wondering whether she would be ended when her body forced her to draw in lungfuls of freezing seawater or when the crushing pressure forced the life out of her.

Neither happened. Eventually, the burning in her chest faded and her need and desire to breathe faded with it. At the same time, the external pressure eased. Gradually the darkness began to brighten as well. A diffuse pearlescent light slowly revealed the ruins of an enormous city that extended to the limits of Cordela's vision. She was descending into what appeared to be a large plaza or public square, surrounded by buildings of an architecture that was strange but vaguely familiar. She came to rest on her feet.

A voice with undertones as deep as the ocean reverberated through her body. "Cordela. You have come."

She turned, slowly, limited in her movement by the water that surrounded her. She saw a human-like figure, giant in size, with a muscular, masculine build but rounded, feminine breasts. There were gill slits in the figure's neck, and its eyes were flat and wide like a fish's.

"I am Wadj-wer, the Great Green Deep. I have removed your need to breathe for the time being, but you may speak."

So this was Wadj-wer, the one Isis had instructed her to meet. Perhaps her encounter on the rope bridge had not been mere happenstance or bad luck. "What is this place?" Cordela didn't understand how she produced sound without expelling any air, but that was yet another question that would have to wait.

"You stand among the ruins of the great city of Arkhum, known to the Greeks as Atlantis, though it was built by people from Egypt."

"Did you bring me here? I mean, thank you for saving me, but why?"

Wadj-wer looked stern. "It was not my choice. Isis has demanded it, and in this case her demands must be met. Follow."

It was not really an answer, but Cordela allowed the blue-green giant to lead her from the plaza down a wide street flanked on both sides by buildings so ruined that their original purpose was impossible to determine.

"Arkhum was once a great kingdom," Wadj-wer described as they walked. "Her people were favored by the gods. They were wise in lore and philosophy, practiced great scholarship, and ruled with justice and fairness. The greatest expression of their wisdom and scholarship was embodied in the Spa-iba-wukh, a powerful artifact of their own craftsmanship, inspired by the gods. With it, the people of Arkhum expanded their influence and ruled much of the world from their small island."

Artifact? "Isis instructed me to find an artifact," Cordela said.

Wadj-wer sighed wearily. "Beware, Cordela, for the people of Arkhum abused their power. Eventually, their greed overcame their wisdom. Their rule became tyrannical. Ultimately, they threatened all of creation and brought down upon themselves the punishment of the gods. These ruins bear witness to their fate.

"If it were my choice, the Spa-iba-wukh would stay hidden for all eternity, so great is its danger and potential for abuse. But Isis has convinced all the gods of Egypt that the need is great enough. And that you, Cordela, will use the Spa-iba-wukh for the task she intends and not beyond."

Be brave, Isis had said. Be true. She had chosen Cordela to safely steward this object of great power that had brought down a mighty empire and threatened the entire fabric of creation. And accomplish her as-yet-unspecified but apparently urgent purpose. You don't have to do it all yourself, Valory had said. But this part was hers to do. She slowly nodded in response to Wadj-wer.

The ocean deity had stopped before the remains of what appeared to be a great temple. Among the fallen pillars and collapsed walls an obelisk stood, uniquely undisturbed in the smashed cityscape. "I find it difficult to interact with the physical world," Wadj-wer explained. "It will be more expedient if you do what needs to be done."

"And what would that be?" Cordela barely noticed that she still somehow spoke without breath.

"Under the obelisk is the chamber of the Spa-iba-wukh. It must be pushed back to reveal the entrance."

Of course, thought Cordela. Powerful, giant god of the sea standing right there, and the little half-elf has to do all the heavy lifting. Just about right. She would have breathed a heavy sigh, if she had been breathing at all. Instead, she just leaned into the obelisk with her shoulder and shoved. The obelisk moved a little at a time, but six good shoves had revealed an opening big enough for her to fit through. Steep stairs led down into the stone floor of the former temple. Her shield emitted enough illumination for her to see the inside of the chamber at the base of the stairs. It was small, and the only feature was a stone pedestal decorated with hieroglyphics. She recognized some of the symbols, as they were more primitive versions of the designs she was familiar with. The pedestal, and the chamber, must have been very old.

Atop the pedestal was some sort of brass apparatus. It was small, but very finely crafted. Hundreds of gears interlocked within it, controlled somehow by six knobs on the front. Each knob had a raised triangular design carved into its face, and was surrounded by a ring divided into sections by radial lines etched into its surface. The back face held a handle connected to the device by a hinge. She gingerly picked up the apparatus. It fit easily in her hand. There was nothing else in the chamber, so she mounted the steps back to where Wadj-wer waited.

"Is this it?" Cordela held the object up to show the Great Blue-green.

"The Spa-iba-wukh," Wadj-wer said reverently.

"Looks pretty interesting."

Wadj-wer scoffed. "You hold in your hand the most powerful object in the world, capable of turning all of creation to lifeless dust. You must conceal it and protect it with all your capability. Speak of it to no one but those most closely trusted by Isis. She will instruct you further."

Cordela shrugged, placed the artifact into a sack attached securely to her waist. "Now what?"

"Now you must return to the surface. You do not belong here in the deep."

No kidding, Cordela thought. "Any way you can help out with that? The way I got down here only works one way."

"Farewell, Cordela. I hope that the trust that Isis places in you is not mistaken. May fortune favor your mission." With the last words, Wadj-wer faded from Cordela's view. As that happened, the water lifted away from Cordela, and she began to breathe again. Despite feeling heavier without the buoyant effects of water around her, she felt herself being lifted off of the stone floor of the ruined temple. She was accelerated upwards, surrounded by the bubble of air that had formed around her. Away from the illuminated city, the blackness of the deep ocean surrounded her again. The light from her shield just reflected off of the inside surface of her bubble. The return of dim lighting to the sea outside presaged her return to the surface by just a few seconds. The bubble burst through the waves, and Cordela saw the Rowan Grouse and the pirate ship below her, still locked in combat. The battle seemed to have a focus on the rear upper deck of the attacking pirate ship, but Cordela couldn't quite see what was happening there. A minor shift of her weight toward the Grouse induced the bubble to slide in that direction as it gently sank back down. With a nearly silent pop the bubble burst, depositing Cordela on the deck of the Rowan Grouse. Valory's eyes were teary as she ran to greet her friend.

Fifty Six

CAPTAIN Krazen surrendered to Rizo forthwith. Cap' Kenna's crew, led by Bonshpiel, soon arrived to take control of Krazen's men. His ship, the Dread Catoblepas, was lashed to the side of the Rowan Grouse. Rizo was hoping to lay his hands on any booty that Krazen had on board, but was disappointed that all they had was some silk and spices. Valuable, but low cost-to-weight ratio. The captured pirates were all stashed in the lower hold of the Grouse, except for Krazen, who was accommodated a bit more luxuriously in the cabin next to the one Rizo shared with his fellows.

Toward that evening, Rizo was on deck, listening to Cordela tell a knot of crewmen the story of how she survived sinking in the ocean. She described meeting a tribe of intelligent giant clams who were engaged in a battle with a band of starfish over a magic pearl. Rizo heard the tale grow more fantastic the longer it went on.

"Right, so the oysters had this magic, ruby pearl — "

"I thought ye said they was clams," interrupted a crewman.

"Yeah, that's right!" Cordela went on without hesitating. "They were a sort of hybrid between clams and oysters — cloysters! A society of intelligent magic-using cloysters. And they needed my assistance. I helped them fight off the starfish army to protect their pearl." She took a deep breath. "It was really hard! If we broke or cut off a starfish's arm, it just grew it back. And the severed arm grew a whole new star!" She paused as her audience gasped. "We needed reinforcements. I negotiated an alliance with the Crab Kingdom."

"Don't crabs like to eat clams?" someone asked.

"That's right," Cordela pointed at the questioner. "But they were both under threat from the octopuses. The combined force was able to vanquish the starfish and provide ongoing defense against the octopus."

"What about the big bubble?" asked another listener.

"Right, I'm getting to that." Cordela really seemed to be enjoying herself. "They were so grateful for my help. Once the pearl was safe, they all gathered together and blew air from within their shells. All the expelled air coalesced into an enormous bubble that surrounded me and carried me back to the surface."

Rizo shook his head. Intelligent cloysters? A ruby pearl? Battle with a starfish army? A crab alliance? He was very skeptical. He figured he would get the real story out of her later.

Finnlar approached Rizo. "Captain wants to see ya. In her quarters, if yer not too busy."

"Thanks." Rizo went right away. He was hoping to get a share of the booty, whatever value it had.

"Come in Rizo," Cap' Kenna said as soon as he poked his head in. She poured a drink and slid it toward him on the table. "Have a seat. Care for some whiskey?"

Rizo sat and took a sip from the proffered cup. It had a strong smokey aroma with hints of lavender. "Thanks."

"I'm impressed with your resourcefulness. Krazen is one of the area's most ruthless and lethal pirates." She sipped her own drink. "He's also one of the most wanted. Authorities all along the coast have posted a bounty on his head."

Rizo's ears twitched. "How big a bounty?"

"Big enough. But not your concern. I plan to claim the bounty meself."

"Even though technically I'm the one who brought him in."

"I thought you might feel that way." She twirled her cup in

her fingers. "Which is why I have a proposition for ye."

Rizo put his cup down. He preferred to be as sober as possible when there was dealing to be done. "Go on," he said with steely eyes.

"Maritime law has many — well, peculiarities. One that is not well known, even among sailors, is the Law of Salvage."

Rizo wasn't sure where the Captain was going with this. "Law of Salvage?"

"Yes. It provides incentive for recovery of derelicts. Under its terms, the one who finds anything on or under the sea can claim it, with no obligation to seek out a prior owner."

"The Dread Catoblepas." Krazen's ship, currently lashed to the side of the Rowan Grouse.

"Indeed. Certainly, it is well known that it belongs to Krazen, and it would arouse suspicions were I to attempt to claim it AND the bounty on Krazen. However, if you claim the ship, and I vouch for your recovery of it as a derelict, authorities will not gainsay us, despite how suspicious it looks."

"And all I have to do is keep quiet about who really captured Krazen."

"Exactly. His ship is worth at least 10,000 gold, maybe more if you fix it up a bit. What do you say? Do we have a deal?"

Rizo wasn't even listening to Cap' Kenna's appraisal of the vessel. His mind was already churning away. This could be the entree to a nautical career that he had been looking for. He picked up his cup and offered a toast. "To Maritime Law. Deal!"

Fifty Seven

THE Beaver Lodge was packed. Willie's father had been trying to talk people into sharing rooms all morning. A couple of times he tried letting out Cordela and Valory's rooms, but Willie reminded him that they were, at least officially, back in town and potentially using the rooms. Ultimately, he had to turn a few away. Word had apparently gone around that the shearings were particularly high in quality this season, which had attracted even more than the usual number of buyers. Willie was whipping a biscuit batter, directing diners toward open tables, and listening to Rizo's latest story all at once, and in truth was only paying attention to Rizo with one ear.

"Wait! Did you say 'cloysters'?"

"That's what she said," Rizo was practically shouting over the dinner noise.

"What in Hestia's name is a cloyster?" Her batter was thickening nicely.

"Some kind of giant intelligent hybrid of clams and oysters."

Willie had heard some pretty far-fetched tales here in the Beaver Lodge, but she had never heard of these cloysters or anything like them. Still, a story was a story, and if Willie was going to take her hobby as a story collector seriously, she couldn't be too judgmental.

"If you ask me, it's a load of dragon poo," said Rizo, scowling. "But I haven't been able to get her to cough up any other account of her time underwater, or how she ended up in that bubble."

"Well, I'll let you know if she tells me anything different." She spooned the batter onto the hot griddle one spot at a time.

"What happened next?"

"Maybe Cordela can tell you. Here she is now."

"Hi Rizo!" Cordela greeted the halfling. "Forescythe is about ready for the enlargement. Did you get the scroll?"

Rizo nodded.

"Can you get to Fallonfael this afternoon?"

"I guess. I'll need to head back to Miletos soon after, though."

"What's going on in Miletos?" Willie asked after hoisting the griddle back on the hearth to finish baking the biscuits.

"Hi, Willie," said Cordela. "I guess Rizo hasn't told you that part of our adventure yet. He needs to get going, so I'll fill you in. Ok, Rizo?"

"Going. I can take a hint."

"See you back in Fallonfael in a few days. Now, how far did Rizo get?"

"He had just finished telling me about you and the cloysters."

"Right. The cloysters. Hey, are those biscuits up for grabs? They smell delicious."

With a huff, Willie grabbed one right out of the fire with a pair of tongs and set it in front of Cordela, followed by a pat of butter laid down with a skill acquired over years of serving at the Beaver Lodge.

"Mmmm. Amazing." Cordela licked her lips. "Anyhow, after the pirate attack we had good wind and smooth sailing. I checked on the captives once or twice when they were being fed. They were surprised at how few rats there were down in the hold."

"Rizo's cat must have been very busy." Willie hefted the griddle back out of the fire and transferred the biscuits to a basket for distribution.

"Yes, they also were impressed by the fresh coat of tar. Things got interesting again when we arrived in Amorium ..."

Fifty Eight

CORDELA had never approached Amorium by sea, and was looking forward to seeing the city from that side. She knew that the harbor entrance could be closed off by massive gates hung from twin towers that stood at the ends of sea walls bracketing the harbor. The sea walls were extensions of the city walls that curved out from the coast, hugging the harbor to the city like the arms of a mother cradling her baby. Within, the city climbed up the cliff face so that it could always view the harbor.

Finnlar ordered the Rowan Grouse to a stop adjacent to one of the gate towers. Calls were exchanged, and soon a harbor master arrived to question the Captain about her business. He confronted her on the upper aft deck, with Rizo standing right next to her for some reason. Cordela stood on the main deck below, where she could hear and see them.

"Oil, wine, some bolts of silk," Cap' Kenna was telling the harbor master. "Ye can review our manifest if ye like. Also, six passengers, their mounts, and personal effects."

The harbor master scribbled in a small notebook.

"Where are the passengers from?"

"On their way back to Palmyra."

More scribbling.

"Anything else?"

"Aye. We have some maritime outlaws that attacked us, including one ye might have an interest in. The notorious Krazen."

The harbor master nearly dropped his charcoal pencil. *"The*

Krazen? There is a substantial bounty on his head if his identity can be verified. You intend to collect?"

"Indeed I do."

The harbor master wrote something on a new page and underlined it twice.

"And what about this other ship you have tied alongside?"

Rizo spoke up. "That is a derelict we found abandoned. I claim it by right of salvage."

Rizo was claiming the pirate ship? What was he planning to do with that?

The harbor master narrowed his eyes. "Isn't that Krazen's ship?"

"Could be," Rizo lilted.

"If it is, he wasn't on it when we found it," Cap' Kenna added. Not precisely true, but Cordela supposed that after they had taken all the pirates into custody, the ship was pretty empty.

The harbor master seemed as skeptical as Cordela would have been. He looked from Rizo to the Captain, and back again. He jotted something in his notebook and said, "If you intend to dock it, that will be 15 gold per day. You must pay for five days at once, with a refund for any unused days."

Rizo crossed his arms. After a moment, he said, "Any less expensive options?"

"You may anchor in the harbor for 3 gold per day."

"That sounds more appropriate for this wreck."

"I'll have my deputy assign you an anchorage." Some final scribbles in the notebook. "Everything seems in order. You are cleared to moor at slip 23. Raise the commerce flag as you enter. The constabulary will meet you to take custody of the fugitive. Welcome back to Amorium, Captain Aylson."

"Thank you, Master Hobson."

When Rizo slid down the ladder to the main deck, Cordela was waiting for him.

"What just happened there? You have a ship now?"

"Cap' Kenna wanted to keep the bounty on Krazen herself. Seems like maybe they have some history between them. Since I'm actually the one Krazen surrendered to, she couldn't just cut me out. So she bought me off by letting me take the ship. It's worth plenty."

"What do you plan to do with it until you find a buyer?"

"Still working on that." Rizo had on one of his 'I'm up to something' looks, but Cordela didn't want to press him on the subject. It would just give him another opportunity to press her on what had happened to her at the bottom of the sea, and she wasn't sure she was permitted to tell even Rizo the truth about that.

"I'm trying to organize us so we don't waste any time once we go ashore," Cordela moved on quickly. "I put Valory and Markham in charge of finding us lodging. Forescythe says we'll need special tackle for — our project. I'm planning to see Lanthanum. I'm hoping he can write us a scroll to re-size our — our project. Is there anything you need to do?"

"Assuming Cap' Kenna can help me get my ship to its anchorage, I should be set for now. Other business can wait. I'd like to see Lanthanum as well. We could use something to eat for our 'project.'"

"I hadn't thought of that. Maybe Forescythe will want to do that. After all, he's going to have to find out what the project likes to eat." They put ashore while it was still mid-morning. Valory and Markham took their mounts and packs with them to secure lodging. "We're going to check at the Keep Inn," Valory explained. "The city isn't nearly as full as it was the last time we were here, so they should have plenty of room."

"True. The last time we were here was in the middle of a

The Amulet and the Dragon

refugee crisis," Cordela observed. "Sounds like a good idea. The Keep area should be really secure. Say, since you are going that way, can you deliver the letter from Sintros and Athera to the House of Poseidon?" She handed Valory the missive. "We will meet you at the inn this afternoon."

Cordela and Rizo both knew the way to the home of the great wizard Lanthanum. Bowe, however, had never met the magic user and was excited and a little nervous. "He's very friendly," Cordela assured him. "Really the most easy going fellow you've ever met."

"But don't forget, he can turn you into a lizard in an instant," Rizo added.

"You're not helping Bowe calm down," Cordela frowned at the halfling. "It *is* really easy to forget how powerful he is. Just be respectful."

Bowe continued to fidget.

They led Bowe to the modest door in the stone cliff that was the entrance to Lanthanum's abode. Rizo knocked, and after a moment Lanthanum himself answered the knock. Cordela was a bit surprised, since he usually had his Brownie servant Math greet visitors for him. The elderly wizard's friendly eyes opened wide when he saw them.

"Rizo, Cordela! What a surprise. I was not expecting you for at least two more days."

"We hit some particularly favorable winds," Rizo commented.

"Well, I suppose there is no accounting for divine intervention." Lanthanum took a step back. "Won't you come in? And you may introduce me to your friend here."

While Rizo introduced Bowe, Cordela looked around Lanthanum's home and mused silently. Had their favorable winds been of divine origin? Had it been Wadj-wer speeding her along to whatever mission Isis had planned for her? There was no answer to the question. But, as usual, Lanthanum seemed to have an unnatural level of interest

291

and knowledge of her movements and activities. She was going to have to figure out a way to get that crystal ball away from him.

Lanthanum's home was familiarly mundane, and much like it had been the last time she had seen it. A small table near the door held a few knick-knacks. Simple chairs and a sofa in need of repair or maybe a full reupholstering provided seating. To the right, Math was in the kitchen preparing dinner, which explained why he was unavailable to answer the door.

Lanthanum sat himself in one of the chairs and waved from his guests to the other seats. Rizo and Bowe took the other two chairs, leaving Cordela the worn sofa. It gave pleasantly to her weight without sagging.

"I see that you were able to use the scroll I made for you, Rizo," the wizard began.

"Yes. It made a lot more sense than the version they tried to teach me at PIMNA." Rizo replied, and stroked the cat on his shoulder. Cordela had become so accustomed to the feline's presence, she often didn't even notice him loitering in Rizo's vicinity.

"Perhaps you've had enough of their teaching methods? I find that I have an opening for an apprentice, if you'd like to advance your studies?"

"Well, I have certainly had enough of PIMNA," said Rizo, "but I'm also not interested in an apprenticeship right now." He paused. "In fact, I'm starting a sailing career. I'll be the captain of my own ship."

"You're what?" Cordela blurted out. Bowe's jaw dropped. The one who seemed the least surprised was Lanthanum.

"And how did you arrive at that plan?" the elderly wizard asked calmly.

"I've recently come into the possession of a seaworthy vessel, and I have a notion of how to turn it into a profitable business."

"I see," Lanthanum tapped the side of his nose. He looked at Bowe. "How about you, young man? Looking for an advanced apprenticeship?"

"That. That would be great," Bowe stammered. "I'll, um. I'll have to let PIMNA know I'll be leaving. Uh, does it cost much? The instruction, I mean."

Lanthanum laughed. "Apprenticeship doesn't work quite the same way as a school such as PIMNA. As an apprentice, you work for me, and instead of wages I share my magical secrets with you. And dinner, of course, can't have you starving when I need you to work. Speaking of which, here's Math with some victuals."

The brownie set a tray-table among the seats. "Anything else master?"

"Some wine, I think. Thank you, Math. Oh, and have we got any of that smoked fish left? Rizo's cat looks a bit hungry as well."

Cordela helped herself to a stuffed pastry. It was still too hot to eat. "We did have another favor to ask of you, if it isn't too much trouble."

"Do you now?" said Lanthanum around his pastry. "What sort of favor?"

"Well, you see, we have this dragon, and — "

"Dragon?" Lanthanum's bushy eyebrows rose like they were going to levitate right off his face. "You two are full of surprises today. Speak."

"Yes, you see, it's a very small dragon — well, it didn't start out small, but ..." Eventually, Cordela found herself telling Lanthanum the entire story of their journey from Palmyra to Ismara, and up to their encounter with Klepsis. Much of the story seemed like news to Lanthanum, so perhaps he hadn't been constantly spying on her.

"I'm acquainted with this Klepsis," Lanthanum said finally. "Very unorthodox methods. The effects he achieves should not be possible by my understanding of magic. Perhaps my theories could use some revision. But I understand that you would like a powerful spell to negate the diminution effect on the dragon?"

Cordela and Rizo nodded.

"Assuming that the magic is a normal shrinkage spell that Klepsis has somehow made semipermanent, that should be straightforward. I can write you a scroll. It will take a few days."

Cordela looked at Rizo.

"I'll have to come back in a few days to make arrangements for my ship," he said. "I can pick up the scroll then."

She nodded. "Thank you, Lanthanum. I was hoping you could help out."

"While we're asking for favors," Rizo reached into his vest and took out the slender piece of wood, "you said you could recharge this."

Lanthanum smiled crookedly. "I did say that, didn't I? Wait here." The elderly but nimble wizard exited the room through a door in the back that led to his workshop. He returned shortly with a box similar if not identical to the one he had given Rizo with the wand, nearly a year ago. It had the same stylized "L" carved into its top. He undid the latches, swung it open, grasped the wand inside, and traded with Rizo. "There. That one should have about ten charges on it."

"About?"

"Sure. Ten, twelve maybe? Just don't depend on it too much when you're close to the end."

"Thanks." Rizo rolled his eyes, but tucked the replacement wand into his vest.

"Thank you so much for dinner," Cordela stood up to go. "It was wonderful seeing you again."

"Yes, you are always welcome here, Miss Shent. I wouldn't be concerned about Rizo moving on. I should think you will soon be getting some new assistance."

"That's very reassuring." Once again, Lanthanum was being creepy and cryptic.

"And good luck to you, Rizo. I think I shall have to wheedle an invitation to the Prince's wedding. I would dearly love to see his reaction when he receives his gift!" He looked at Bowe. "You and I will be seeing much more of each other very soon. We will see how well PIMNA has prepared you."

Fifty Nine

THEY rented a cart in Amorium to carry all of their luggage including the barrel with Snowball still safely sealed inside. They had all the animals take turns hauling it, although they seemed to make much better time when Valory's stallion was strapped to the wagon. They reached Kandahar early in the morning after riding for much of the night under a clear sky and nearly full moon. While there, Cordela wanted to check the progress of the construction of the new Isis temple. It was nearly complete. They picked up a quick breakfast of pretzels at Mario and Luigi's bakery before setting off again.

"Hey, Cordela," Valory called as they cantered northward. "What do you plan to do with our little friend?"

"I'm going to try to convince my father to let us use his barn in Fallonfael."

"So, you and Rizo can probably take care of that, right?"

"Why?"

"I thought the rest of us can just go directly to Palmyra."

"I don't see a problem with that." Cordela said. "Wait, maybe there is something you can do for us, though. Forescythe," she turned in her saddle to address the trainer. "Can you write down the specifications for the tackle we're going to need?"

"If I had something to write on, maybe."

"Hey, Rizo," she called, "do you still have that paper you were using to map the structure under Eridu?"

"Let me check." He fished a pen, ink, and parchment out of

his saddlebag. "Here. Try these "

"When you get to Palmyra, you can take these specifications to Mallaher the saddler," Cordela instructed Valory. "See if he can make it for a reasonable price."

"What's reasonable?" asked Bowe.

Cordela shrugged. "Less than 200 gold?"

"We'll have to stop. I can't draw while riding." Forescythe complained.

"We should stop up ahead, where the road to Fallonfael diverges," Cordela said.

They approached the familiar crossroads late in the afternoon. Markham helped to transfer items that she and Rizo would need, including Snowball's barrel, to their horses.

Forescythe handed over a fairly detailed rendering of the complex system of straps and harnesses they needed. "What should these fittings be made of?" she pointed to some clasps he had drawn.

Forescythe wrinkled his nose. "Probably brass. Should I write that?"

Cordela nodded, handed the page back. Notation updated, Cordela gave the specification a final look and passed it to Valory. "Tell Mallaher we need this tackle in two weeks." Then she hugged her friend, and waved to the other two.

Rizo addressed Bowe. "If you are heading back to Amorium in the next few days, come get me in Fallonfael and we can ride together." They shook hands, and with a final wave the three of them were on their way.

Cordela, Rizo, and Forescythe were soon on their way eastward to Fallonfael. Moon didn't seem to mind the extra weight of the barrel. Cordela was more concerned with whether Snowball would tolerate the jouncing. She kept the pace slow to smooth out the ride.

Cordela's parents greeted them warmly on their arrival. They already knew Rizo, and Cordela introduced Forescythe without being too specific about why he was there. As Cordela had anticipated, the cordiality dried up as soon as she mentioned what they were there for.

"Cordela, dear," her father's voice was strained and stern, "I spent ten years fighting a war against those things. And now you want me to keep one in my house?"

"I heard recently that the white dragons didn't participate in the war." Cordela hoped she could reason with her father. If not, she had one more tactic.

"A dragon is a dragon," Cordono Shent crossed his arms.

"He only needs to be here until he's trained. Just a few weeks."

"Trained? You think you can train one of those things?"

"Forescythe here has had lots of success in the past." Cordela hoped that was true.

"What do you intend to do with it once it is trained?"

"Promise you won't tell?"

Cordela's father tilted his head to one side. Cordela could see that he was going through his "What is she up to now?" thought process. He was the only person in the world who could always tell when she was planning something devious — although Rizo was getting to be a close second.

"Okay, I promise. This had better be good."

"It's a wedding gift for the Prince of Kandahar."

"The one getting married next month?"

"Yes. So he won't need to be here past the wedding. And, just take a look at him!" She motioned to Rizo to take the lid off of the barrel that had been next to them in the sitting room the whole time. Her father's eyes nearly popped out of his head at the sight of the tiny dragon. But it was her mother's reaction that she had been counting on.

"Oh, how adorable! So cute. He can definitely stay!"

It was Cordela's secret weapon. And the matter was settled. She would tell them later that he wasn't going to stay small.

Cordela replaced the lid, picked up the barrel, and led Rizo and Forescythe out to the barn. Forescythe looked around, nodding and stroking his chin.

"This will make an excellent flight cage while he is small. We can use that time to train him on the whistle. Once he's big, we'll have to move him outside for flight operations, but by then he should be responding to the whistle and voice commands. Do you think he'll fit in here once you restore him to full size?"

"He'll have to watch his tail," Rizo said, " but otherwise he'll fit."

"We need to make sure we can feed him," Cordela said. "Our neighbors the Pioullous have a sizeable herd of goats. That will keep him busy once he's restored. But we need smaller prey until then."

"It looks like Iko-Iko has one solution," Rizo bent down to receive a mouse from the cat's jaws.

"We probably want a backup alternative, in case Iko-Iko isn't in the mood to hunt," Cordela observed.

"I'm also going to need some kind of small treat for rewarding proper behaviors during training." Forescythe shook his head. "Even a whole small mouse is going to be too big for that. And you aren't paying me enough to get me to cut up dead mouse. Also, it should be something he really likes."

"Hmmm." Cordela held up a finger. "Wait here." She ducked out of the barn and found Moon grazing nearby in the dusk. She rummaged in her saddlebag and found what she was looking for — a package of Mario and Luigi's goat jerky that she had picked up in Kandahar.

Back in the barn she handed Forescythe the paper-wrapped package. "If he likes these, they'll be perfect as treats. You can break off little pieces one at a time."

"Yes, perfect — if he likes them. Hmmm, they smell good."

"Just be sure to save enough for the dragon.

"What are we going to do for sleeping? I don't think my parents have room for all of us."

"As uncomfortable as it likely will be," Forescythe sighed, "I should stay in the barn here with the trainee, at least initially."

"I'll only be here part time, but I'd like my own place, if possible," Rizo said.

"I have an idea," Cordela said. "Forescythe, why don't you stay here and arrange the barn however you need it, and maybe introduce Snowball to his new accommodations. Rizo, come with me."

The Mallow family lived a short distance from the Shents and had a detached building that they sometimes used when they had visitors. Cordela had known them since she was a small child, and they were happy to lease the building to Rizo for the few weeks that he would need it. The two of them walked back to Cordela's parents' house in the deepening twilight to collect Rizo's pony and packs.

"Rizo, I really need to visit the temple in Palmyra." She hoped Rizo wouldn't probe for details. "Can you supervise Forescythe for a few days until I get back?"

"Make it two. I need to get back to Amorium and make arrangements for my ship. It's costing me gold to park it in the harbor every day."

"Two days. You got it." She said goodnight to him at his new apartment and returned to her parents' house for supper and sleep.

Sixty

CORDELA was on the road at first light the next day, after assuring her parents that Rizo was more than capable of overseeing Forescythe and keeping Snowball under control. She assumed that was true. Her mission for Isis seemed much more urgent. If the artifact she had wrapped up in her belt pouch was as powerful as Wadj-wer said, the sooner she could make it someone else's responsibility, the better.

It was still early when she arrived at the temple. She paused a moment just inside the entrance to glare at the large relief carving of Isis on the opposite wall. It still held the faceted garnet that Cordela had retrieved as her very first mission for the goddess. Morrie, the temple's elderly seer, met her there.

"Thank Isis you arrived safely," she said without prelude. "Soussi awaits you in her private chamber."

"I should have guessed that you would be expecting me." Morrie's visions were often uncanny, if mostly non-specific. She followed the aged priestess through the temple hallways. Acolytes were just beginning their daily cleaning and maintenance chores. A few that she knew smiled as she passed, and she could hear them whispering her name to their fellows, often in connection with "Chosen of Isis." Cordela might have been flattered or proud, if she weren't aware of all that being Chosen of Isis entailed. Instead, her attention was focused on her current mission for Isis, which right now consisted of securing the artifact.

Morrie ushered Cordela into the High Daughter's private room. Soussi sat cross-legged on a reed mat with eyes closed. Morrie sat across from her and motioned for Cordela to do the same. They waited for what seemed like a long time, but was probably only a minute.

"Do you have the object?" She finally said, opening her eyes.

Cordela took the artifact from her pouch but did not unwrap it.

"Can you tell us how you acquired this?" Soussi stared at the cloth-covered artifact reverently.

Cordela gave a brief synopsis of her experience under the sea, then revealed the item.

"It is indeed the Spa-iba-wukh. It is only even mentioned in a few of our histories. But legends of its power — and danger — are still told among the highest initiates of the Daughters of Isis." She glanced at Morrie. "You should tell Cordela of the message you received from Isis."

"In my vision," Morrie began, "Isis was before me on the road to Luxor. She told me that her chosen one would soon bring the lost Spa-iba-wukh. It will be needed for a mission of great importance for the future of all of Egypt. Until that mission begins, it must be guarded carefully, since in the wrong hands it can bring about the destruction of everything. And most hands are the wrong ones."

A storm from the east, Isis had told her in her dream. A crisis for all of Egypt. At least it wasn't the entire world this time. "Who is to carry out this mission?" Cordela assumed she knew the answer to that, but asked anyway.

"Only Isis' Chosen can complete the task," Morrie said. As she had suspected. "But she will have assistance."

Well, that was a bit of good news. "I guess I need to get ready to travel again," Cordela sighed.

"Not necessarily right away," Morrie waved a finger at her. "Isis seems to say that the mission is important, but not urgent."

"How can that be? If something is threatening all of Egypt, we need to do something right away, right?"

"I do not know. But it seems that it does not matter when

you go, just that it is important that you do go."

Cordela breathed in relief. She would be available to attend the Prince's wedding after all. She really didn't want Rizo getting all the credit for their gift.

"On the subject of assistance," Soussi rewrapped the eldritch machine, "there is a new acolyte in the temple that seems to be having some problems fitting in." She stood and invited the others to do so. "Place this in our most secure vault," she handed Morrie the item. "Of course, you must not speak of it to anyone else." Morrie left with the Spa-iba-wukh, and Soussi draped her arm over Cordela's shoulder. "I think you may have a bit in common with our new acolyte. I'd like you to take her on as a personal project."

"Is it anyone I know?"

"I believe you have met her. Her name is A'aleisa, and she is half elven, like yourself."

Oh no. Her one encounter with A'aleisa had been a heated argument about the correct procedure for compounding the incense used in most temple rituals. Cordela had to shut her down with a stern warning and threaten her with stable duty for a month to end the discussion. Cordela thought about refusing, but she supposed that missions from Isis came in all forms and along many paths, and as the Chosen one she couldn't really pick and choose. She recalled again Lady Karela of Loerhold, saving the world every day through her sacrifice. She nodded to Soussi. "Anything else?"

"No, child." Soussi guided Cordela to the main gallery of the temple. "I know that Isis asks much of you. You bear it well. I can offer little counsel, other than to be true to yourself while doing the will of Isis."

Be brave. Be true. She was trying. She stood and bowed to Soussi as she took her leave.

On her way back to the main temple vestibule she met Valory, who was as uptight as Cordela had ever seen her. Her shoulders were hunched up, her fingers locked and unlocked at a rabbit's place, and Cordela even thought she saw her left eye twitching. She brightened a bit when she noticed Cordela.

"You're here! I am so glad to see you." Her voice was almost a screech, as though her throat was too tight to let out the words properly.

"Yes, hello. What is going on with you? Is everything alright?"

"Yes! Everything is just great!" Valory did not sound convinced that everything was indeed great. Her forced smile seemed to unnaturally stretch the corners of her face.

"Valory. Something is wrong. I've never seen you so wound up."

Valory took Cordela by the hand and led her to an unoccupied corner of the temple. "I have some news."

"Go on." What news could have her friend in such a state?

Valory spoke in practically a whisper. "Markham asked me to marry him."

"That's fantastic." Not a total surprise, but great news nonetheless. "What did you say?"

"I said yes!"

"Oh, congratulations!" Cordela gave her a huge hug, which Valory seemed to pull away from. "So what's wrong?"

"I'm so scared, Cordela. What if it's a mistake? I don't know what to do."

"Valory." Cordela put her hands on the taller woman's shoulders. "This is what you want. And you are so strong of heart. You faced the army of Amorium. You went toe-to-toe with an enormous bugbear. You took on a giant spider, and who knows what else. This should be easy."

"All those times I had you beside me."

"And I'll be beside you for this, too." Cordela thought for a second. "Well, I'll be beside you for the wedding. What you and Markham get up to after that is your own business."

Valory laughed, and visibly relaxed. "It's definitely what I want. As much as I wanted to serve Isis. And Markham is amazing."

"When are you thinking of having the ceremony?"

"The night of the summer solstice is auspicious for Isis. We would want her blessing for our marriage."

"Okay, that gives us about eight weeks to plan. And I think I can rope in another Daughter of Isis to help us."

"What do you mean?"

"Soussi has given me a project to focus on. A'aleisa. I'm supposed to guide her in fitting in."

"Yes, she seems to be having some issues. You don't sound too happy about it."

"I'm not. She's headstrong, argumentative, undisciplined, and has no respect for authority or experience."

"Kind of like how you were when you first arrived?"

Cordela thought about that. She remembered butting heads with Gille Scarlet, the more experienced Daughter she had been paired with when she first arrived. Had she been a special 'project' that Soussi had assigned to Gille? To Valory, she just said, "Like you told me, sometimes the world just needs a little help. In this case, the world can also help us out. I think I'll put A'aleisa in charge of flowers."

"If she's anything like you, she won't appreciate that."

"But if she's anything like me," Cordela winked, "you'll have the most amazing floral arrangements for your wedding."

Sixty One

RIZO and Forescythe worked together to fully prepare the barn for dragon flight. There was a window in the hay loft that they had to get closed and sealed — it would have been bad if Snowball had found that open before Rizo did. At Forescythe's request, Rizo manufactured a little harness that could be tied to a line, to keep the dragon from getting lost before he was reliably answering to the whistle. Later, Rizo set traps around the Shent's farm for small rodents, so they wouldn't have to rely on Iko-Iko being in the mood to hunt.

Snowball really liked the goat jerky. By the end of the second day Forescythe was able to get the little dragon to fly to him when he heard the whistle, and even respond to some simple voice commands. Rizo watched as Forescythe placed the tiny white dragon on a bale of hay, uttered a stay command, and walked back to where Rizo stood near the small entry door. He raised a hand and blew the whistle, and Snowball immediately flew toward them, landing at Forescythe's feet.

"Looks like you're making pretty good progress," Rizo commented.

"He's in a good mood today since we let him out of the barrel. We'll see how much he cares to cooperate tomorrow."

Rizo nodded.

"Wasn't Cordela supposed to be back today?"

"Yes." Rizo was irked. He had told her of his own urgency. He wasn't sure what her important activities were — although he suspected it had to do with the thing she always kept carefully wrapped and near her. She had better show tomorrow he thought. If not, he had a good mind to make her get her own gift for the Prince.

As it happened, she arrived with Bowe just after midday on the morrow. Cordela was nonchalant. "You said two days." She shrugged. "I wasn't counting our first day here since it was basically over."

As much as he wanted to, Rizo couldn't complain. "Forescythe has made some progress, but Snowball has developed a stubborn streak. He seems to behave better when I'm there. Maybe you'll have the same effect."

"I hope he gets over that. One of us can't be with the Prince every time he wants to take his dragon for a spin."

"Forescythe thinks he'll come out of it. Here, let me show you where I've set some traps for small game, so we'll have enough small dragon food. Bowe, you can relax for a while. After I show Cordela around I still need to stop by my apartment and grab a few things."

It took less than an hour to catch Cordela up and pack. He took a bit more than his share of the remaining gold. He hoped Cordela wouldn't mind. If he had any left, he would pay the leather worker in Palmyra for the tackle. Meanwhile, he had no idea what the work on his vessel was going to cost. He resolved to make it up to Cordela later, somehow.

Bowe tried setting an easy pace, but Rizo was eager to reach his destination and pushed his little pony as hard as he dared. Bowe had little trouble keeping up on his larger animal, and used the opportunity to pepper Rizo with questions about Lanthanum and what he might be getting himself into. Rizo told the story of how they had met Lanthanum, first via Math's Brownie brothers who were trying to reach him, and then after the Battle of Kandahar when they met him near the battlefield. Even though Rizo had known the wizard for many months, there was much that he didn't know. Many of Bowe's questions went unanswered.

"What made you want to become captain of your own ship?" Bowe asked abruptly.

"I find that the wizard life doesn't really suit me," Rizo began. "I've been looking for something else to do, and this boat just sort of fell into my knapsack."

"It's too bad. You're really good at magic. You could really make a difference if you developed some real power."

"It's hard to make any sort of difference when you spend all your time with your nose in a scroll."

"Hmm. I guess so. I'm hoping my time with Lanthanum provides some balance."

"It should. He apparently still gets around a bit, and if you believe the stories he was quite the adventurer in his younger days."

They arrived at Amorium just as they were closing the gates for the night. Since Rizo and Bowe were both in Amorium to see Lanthanum, they gave that answer when asked their business. The wizard was taking his supper when they arrived at his door.

"We can come back later if we're interrupting," Bowe called from the door.

"Nonsense." Lanthanum said within. "Show them in please, Math. And pull up two chairs."

Rizo and Bowe watched him eat for a minute. Rizo got bored first. "Did you finish that scroll you offered to write for Cordela and me?"

"Hmm?" The wizard was chewing a carrot. "How do you like the bean salad?"

"Leaves a bit to be desired."

"What? Oh! Silly me. Math, would you please bring our guests some supper?"

"Right away, Master." Rizo remained composed. He had seen the "absent minded wizard" act before.

The Brownie was just leaving the kitchen with a tray of food when, with a wave of his hand, their host dropped the room into complete darkness. Rizo felt Lanthanum's hand on his shoulder, and heard him say very softly, "wait."

About ten long seconds passed. Eventually, Lanthanum said out loud, "Bowe, do you think you might help Math find his way here with the food?"

"Me? I can't see a thing."

"Surely there must be something useful you can do."

"Um." Bowe's breathing accelerated. "Um." Then, "Wait. How about this."

Rizo couldn't see Bowe's hands, but he recognized Bowe's words as a dancing light spell. Created as a diversionary tactic by an unknown mage perhaps a thousand years ago, it called into existence several glowing spots of no substance that flickered like torch flames and bobbed as if being carried. It was a simple spell that all new students at PIMNA learned. Bowe's lights formed near the kitchen in front of where Math stood waiting with the food. Under Bowe's command, the lights slowly bobbed toward the table where they sat, leading Math along to deliver the food. The moment he arrived at the table, Lanthanum dispelled the magical darkness.

"Your first lesson," Lanthanum addressed Bowe. "The ideal spell to use depends upon the situation. Don't always just cast the most powerful one at your disposal."

Rizo smiled as he sampled the bean salad that Math placed before him. He could see that Bowe was going to be very busy for the duration of his apprenticeship. But he didn't let Lanthanum distract him. "About that scroll..."

"Yes, it is done. I will fetch it for you after supper. It should work, though there might be some," pause, "unusual side effects."

"You mean like his body is back to normal but his voice is still a little squeak?"

Lanthanum laughed. "Something like that. I'm sure it will be fine, but I wanted to warn you, just in case."

"I appreciate that."

Iko-Iko was not interested in the bean salad, nor anything else Lanthanum was serving. Rizo slipped him some smoked fish that he had acquired in Kandahar, which kept the cat busy for the duration.

When they finished eating, Lanthanum delivered the scroll as promised. "Thank you again. Say, do you know of anywhere in town to stay that is cheaper than the Keep Inn?"

"Try the Port of Call, down by the harbor. It is usually clean, or at least not too dirty, and much more affordable.

"That reminds me. Bowe, I have reserved rooms for you nearby. I hope they meet with your satisfaction. Math will show you them as soon as he has finished cleaning from supper."

"Goodnight to you both," Rizo bowed slightly. "Thank you again for supper. I'll be very busy for the next few days, but I'll try to stop by on my way out."

Rizo found the Port of Call without any problem. It was certainly cheaper than the Keep Inn, just a few silver per night, including stabling for his pony. The room was adequate, and Rizo slept well.

His first act upon waking was to head to the harbor to verify that his ship was still at its assigned anchorage, which it was. Next up, after a quick breakfast, was to seek out a competent shipbuilder and see what sort of refit was within his budget.

There were several in Amorium that seemed to have equally good reputations and similar fee scales, so he picked one at random.

"I want to fix up the galley anchored over there in the harbor," he began once the master builder invited him into his shop. "I really want an option to carry a smaller crew. Can I get a sail on it?"

"Sure," said the builder, "We do that sort of work all the time. You just need a mast or two plus some cleats for rigging. But you'll probably want a steppable mast."

"What does that mean?"

"That galley looks to have a reinforced bow made for ramming. If you plan to use it, you'll need to take down the mast first. Otherwise, the momentum will rip your ship apart."

"I see."

"That sort of work will require a drydock."

"Do you have one?"

"There's just one in Amorium. You'll have to deal with them directly."

Rizo got similar price estimates from three shipbuilders. Then he spoke to the manager of the drydock. He began to realize that the refit plus drydock fees were going to exceed his budget. He had heard from a couple of the builders that things were often cheaper in Miletos, up the coast to the north, if you could handle the risk of finding a knife in you and your purse missing. That didn't bother Rizo (much), so he instead began to inquire into towing services. Before he committed, he needed to talk to a builder in Miletos. He left Amorium right after dinner.

Sixty Two

CORDELA awoke in a strange room. The pale predawn light that filtered in through the partially covered window revealed furniture that seemed vaguely familiar, but unaccustomed. As she gradually regained more of her waking faculties, she began to recognize things from her childhood — a wall hanging knitted by her mother, a clay tablet she decorated when she was 10. Once she was fully conscious she remembered that she was in her old bedroom in her parents' house. She had only been gone a bit more than a year. When had it become so strange to her?

She sat in bed and thought over the events of the past few days. She had sought out A'aleissa at the temple, and informed her that she would be Cordela's ward for the next few months. As Cordela expected, the girl was not terribly receptive. Cordela tried establishing some sort of bond by talking about growing up in a mixed race household, and got A'aleisa to share that she was elven on her mother's side, but that was about all. She certainly wasn't very excited about being responsible for securing flowers for Valory's wedding.

"I came here to fight against the forces of chaos and save the world, not assemble floral arrangements."

"You haven't seen how chaotic Valory has been since she started planning this wedding," Cordela replied. A'aleisa grinned a bit at that, the first time Cordela had seen anything other than a scowl on her face. A'aleissa begrudgingly agreed.

That left food, invitations, and music for Cordela. She decided to tackle music first. She would have to audition some musicians. She wrote an announcement and was pinning it to the cork board between the market square and the tetrapylon when a man, reading over her shoulder, said he was available.

"Great. Meet me at the Beaver Lodge Inn this afternoon, and be ready to play." She had truly meant to at least warn Willie before the musician arrived.

Invitations she could write herself, but she really wanted to spend some time writing some magical scrolls to supplement the spells she was able to retain in memory. She would hire a scribe, once Valory and Markham provided the guest list.

A crowing rooster brought her back to her old bedroom.

While she dressed she reflected on her new responsibilities. She was helping Valory plan her nuptials, she had A'aleisa to shepherd, and beyond all that she had whatever Isis had in mind to do with the strange mechanical artifact she had retrieved from the bottom of the sea. Valory, at least, would appreciate her efforts. She wasn't so sure about A'aleisa or Isis. But she resolved to do her best, rely on the support of her friends, and not worry about fame or recognition. Much.

Before all that, though, she needed to make sure that the Prince's gift was trained and fed properly. To address the second, she went to check on Rizo's traps. One had caught a squirrel. Many people would balk at keeping a trapped squirrel, since they seem so cute. Cordela, however, knew that squirrels were the absolute worst. They were mean, vindictive, selfish, rude, and absolutely incorrigible. Just to prove her right, this one bit her finger as she was pulling it out of the trap. Yep, dragon food for sure. Her regard for all living things only extended so far. She placed it in a hard leather pouch that the animal wouldn't be able to gnaw through, wrapped her finger in a bandage, and continued on her rounds.

She released the dragon dinner into a cage in the barn set up for the purpose. Forescythe was coiling a line in preparation for the day's training. When he saw the squirrel, he modified his plans to include "playing fetch." He asked how much Cordela would be available to assist in the training.

"I should be around from before dinner through the rest of the day. I just want to check with the neighbors on the supply of goats we will need in a week or so."

"Good," the trainer hung the coiled line on a nail. "I'll see what I can do with the trainee before then."

She stopped by her mother's kitchen for a warm bowl of meal before heading to the Pioullous', one farm over.

"Oh, hello, Cordela," Mrs. Pioullous greeted her at the door. "We've missed seeing you around. We're so glad you're back for a while."

"It's good to be back," Cordela brushed back a strand of hair that had crept up to her face. "Though, a little awkward. Seems I've changed a lot since I left."

"We've noticed." The woman ducked her head a bit. "Say, will you be bringing us any more of that delicious frozen creamy dessert today?"

"Um, excuse me?"

"That nice halfling fellow came by to pick up fresh goat milk for your parents. An hour later, he was back with this freezing cold but sweet and delicious treat he had made with some of the milk. He said that he had a dragon in your parents' barn with ice breath that made it for us. Is that true?"

"He told you that?" Cordela sighed. They were supposed to remain discreet. "Yes, it's true. I hope you don't mind."

"Mind?" Mrs. Pioullous waved her hand at Cordela, and leaned forward with the same hand next to her mouth. "We wouldn't care if you had a Chimera in there as long as we got frozen cream out of the deal."

"I'm glad you said that," Cordela set aside her surprise for the moment, "because he's going to be getting bigger, and we'll need to feed him. I was hoping we could buy some of your goats for that purpose."

"Oh, sure. That should be no problem, dear. Not too many, I hope? I mean, how hungry is it?"

"Maybe three per week, for a few weeks?"

"Hmmm. That's a chunk of our herd."

"We can pay a little over market."

"That won't be necessary. You're a long term friend of our family. Plus, you saved our town from the wolves, so we owe you."

Cordela thanked her and promised to try to get her some more iced cream later. She took her leave, shaking her head. Leave it to Rizo to bribe the neighbors into going along with this plan. She hoped Forescythe knew the process, otherwise Mrs. Pioullous was going to have to wait until Rizo returned.

Cordela's presence in the barn seemed to calm down Snowball just a bit, and he became very adept at targeting stationary or moving objects, pouncing on them, and returning them to Forescythe. Over the next several days, she was needed there less and less. She helped Forescythe with the process of freezing the milk with sugar, and experimented with adding in fresh blueberries and crushed nuts. These she shared with the people of Fallonfael, taking Rizo's lead in winning over the good will of the neighbors. At the end of the third day, Forescythe announced that he had done all he could with the miniature dragon, and it was time to bring him back to full size and to get him used to the saddle and a human rider. Cordela planned to ride into Palmyra the next day. She hoped Rizo was done with whatever business he had been up to.

Sixty Three

MIDSPRING Day finally arrived — the day of the Prince's wedding. Cordela wore emerald green. Rizo couldn't remember her ever not wearing emerald green. He assumed it was some elven or family custom, but it was just as likely that she just liked the color green. It certainly highlighted her eyes.

Rizo wore a freshly pressed black waistcoat over his cleaned and polished leathers. He left his bandolier of throwing daggers at home. He hoped he wouldn't need it.

He and Cordela rode at the head of the small Palmyra delegation to the Prince's wedding. Valory and Markham were with them, and also Gille Scarlet and a few other heroes of the Battle of Kandahar. A Palmyran honor guard of city reserves rode before and after them.

"That was brilliant of you to win over the townsfolk with that creamy frozen dessert," Cordela said.

Rizo checked to make sure that they were out of earshot of most of the others. "Thank you. I like what you did with adding the fruit and nuts."

"I'm really glad the tackle we had made worked out so well."

"It better have. It cost us enough." Rizo huffed. "Good thing I had some cash left after funding my ship's refit."

"What made you move it to Miletos?"

"Amorium was too expensive. Just the drydock fees would have eaten all of my budget. I had to move it to Miletos. Even after paying for the tow, it was still way cheaper to have the work done there."

"Miletos doesn't have the best reputation."

"The shipbuilders there are competent enough — I've seen their work. You just have to watch your back in the streets. I'm used to handling myself in that environment."

"How long will this refit take?"

"Several months. Long enough for me to learn a bit about sailing."

"So, you'll be making use of the research habits you learned from me and at PIMNA?"

"No, I'll be hanging out in the portside taverns and finding a crew that knows what they are doing." He flashed Cordela a smile calibrated to annoy her. Her rolling eyes let him know he had hit his mark, but she quickly shrugged off his teasing.

"What do you plan to do with this ship once it's ready? Hauling wine and olive oil doesn't seem like your speed."

"It turns out that merchant communities will pay a lot to rid themselves of nuisance piracy." He paused as a small animal darted across the road in front of them. "I think I can turn a tidy profit collecting the bounties offered for various buccaneers and outlaws, plus salvaging their ships and any booty they happen to have already made off with."

"That sounds like you," Cordela smirked. "Well, good luck on your new career."

They slowed to let the others catch up.

"Congratulations on your promotions," Rizo looked past Cordela to take in Valory as well. They had both been elevated to the rank of Matriarch in the Daughters of Isis.

"Thank you, Rizo," Valory nodded.

"Valory deserves it," Cordela said. "She and Markham are off to head their own temple right after their wedding."

"Where will you be?"

"The people of Pistros invited us," Valory explained. "I guess we made some sort of impression on our way through there." She shrugged.

"Sounds like a different sort of adventure," Rizo mused.

"It won't be easy," Markham rode beside Valory, opposite Rizo. "Soussi said she could provide a small stipend for a few months, but it will be up to us to attract followers — and funds."

"PIMNA paid you handsomely for those Harpy feathers. That stack of coin should help get you started."

"Most of that is going to pay for the wedding," Valory said. "However, they were very happy to take the whole lot off of our hands."

"Well, I wish you luck."

"We'll see you at the wedding, won't we?" Valory plainted.

"I wouldn't miss it."

"Cordela," Valory continued, "Don't you think you deserve your title, too, after all you've done for Isis?"

"I suppose," Cordela hunched down in her saddle. "But I'm trying to practice humility."

"Is that what that is?" said Rizo sardonically. "I was wondering why it didn't sound like you. Keep practicing, I guess."

Cordela humphed. Rizo was going to miss ribbing her.

"What did you end up getting the Prince for his wedding?" Rizo asked Valory.

"Well, for the Princess I had the jewelry I got from the sphinx. But I was stumped on what to get for Prince Prothar. Markham's parents sent a beautiful hunting horn. They insisted that they would be honored to have the Prince accept it with their regards."

"It has been in our family for generations," Markham added.

"I'm sure Prince Prothar will treasure it."

"How is your gift doing? Are you going to deliver it on time?"

Rizo smiled at Valory. "Yes, I think our gift is well in hand."

They left their mounts at a makeshift stable constructed just for the wedding at the edge of the assembly ground. The large area off the main road and adjacent to the Royal Residence was used most days for viewing the Prince's daily appearances on the balcony of his Residence. Today it would host the reception, gift line, and festivities that most of Kandahar would be participating in.

Rizo told Cordela he would meet her inside the Residence, where very special invitees such as themselves would witness the actual ceremony. He had a bit of preparation to take care of first. He went to look at the security arrangements for the day. He first met Captain Kirloo, the Prince's military chief.

"Hello Captain. I hope things will be very secure for the Prince's nuptials."

"Hello Rizo." The Captain said flatly, barely glancing at Rizo. "I'm very busy, so I don't have time to chat." She deliberately fingered her sword.

"Of course." Rizo pretended not to notice the implied threat. "I'm looking for Stonefoot. Where might I find him?"

"He is coordinating security from the roof of the Residence. I hear you know your way there?"

"I do, but I think I'd prefer to take a different route to get there than I used last time."

He wasn't sure if Kirloo laughed, but it was about the closest thing to it Rizo had ever seen out of her. "Thanks."

The last time Rizo had been on the roof of the Royal Residence, he had climbed the wall in the dark to get there.

He didn't want to scuff up his waistcoat or polished leather, so he tried the stairs. He was stopped several times, but he always managed to find someone who recognized him to wave him through. Finally he was standing next to his friend Stonefoot the dwarf.

"How goes the security detail?" he opened.

"The Prince insists on being close to his people. We will protect him and his bride the best we can." He took a long look at Rizo. "You look awfully handsome for the occasion."

"Why thank you." He bowed slightly. "The reason I came up here was to let you know that if you see something approaching through the air, please try to have your archers hold their fire. It wouldn't be very nice to ruin the Prince's wedding gift before he even gets a chance to enjoy it."

"What are you up to, Rizo?"

"Who, me? I'm just delivering a helpful message."

"Thanks for the warning," Stonefoot said sternly. He stared Rizo down for a few more seconds, but Rizo just smiled and squeezed his shoulder.

"We'll see you after the festivities."

"We?"

"All of us from Palmyra. Me, Cordela, Valory, Markham. We're glad you're up here keeping an eye on things."

Stonefoot sighed. "If you weren't such a steadfast and dependable friend, I don't think I would ever put up with you."

"Sure you would. What you really like the most about me is my smile!" He flashed one at Stonefoot and headed downstairs.

The ceremony was held in the Grand Foyer of the Royal Residence, after which the Prince and his new bride appeared briefly on the balcony for the first time as a couple.

After a short break, a guard detail accompanied them in an open carriage out to the assembly ground, where a pair of throne-like chairs were set up atop a dais. A long line of guests, admirers, and subjects presented the new couple with all manner of gifts from near and far. Cordela and Rizo waited until the very end. Rizo had prepared a mind-reading spell, just so that he could get the Prince's full reaction to his gift.

As they approached, Rizo was picking up that the Prince was very worn out from the day's events and having to spend several hours sitting in the hot sun and smiling and thanking everyone regardless of what sort of gift was brought.

"What in the world could that ambassador from Susa have possibly been thinking?" Prothar thought. "Who needs a jewel-encrusted chamber pot?" And a short while later, "I am grateful that so many Kandahari have appeared to offer congratulations and blessings. Particularly those that can afford little else."

Gradually Cordela and Rizo moved closer to the dais. The Prince noticed them and thought, "Ah, Rizo and Cordela. I'm certainly pleased to see them." The Princess, however, was not nearly in such high spirits. "Ugh, it's so hot," her impassive smile contrasted with the thoughts Rizo received. "This is boring. I don't know these people," and, "this dress is digging into my hips," and, "Almost the end of the line. Can't be too soon. I have to pee."

She clearly had no idea who he and Cordela were, even when the Prince introduced them as friends of Stonefoot and defenders of Kandahar. Rizo detected that she actually wasn't listening at all. She perked up a bit when Cordela approached with the half of their joint gift meant specifically for the Princess. She was very confused about why anyone would want a plush bugbear. She did find it cute and cuddly, however. And she liked the bracelet that it wore as a necklace. Rizo heard her think, "Should I wear this bracelet? Or just leave it? This will be the best-dressed bugbear doll anywhere."

Then it was his turn to present. He stepped forward and placed the wooden box in the hands of the Prince.

He undid the latch, opened it, and withdrew the silver cylinder. He inspected it, saw the inscription, and looked at Rizo with a furrowed brow.

"It's a whistle. You blow on it." Rizo brought his fingers to his lips.

"What are you up to?" was what Rizo read from the Prince, but he followed Rizo's lead and put the whistle to his lips and blew. "Should I be hearing something?"

"Not just yet. Wait."

More confusion from the Prince. Then, Rizo heard the sound he was expecting. Screaming. People shouting, "Look out!" and "Run!" and "Hide!" It was perfect. The Prince and his guards saw the approaching dragon at the same time. The guards quickly closed ranks around the Royal couple. The Prince drew his not just ceremonial sword and moved to ward his new bride from the threat, while Rizo read from his mind "What did you do, Rizo?"

Snowball soared above the assembly field majestically, and swooped low in front of where the newlyweds now stood. "Is that a man on the dragon's back?" Rizo read from the Prince. He was still confused, but realized that there was no actual threat and began to relax. Forescythe landed the dragon elegantly before the Prince, and climbed down from the saddle.

"Greetings, your highness," said Forescythe, bowing low. "I present to you your gift from the Lady Cordela Shent and Sir Rizo Malkin, on the occasion of your wedding. As you see, he is fully flight trained. His training could continue to full battle readiness if you desire. I humbly offer my services as Royal Dragon Trainer for the duration, as you wish. Come greet your new pet." He beckoned to the Prince.

"This is astonishing, Rizo, Cordela," said the Prince. "I don't know whether to have you both killed or to confer upon you even greater honors than you already have. This is a gift beyond compare. Come, beloved. Have you ever been so close to a dragon?"

The eyes of the Princess were huge white circles with a spot of blue. All Rizo got from her mind was "BIG, BIG, BIG DRAGON." She had wet herself in the commotion. The Prince tenderly brought her hand up to the dragon's neck while Forescythe held him steady. Her terror turned to wonder and she smiled at the Prince.

"Thank you, Cordela and Rizo. Your gift is truly unique, but not nearly so unique and special as the two of you. May you both have long life and success in all you do."

The Prince called the chief of his personal guard. "Please work with Forescythe here to find a suitable place for the creature to reside until we can construct a more suitable permanent home for him. Forescythe, we will discuss terms for your services later, but I accept your kind offer to continue the dragon's training." The Prince curled his nose a bit. "And now I am afraid that my bride has had enough excitement for one day. We will retire to the Royal Residence to rest."

"And get a change of clothes," Rizo got from his mind, just as his spell was wearing off.

Epilogue

WITH the height of the shearing season over, the dining room of the Beaver Lodge was beginning to thin out. Willie wasn't nearly as busy serving and had time to catch up on some of her other tasks, which now included planning a menu for a catered wedding. Valory and Cordela were there to audition one more musician, with Cordela's new tag-along A'aleisa nearby. The artist had not arrived yet.

"Cordela, I can't believe you were auditioning players here for over a week without telling Willie what for," Valory laughed.

"Well, it was your news to deliver, and I didn't want to spoil it if you wanted it to be a surprise."

It hadn't been a surprise, since almost nothing happens in Palmyra without Willie knowing about it. But she had put on a good act when Valory finally spilled her stew.

"Thank you, Cordela." Valory dropped her voice a bit. "For everything. Now, who are we here to listen to?"

"Well," Cordela fiddled with the crossbow bolt that pinned her hair in place, "I have a very good ensemble lined up. They can play most types of music. But they really need a luthier to fill out their sound. The fellow I have coming in arrives highly recommended. I look forward to meeting him."

"And what progress on the flowers, A'aleisa?"

The young woman pouted and slumped in her chair, but at a stern look from Cordela straightened out. "I'm trying to find a way to decorate the entire circle while staying within your budget. It seems like if we use potted periwinkles we can have as many as we want, since they can be planted afterwards."

"Hmm. Purple doesn't really go with our other colors. But I like the idea of part of our wedding growing in the future. I'll talk to Markham."

"Here is our luthier," Cordela stood.

As soon as Willie saw the musician, she was immediately on edge. It was the same fellow that had come to the inn just after Cordela left on her great adventure. Willie decided she had better warn Cordela about this stranger. She waited until he started playing and approached to whisper in Cordela's ear.

"That man was in here a month or so ago, asking for you by name. I think he's up to something. You should be careful of him."

"Thanks for the warning," Cordela replied. "I'm glad you're watching out for me."

When he finished his song and sat down next to Cordela and Valory, Willie cleaned the next table over as a pretext so that she could hear the discussion.

"That was a beautiful ballad," Cordela opened, "but I couldn't help noticing that some of the events described in the lyrics seemed — familiar?"

"Well, yes my Lady. They are about you and your great deeds."

"Your own composition, I presume?"

"Yes, my Lady. But I am afraid that I only heard your tales second hand. I would be honored to incorporate your own telling into the composition."

"Is that why you have been looking for me for the past month?"

"Indeed. I have followed you across the Middle Territory, from Ismara to Ilium, just for the chance to hear the story from your own lips."

"Well," Cordela folded her hands on the table, "I would say that is dedication to art. Wouldn't you, Valory?"

"Maybe. A bit creepy, too."

"Nonsense! What is your name, sir?"

"I am Garynd DiMarco, at your service."

"Can you play in ensemble as well as solo?"

"Pardon?"

"I have arranged with the Badrewly group already, but I think they need some strings to create the right mood for our event."

"I see. Well, I have played with them on at least one occasion that I remember. I can hold my own in a group as well as I play solo. And my Lady?"

"Yes, Garynd DiMarco?"

"I would also make myself available for any future adventures you undertake. Such that I might witness them firsthand and compose the authoritative ballads of your great deeds that bards will sing of for centuries to come."

"Hmmm. Well, that certainly sounds appealing," Cordela extended a hand to shake. "I'll tell you what. You're hired for the wedding. As for future adventures, well, we will have to see..."

About the Author

R. A. Klepsis, author and Wizard Extraordinaire, spends most of his time at his residence outside of Ilium, where he writes and tends his collection of tiny monsters. His previous works include *Water Against Chaos*, the first volume in this series; *Dragonslayer: A Young Wizard's Tale*; and *Lair of Tellenioc*. He insists that the stories that blame him for inciting the Dragon Wars are very much exaggerated.

Keep up with Klepsis from the Material Plane at his website Klepsis.com, where you can sign up for his newsletter or read his blog about reduced monster care and other topics. Find him on Mastodon @Klepsis@mastodonbooks.net, in Bluesky @klepsis.bsky.social, and on the X service @RKlepsis. Interview requests should be directed to wizard@klepsis.com.

Milton Keynes UK
Ingram Content Group UK Ltd.
UKHW020644201123
432908UK00019B/2567